Four major powers who never m
gather in one

Güliedistodiez
Administrator

Ariel
Ancient Divine B

ingle with one another now
spot—

Potimas
Leader of the Elves

Dustin
Word of God Pontiff

So I'm a Spider, So What?

OKINA BABA

Illustration by
TSUKASA KIRYU

7

YEN ON

New York

So I'm a Spider, So What?, Vol. 7

Okina Baba

Translation by Jenny McKeon
Cover art by Tsukasa Kiryu

This book is a work of fiction. Names, characters, places, and incidents are the product of the author's imagination or are used fictitiously. Any resemblance to actual events, locales, or persons, living or dead, is coincidental.

KUMO DESUGA, NANIKA? Vol. 7
©Okina Baba, Tsukasa Kiryu 2017
First published in Japan in 2017 by KADOKAWA CORPORATION, Tokyo.
English translation rights arranged with KADOKAWA CORPORATION, Tokyo through
TUTTLE-MORI AGENCY, INC., Tokyo.

English translation © 2019 by Yen Press, LLC

Yen On
150 West 30th Street, 19th Floor
New York, NY 10001

Visit us at yenpress.com
facebook.com/yenpress
twitter.com/yenpress
yenpress.tumblr.com
instagram.com/yenpress

First Yen On Edition: December 2019

Yen On is an imprint of Yen Press, LLC.
The Yen On name and logo are trademarks of Yen Press, LLC.

The publisher is not responsible for websites (or their content) that are not owned by the publisher.

Library of Congress Cataloging-in-Publication Data
Names: Baba, Okina, author. | Kiryu, Tsukasa, illustrator. | McKeon, Jenny, translator.
Title: So I'm a spider, so what? / Okina Baba ; illustration by Tsukasa Kiryu ;
    translation by Jenny McKeon.
Other titles: Kumo desuga nanika. English | So I am a spider, so what?
Description: First Yen On edition. | New York, NY : Yen On, 2017–
Identifiers: LCCN 2017034911 | ISBN 9780316412896 (v. 1 : pbk.) | ISBN 9780316442886 (v. 2 : pbk.) |
    ISBN 9780316442909 (v. 3 : pbk.) | ISBN 9780316442916 (v. 4 : pbk.) |
    ISBN 9781975301941 (v. 5 : pbk.) | ISBN 9781975301965 (v. 6 : pbk.) |
    ISBN 9781975301996 (v. 7 : pbk.)
Subjects: CYAC: Magic—Fiction. | Spiders—Fiction. | Monsters—Fiction. |
    Prisons—Fiction. | Escapes—Fiction. | Fantasy.
Classification: LCC PZ7.1.O44 So 2017 | DDC [Fic]—dc23
LC record available at https://lccn.loc.gov/2017034911

ISBNs: 978-1-9753-0199-6 (paperback)
       978-1-9753-0198-9 (ebook)

10 9 8 7 6 5 4 3 2 1

LSC-C

Printed in the United States of America

contents

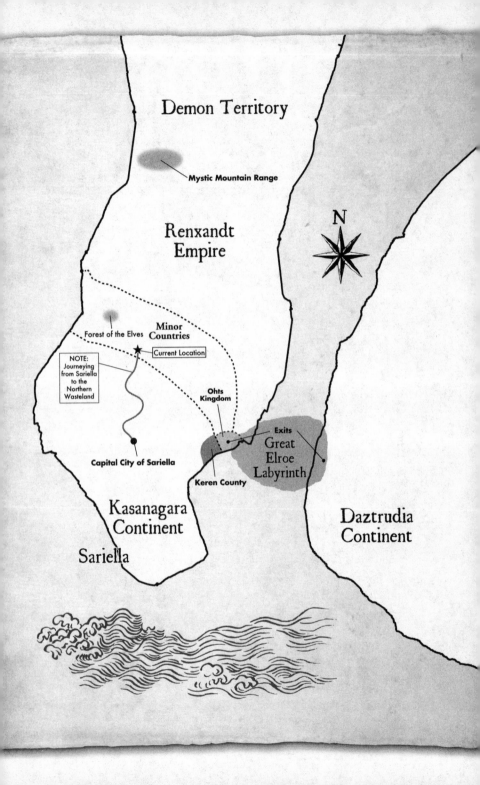

1   Transcontinental Journey Progress Report

"Okay. Say 'aaaah.'"

"""""Aaaah.""""""

"Now say 'eeee.'"

"""""Eeeee.""""""

A chorus of young girls' voices echoes across the barren wasteland.

They're not actually singing, but when you hear a bunch of people repeating things in unison, it sort of sounds like a song, doesn't it?

And no, don't point out that none of them are human. That's rude.

Right now, we're in the middle of a huge wasteland in the cluster of small countries north of Sariella.

When we arrived at the initial destination of our little journey, the capital of Sariella, Vampy and Mera decided to leave their homeland behind and go to the demon territory.

These two were driven out of their hometown by a war with the Word of God religion and Potimas's machinations.

The fact that they're both vampires, not humans, probably played a big role in their decision to take things a step further and leave their home behind.

Vampy is a Progenitor who was born as a vampire, and Mera was turned into one when Vampy drank his blood.

If they want to live in the human world without anyone protecting them, they'll have to hide that fact.

That's why they decided to follow their protector, the Demon Lord, into demon territory. That decision took guts, if you ask me.

It's been about a year since they made that decision.

We headed straight north from the capital of Sariella and crossed the border.

It's been a pretty peaceful journey since we left the capital, without any notable incidents.

In fact, the biggest incident since we started this journey was my Parallel Minds going rogue.

I kept bracing myself for Potimas to attack, but he hasn't. Things are going so smoothly, it's almost anticlimactic.

Still, we can't let our guard down.

Just to be safe, we've been avoiding any regular routes where we might be seen, taking the roads less traveled, to the point where there aren't even any roads.

People don't normally cross through this wasteland, so it's a perfect place for us to travel.

It's easy to see why nobody else is here when you look up at the sky.

Countless black shadows fly about in the air.

Birds? You wish.

Some of them look a bit like birds, but most resemble reptiles.

A bunch actually look like feathered dinosaurs, so somewhere between birds and reptiles, I guess.

The creatures flying through the air are wyrms or maybe even dragons.

They're the rulers of this wasteland.

Yeah. With that many wyrms and dragons loitering in these parts, it's no wonder humans don't set foot in this place.

A single dragon or higher-ranked wyrm could destroy an entire army of humans.

The only people who would be reckless enough to walk into this nightmare territory must either be suicidal or hoping to go down in history as legends.

But we're neither of those things.

Because we've got a demon lord, who happens to be far stronger than any dragon.

If she felt like it, the Demon Lord could probably wipe out all the dragons flying overhead without breaking a sweat.

Dragons can wipe out an entire army of humans, and the Demon Lord can wipe out an entire army of dragons.

This is just getting stupid.

Even power creep should have a limit, if you ask me.

But that being said, we've got Vampy and Mera in our entourage.

If we got caught in a cataclysmic battle between the Demon Lord and the dragons, those two might not survive.

Of course, it's highly possible that the Demon Lord could protect them both while defeating all the dragons. But there's no need to get into a dangerous situation like that deliberately.

Before we entered the wasteland, the Demon Lord yelled to the dragons, "We're just passing through!"

I don't know whether they heard that and understood her or not, but they've only been flying around above us the entire time, not paying us any mind.

Maybe they decided to keep an eye on us but not interfere unless they had to.

With that, we get to dodge a pointless battle and avoid the possibility of Vampy and Mera dying.

Plus, this way the dragons won't have to be totally obliterated.

Fighting wouldn't benefit either party, so they made the right call there.

And so we're just walking along normally, not bothering the native wildlife, either.

Maybe crooning as we walk isn't really normal, but don't worry about that.

There's a reason for this chorus, okay?

Otherwise we wouldn't be doing it.

To clarify, what we're doing is vocal training.

The baby bloodsucker's gotten so big, she can barely be called a baby anymore.

Guess you could say she's evolved into a toddler.

But there's one little problem.

Since she's been using Telepathy to communicate this whole time, she's not very good at speaking out loud.

She's a little vampire girl with a lisp.

I guess that has appeal for a very specific audience.

Considering her physical age, it's not *that* weird for her to have a lisp, but in her case, it could be a bit of a problem.

On top of using Telepathy instead of talking, she's never screamed and cried like a normal baby, so her vocal cords are close to unused.

It's led to a vicious cycle: She can't fix her lisp, so she gets embarrassed and uses Telepathy, which means her vocal cords continue to go unused.

If it keeps up like this, we can't expect her lisp to simply go away with age.

The solution we hurriedly came up with was these vocal training exercises.

Watching a little toddler traipse through a wasteland while shouting weird phrases is surreal.

But it actually seems to be fairly effective.

For the vocal training and for her stats.

Generally, stats go up more as you utilize them, but there are limits to that.

To really get results, you have to do training that most people will find hard or even painful.

And the Vampy's starting as a baby, the lowest physical form imaginable.

For her, even just walking is a tall order, which means it made her stats go up like crazy.

I mean, most babies at this age haven't even learned to walk yet, never mind doing it all day.

No wonder her stats went up so fast at first.

But at this point, since they're so high, walking alone isn't enough to raise them much anymore.

Walking for a whole day isn't even a challenge for her now, making this the perfect time to add another element.

That's why I've got her doing vocal exercises as she walks now.

This training requires a lot of deep inhaling and exhaling, so if you do it while you're already exercising, it can get really hard to breathe.

It might even be sort of like the high-altitude training some athletes do.

On top of that, I've got her practicing what little magic she's capable of while she walks, and all that multitasking is raising her Parallel Minds skill, too.

That's the reason our weird little procession is making so much noise as we walk.

Now, have you noticed anything strange about my little update so far?

Bingo. Vampy's voice alone wouldn't make a chorus.

As it happens, she's not the only one participating in this training.

There are four other girls practicing along with her.

Or four monsters, to be exact.

It's the four puppet spiders, the Demon Lord's underlings.

As the name implies, they're spider monsters that control puppetlike dolls.

Their actual bodies are tiny spiders, but they use these puppets made of thread to fight. Pretty crazy stuff.

The thing is, these puppets used to look like the drabbest mannequins. But I've done so much magical modding on them that now you'd totally think they were human, at least from a distance.

Once I was satisfied with their looks, I tried my hand at crafting some vocal cords for them, but that ended up being fairly difficult, so I was stuck for a while.

Heh-heh. But I finally got it done!

It was hard.

It was so hard…

But I think I nailed it!

I spent the past year in an endless cycle of trial and error until I finally produced these vocal cords.

Even now, they don't function all that well.

You've gotta make the thread vibrate to produce something that sounds like a human voice, but accomplishing that is no walk in the park.

Even a single syllable takes a lot of effort.

That's how the puppet spiders started doing vocal training alongside Vampy.

They still seem to have a lot of trouble with even simple sounds, so it'll probably be a long time before they can speak smoothly. They seem determined though, so I'm sure they'll get there eventually.

I figure I can keep trying to improve the artificial vocal cords, too.

By the way, the puppet spiders used to get summoned only when the Demon Lord and the others went into town, but these days they're with us all the time.

Maybe the Demon Lord got sick of summoning and dismissing them over and over.

Whatever the reason, the percentage of girls in this group has certainly skyrocketed.

Congrats, Mera! You've got yourself a harem!

Although there isn't a single normal human girl in the bunch.

I'm a half-human, half-spider arachne; the Demon Lord is…a demon lord; the puppet spiders look cute but they're still just spiders on the inside; and the baby bloodsucker is a toddler.

Okay, yeah. That's not much of a harem.

Plus, Mera's master, Vampy, is always keeping an eye on him, so he has to be careful.

Frankly, if she gets any more attached to Mera, she'll officially be a crazy stalker girlfriend.

She already starts glaring whenever he interacts with the other girls.

Not to mention, her Jealousy skill level's been going up.

Jealousy evolves from the Spite skill, and it's already level 2.

"Sophia, don't get so worked up, okay? You have to make sure you don't raise that skill. The Seven Deadly Sins skills can have a serious effect on your mind, so it's bad news all 'round. Just stay calm, all right? Why is it going up so fast anyway? Those skills are supposed to be really hard to level up…"

That's what the Demon Lord had to say on the matter.

Apparently, Vampy's Jealousy skill is a lesser form of the Seven Deadly Sins skill Envy.

The Demon Lord says the Seven Deadly Sins skills are supposed to be hard to level up, but the baby bloodsucker's making crazy progress.

That can't be good…

Her poor servant can't sleep because of the weight of his master's love.

Hang in there, bud!

Luckily, Mera has a very serious personality and hasn't shown any interest in relationships with women, so Vampy hasn't flipped her lid yet.

If Mera was more of a womanizer, we might all be in big trouble.

He's maintaining a healthy distance between master and servant, even when the bloodsucker keeps shooting him weird looks, so everything seems to be all right.

I mean, she *is* a toddler, so it's not like there's anything to worry about in the first place.

Good thing Mera isn't a creep who goes after little girls.

Speaking of the non-creep, he's actually walking silently in front of me right now.

A heavy thudding sound rings out as he walks along, leaving literal footprints in the bedrock.

I'm applying heavy pressure on him with my Repellent Evil Eye. That's why his feet sink into the rock with every step.

As you may have guessed, this is for Mera's training.

Mera's stats are higher than Vampy's.

It's only natural, since he's an adult man who was recently turned into a vampire, while she's still an toddler.

On top of that, he hasn't missed a single day of training on this journey, so he gets stronger every day.

That's why he has to resort to measures like this or his stats won't go up much.

Even shouting while he walks, the way Vampy and company are doing, wouldn't raise his stats much.

Plus, he doesn't need vocal training in the first place.

Hence the Repellent Evil Eye weight training.

This is way more intensive than the vocal exercises, so his stats have been going up at a decent clip.

They're about as good as the average monster's at this point.

Compared to his stats, though, his skills have been ranking up preeeetty slowly.

Like, they've certainly grown, but when you compare them to my overpowered Pride skill's high-speed leveling, it's not very impressive.

But even I've hit a bit of a wall.

I haven't had many chances to fight monsters on this journey, so my level hasn't gone up, and my stats and skill levels are so high that they barely budge anymore.

If I want to level up at this point, I'd basically have to slaughter enough creatures to wipe out an entire freaking ecosystem.

No wonder my level hasn't gone up.

Since the Demon Lord and I have a ceasefire now, it's not that big of a deal, but I can't help feeling impatient after getting stuck like this.

My ultimate goal is to be strong enough to defeat the Demon Lord or Potimas, but it doesn't look like I'll be accomplishing either of those goals anytime soon.

I've been working on some strategies to deal with Potimas, so I might be able to hold my own against him, but I still don't feel like I could take on the Demon Lord.

"Say 'oooo.'"

"""""Oooo."""""

At the moment, said Demon Lord is happily leading the chorus made up of the baby bloodsucker and the puppet spiders.

Looks like she's having a great time.

Kinda easygoing for a demon lord, isn't she?

If she looked a little older, she could be mistaken for the host of a children's TV show or something.

But unfortunately, the Demon Lord looks like a little— Huh?! I just got a chill!

Um… I should probably cut that train of thought off there.

That particular topic strikes a nerve with the Demon Lord.

Now she's looking right at me, with a smile that's 200 percent scarier than before.

Sorry, sorry. I wasn't thinking about anything, I swear.

I deeefinitely wasn't thinking about how the Demon Lord looks like a little kid.

I think I just saw the Demon Lord's grin widen a little, but I'm sure I'm only imagining things.

Yeah. Let's go with that.

Oh yikes, now even the baby bloodsucker and the puppet spiders look scared.

Let's try not to frighten the children, okay?

A thousand pardons, Madam Demon Lord, but I would be most appreciative if you could forget about me and focus on the kids. Many thanks.

I don't know if my silent plea got through to her, but the Demon Lord goes back to leading the chorus as if nothing happened.

Whew. That was close.

As you can see, my relationship with the Demon Lord hasn't changed much.

On the surface, we don't act like enemies, but sometimes we push each other's buttons.

That's the kind of tentative situation we're in right now.

But it's not like we're seriously provoking each other.

Once in a while, I can tell that the Demon Lord is testing the waters, trying to figure out how I'm feeling.

My guess is she's decided it benefits her more to have me as an ally than to kill me, so she's trying to close the distance between us little by little.

Although it's hard to say whether that's working or not.

I mean, I'm definitely down for whatever if it means I don't have to pointlessly risk my life fighting her, but that doesn't mean I can trust her completely.

Basically, I think we both want to find a middle ground, but neither of us can quite commit to getting closer to each other.

Vampy, Mera, the Demon Lord, the puppet spiders.

We're all traveling together with our own thoughts and feelings.

Overall, the journey's going pretty well.

We haven't been attacked by the elves like we feared.

But I know for a fact that Potimas isn't just sitting around twiddling his thumbs.

"So who exactly is Potimas?"

At some point, Vampy finally asks the Demon Lord the million-dollar question.

"A piece of garbage," the Demon Lord replies immediately.

Okay, you *know* that's not what she was asking. (Everyone else likely had the same internal reaction.)

I'm almost sure the Demon Lord is aware of that, too, though.

Oh, but maybe she wasn't being sarcastic. Maybe that was actually just the first answer that came to mind.

"That's not what I'm asking…," Vampy responds finally.

Her expression is priceless: *I know* is written all over her face.

I guess she's well aware that Potimas is scum.

I mean, he did kill both her parents and tried to kill her, too.

It's only natural that she'd want to know more about him.

To Vampy, Potimas is a mortal enemy who killed her parents and plans to kill her next. She has every right to know who he is.

Still, the Demon Lord doesn't answer right away.

She stays silent for a while, looking pensive.

How much should I tell her?

I'm sure that's what the Demon Lord was thinking.

I want to know more about Potimas, too, so I wait for the reply.

Since my Taboo skill is maxed out, I have some idea of what Potimas might be.

The Demon Lord was once worshipped by the Goddess religion as the goddess's divine beast.

But Potimas knows her and even has the nerve to treat her like a child.

Plus, he had a mechanical body, which absolutely shouldn't be a thing in this world.

If I put together all the pieces, I can guess what he really is.

Still, I'd rather hear the truth from the Demon Lord, who obviously knows the facts.

"All right. White seems interested, too, so I guess I'll tell you the whole story." The Demon Lord glances at me, then sighs. "But there's no going back once you've heard this. That guy's no ordinary villain. He's a threat to this entire world, as rich as that sounds coming from a demon lord. Once you find out what he really is, you won't be able to live peacefully in this world anymore. Well, I guess you *could*, but I'm sure it would weigh on your heart. Now, I can tell you the basic, most harmless facts about him, but that's not what you want to know, is it? If you really want to learn everything, make absolutely certain you're prepared to hear what I have to say."

The Demon Lord's serious attitude seems to catch Vampy by surprise.

She didn't ask about Potimas out of casual curiosity, of course.

But she probably wasn't expecting to hear that the information would change her worldview, either.

Vampy hesitates for just a moment, looks at Mera, and finally seems to make up her mind.

"Please tell me."

Seeing her determination, the Demon Lord nods once and begins to speak.

"Potimas Harrifenas. That's his full name. He's the patriarch of the elves—the head honcho, basically. Elves are one of the demi-human races in this world... Although the only humanoid races are humans, demons, and elves, so I guess the term *demi-human* might not be appropriate. Now, what's special about the elves is that their life spans are ridiculously long. Demons live two or three times longer than humans, but elves live more than ten times longer. They grow a lot slower as a result, about half as quickly as humans do. Once they reach their prime, their bodies stop growing, and after that they slooowly start to age. But the aging process varies among elves: Some get older gradually over the years while others barely change at all, then suddenly age very quickly toward the end of their life spans. But either way, they stick around for a ludicrous amount of time."

These basic facts about elves might be common knowledge to the Demon Lord and Mera, who are from this world, but they're new to Vampy and me.

Elves existed only in fiction back on Earth.

"Since they grow more slowly than humans, they tend to compensate for that by learning magic. When a body's still growing, its physical stats are hard to raise, but magic-related stats have nothing to do with the body, so they can be trained whenever. Oh, but you're an exception, Sophia. Of course your stats are gonna go up, since you've been doing this crazy training as a baby."

The baby bloodsucker screws up her face, unable to respond.

"Once elves become adults, their physical stats can grow normally like a human's. But by that point, it's easier to get strong by focusing on magic stats rather than going out of their way to raise their weak physical attributes, so most elves just stick to magic. That's why elves are generally thought to be better at magic than humans and demons but physically weaker. Doesn't mean they're actually all that weak, though."

Most elves focus on honing their strengths instead of covering their weaknesses, which was how they got that reputation.

"Most elves sequester themselves in a village located in the Great Garam Forest. That forest is swarming with strong monsters, so no normal human could ever reach the village. Even if they did make it, there's a powerful barrier around the place, so they wouldn't be able to get in. That's why people hardly ever meet elves. There are some elves outside the village, of course, but not many, and they don't really like interacting with non-elves. Even if you see one, they'd probably never talk to you. Elves look down on both humans and demons, 'cause they're super-stuck-up."

To summarize, elves have really long life spans, are good at magic, mostly stay in the forest, and don't like other races.

In other words, they're not much different from how elves were usually depicted in pop fiction back on Earth.

Could that really be a coincidence?

"Now, all of that is just society's common knowledge about elves. The rest is the part you guys probably want to know. I'll ask again: Are you sure you want to hear it?"

Vampy nods silently.

"All right. I guess I'll talk about the machines first. The concept is probably already familiar to White and Sophia, but it might not be clear to Merazophis. A machine is the crystallization of highly advanced science and technology... No, you probably don't understand that, either, so I'll break it down a little more. Basically, it's a device that can produce magic-like phenomena without using magic. That's a machine. Get it?"

That was a pretty rough explanation, all right.

I'm not sure if was enough for Mera to get it, but he doesn't comment, although maybe he's just being polite.

But I guess it's not weird to have a hard time explaining machines to someone who doesn't know the first thing about them.

Even if you tried to start with the basics, that would still require some technical knowledge, so it would wind up taking ages to explain.

It's not really the point of this discussion, so maybe it was actually for the best to just glaze over it as a mystery object that makes magic-like stuff happen without using magic.

"The elves are the only race in this world with access to these machines. They have all the materials, the knowledge, and the techniques."

Yeah, I figured.

Potimas's cyborg body made that obvious.

"As for how advanced their engineering is, it's probably ahead of Earth at this point."

Vampy's eyes widen at that.

I can't say I blame her. Who would guess that super-advanced technology exists in a world that seems so stereotypically fantasy based?

But Vampy saw Potimas's cyborg body as well as I did. She must have an idea that this might be the case.

Still, I guess hearing it out loud surprised her.

It must be surprising and confusing if you don't have prior knowledge like I do. Most people would be shocked by the fact that something like that exists in this world.

…Unless the reasoning wasn't actually as strange as you had been led to believe.

"So Potimas has been using this technology to operate behind the scenes. But to be honest, I don't know why he's targeting you specifically, Sophia. From what I've heard, he attacked you knowing you're a reincarnation, so it's probably got something to do with that. But I have no idea what he stands to gain from killing reincarnations, so I can't say for sure. In fact, we don't even know if he really intended to kill you. I got the impression he was planning something else at first."

Like the Demon Lord, I have some doubts about Potimas's motives.

If he wanted to kill Vampy, there were plenty of other ways to do that.

He probably could have killed her regardless of my interference, if that was really all he intended to do.

But since that didn't happen, he must not have planned to kill her at first.

But knowing that doesn't mean I have any idea what his original goal was. Potimas's reasons for going after Vampy are still a mystery.

"*Um, why do the elves have technology like that?*" Vampy asks.

Yeah, that's a reasonable question.

In this stereotypical fantasy world, the elves' machines stick out like a sore thumb.

It's perfectly normal to wonder about it.

"Weird, isn't it? This world's civilizations are way less developed than Earth, but the elves have access to technology way more advanced than anything you'd find on Earth. From your point of view, the elves are probably like O-parts, right?"

O-parts… As in, "out-of-place artifacts," right? What a fitting phrase.

"But it's actually the opposite." The Demon Lord shrugs.

Mera and Vampy don't seem to understand what she means.

"Technology needs a foundation in order to develop. Without someone bringing knowledge from the future or something, it's impossible for technology to suddenly advance out of nowhere. People make tools out of sticks, then advance to stone tools, then improve even further with bronzeware.

Bronze leads to iron, allowing for more complex tools, which leads to gears, then steam engines, then circuits. It all has to happen in order. So the elves' technology must have developed like that, too, right? But they couldn't have done all that alone. It's not entirely impossible, but they hardly ever make contact with other races, and they don't have enough land and resources. Elves should barely be able to preserve civilization, never mind advance it."

Civilizations develop over time, by accumulating history.

No genius stuck in the Stone Age is suddenly gonna skip right to inventing the semiconductor.

In fact, it'd be creepy if that did happen. What would be going on in that person's head?

"What I'm saying is, the elves couldn't have developed such complex technology by themselves. There would have to be others who had the same technology. At least, under normal circumstances."

Mera is the first one to give a gasp of realization.

"I see. So that's why you said it's the opposite...?" he murmurs.

A question mark practically appears over Vampy's head.

...She's a little dumb, isn't she?

"That's right. It's the opposite. The elves haven't independently created highly advanced technology. It's simply that everyone else has moved backward. That's the reality of this world."

Finally, Vampy finally seems to get it.

"Long, long ago, this world had technology far more advanced than that of Earth. But they made a grave mistake and headed down the path of destruction. In doing so, they lost all their technology in the process, and everyone but the elves went into a cultural backslide."

It's not that the elves are advanced. It's that everyone else has fallen behind.

That's why the word "opposite" came up.

The Demon Lord has just revealed part of the truth of this world.

2 ATTACK ON THE ANT HOLE

This so-called fantasy world is actually a postapocalyptic world.

When Vampy realized this, she looked like she finally understood.

It certainly explains a lot.

Really, if you think about it, there were plenty of suspicious signs.

Especially Potimas's cyborg body.

Mera, on the other hand, seems to be having trouble digesting this information.

Unlike Vampy and me, Mera is originally from this world, so it's probably hard for him to keep up with all the new concepts like machines and technology, which he can't even picture.

Seeing is believing, as they say.

Still, he seems to be doing his best to understand the Demon Lord's words despite having little basis for it, and it's not necessarily a big deal if he doesn't fully get it.

We're talking about the distant past, after all. It doesn't really affect us in the present.

…At least, that's what I thought at first.

The Demon Lord party walks through the wasteland in the dead of night.

When I put it that way, it sounds like she's leading her troops on a march. But in reality, we look more like a bunch of young girls and one guy. Mera looks the oldest of any of us, but of course the Demon Lord is actually the oldest by far.

I guess in terms of appearance, I look the second oldest after him.

That doesn't mean I look old, though! I just mean in comparison to the bite-size Demon Lord, the puppet spiders, and the baby bloodsucker!

I've got the same face I had in my old life, which means I look like a high school student, okay?!

Seriously, you'd be digging your own grave if you ever told a high school girl she looks old.

By the way, despite my looks, my real age in this world is roughly the same as Vampy's, so I'm still a minor.

Unlike the Demon Lord, who might seem like a kid but she's gotta be at least a thousand times the legal age of adulthood!

…What was I talking about again? I got a little carried away there.

As my mind wanders, my attention is suddenly drawn back.

Something's entered the range of my Detection.

I use Panoptic Vision to peek at whatever it is.

At first, it just looks like an ordinary bird, but it can't fool my Detection skill.

It's a mechanical surveillance drone in the shape of a bird.

There's only one person who would use something like that.

It must be a surveillance device sent by Potimas.

I activate Warped Evil Eye through my Panoptic Vision.

The space around the bird-shaped device warps, twisting and destroying everything within it. Including the surveillance bird.

The Demon Lord glances over at me as she leads the vampire–spider girl chorus.

I nod silently, and she nods back.

The reason I know Potimas isn't just sitting around is that these surveillance devices have been showing up periodically.

And that's been going on since we first started this journey after the Demon Lord defeated Potimas.

Every time I destroy them before they can get close.

Otherwise he'd get information about us.

By destroying them, I'm giving away our approximate location, but that would happen anyway if I simply left the drones alone and let them see us.

It's better to destroy them and keep the amount of information Potimas gathers as low as possible.

Although the ideal amount would be zero, of course.

We've been trying our best to keep it that way, y'know?

That's why we're using all these routes so far from civilization, to try to keep out of his sight.

But for Mera to sustain himself, we do need to stop by a town or village once in a while.

It's inevitable that we can't quite keep completely out of sight in those situations.

Once in a while Potimas seems to lose track of us, and the surveillance drones will stop showing up for a long period of time. But at that point, he usually resorts to sending drones to anywhere we might possibly be just to find us again.

It's not only Potimas, either. The Demon Lord said the pontiff of the Word of God religion tracked her down with similar methods.

The moment we decided on making the demon territory our destination, the possible routes we could reasonably take were inevitably limited.

No matter how much we try to avoid being seen, we can manage for only so long.

This latest drone was the first surveillance device that's found us in a while.

I guess Potimas had this wasteland on his radar. Since we've been avoiding populated areas, he probably predicted we might come through here and set up surveillance in advance.

Still, even now that he knows roughly where we are, it's not like he can act immediately.

Judging by his actions up to this point and his words when I ran into him back at Vampy's mansion, Potimas seems to be the kinda guy who plans carefully before he acts. Also, he's stingy.

He won't pick any fights he might lose.

And we've got the super-powerful Demon Lord on our side, so he's not going to come after us without a solid plan.

Especially when he can't even spy on us successfully with his surveillance devices.

If he does attack us, it'll be when he's confident he can win.

That would probably be when he musters enough power to take the Demon Lord down or if something happens to put us in serious trouble.

If Potimas has the military strength to beat us outright, then we're screwed. The only victory left for us would be successfully running away.

But I don't think that's the case.

It wouldn't be easy to find something that can surpass the Demon Lord's power, and if Potimas had something like that up his sleeves, he would've made his move ages ago.

Since he hasn't done that, I have to assume he either doesn't have the power in the first place or he does but he's reluctant to use it.

The scary thing is that the latter could actually be true. That guy is so stingy that he didn't want to use his machine gun in our battle because he hates wasting ammo. It's not hard to believe he'd hold stuff back.

But there's no point worrying about whether he has some secret weapon or not.

All we can do is be careful and not give him the opportunity to strike.

As long as Potimas thinks it's too risky to attack us, he's much less likely to try anything.

If I keep destroying his surveillance drones, it'll give the impression that we're not letting our guard down... I hope.

With my Detection skill, I can pick up on anything that's approaching us before it gets too close, which means we always have the initiative, whether it's getting the jump on a surveillance bot or a would-be attacker.

Find them with Detection, identify them with Panoptic Vision, and attack them with one of my Evil Eyes.

If it looks like a particularly troublesome opponent, I can just replace attacking with fleeing via Teleport.

Frankly, it'd be pretty tough for an enemy to get near me at this point.

Detection can even sense the signs of an approaching Teleport before it happens.

Sure, maybe a certain Demon Lord has managed to dupe me by moving so fast that Detection doesn't even have time to notice, but that's an exception, okay? A rare exception!

Besides, my Detection's range has improved a lot since then.

At this point, I would notice someone approaching even at demon-lord speed, I think!

Although whether I'd be able to get away in time is another story!

Come to think of it, I could just use the Demon Lord as a decoy while I run away.

But my Detection range is big, and my speed is high as hell, so I'm confident I could escape just about any opponent if I had to.

By the way, the reason that my Detection range improved despite it already being maxed out as part of the mega-broken skill Wisdom is all because I wasn't using Detection very well, turns out.

Actually, I guess the past tense might not be appropriate there. I'm still not using Detection to its max potential.

Detection is a crazy skill, containing all the Perception-type skills in one.

As a result, though, it's so high-performance I can't even process the information that's coming in all at once.

Just like how humans aren't really aware of every single thing in their range of vision, my brain subconsciously rejects seemingly unnecessary information, like the number of rocks on the side of the road.

In fact, if I don't do that, I get a headache from the surplus of information.

But as it turns out, the range is basically limited only to how much information I can process.

In other words, if I'm able to process more, my range expands to match.

But it's not as easy as it sounds.

My most obviously related skill, High-Speed Processing, is already maxed out. The only option left now is to raise my own innate processing power without relying on skills.

So I have to train my already skill-enhanced brain even further.

It's like telling an abacus master to get better at calculating!

That's not the kinda thing you can do in one day.

So I've been trying to unconsciously shut out any unnecessary details and focus on picking up only the most important information.

If I feel like it, I can check out the shut-out information, too, but it's tiring to concentrate that much.

Like right now, for instance. If I really wanted to, I could tell there's some kind of underground cave here.

Huh? An underground cave?

What's this doing here?

But right as I finally notice it, Mera steps onto the patch of ground right on top of the cave.

While enduring the pressure of the extra gravity that my Repellent Evil Eye is putting on him.

I can barely manage an "uh-oh" before Mera breaks through the ground and starts to sink.

The thin part of the surface above the cave couldn't take the extra weight.

The Demon Lord and company stop their reciting and turn around.

Peering down into the rubble, I can spot Mera, without a scratch on him.

With his heightened stats, falling into a hole doesn't hurt him at all.

But it's too early to be relieved.

I sense something approaching Mera in the hole.

An ant!

And not just any ant—this one is practically human size.

Turns out this cave is actually part of some ant-type monsters' nest.

One by one, they start coming toward Mera, the intruder who's busted into their home.

Still, these ants aren't particularly strong. Their stats barely break a hundred, so Mera could easily take them alone. Sure, there are a lot of them, but I think Mera can handle it.

Hmm. Maybe I should let him fight the ants alone so he can level up.

But before I can enact my master plan, one of the puppet taratects—Ael, who's sort of like the eldest sister among the spider siblings—hops right into the hole.

Ael is the most proactive of the puppet spiders and has basically become their leader.

Her tendency to act quickly means she also has a bad habit of stealing the spotlight.

Not to mention the tastiest cuts of meat whenever we're eating dinner!

In other words, she's my rival when it comes to mealtime.

But other than that, she's smart and dependable.

She's rushing to Mera's aid right now, for example.

...She *is* doing it to help him, not just because she wants the experience points, right?

Knowing how crafty Ael can be, it's totally possible.

Ael lands right on top a giant ant, crushing its head.

Then she unsheathes one of her swords with a slash, instantly slicing another ant in two.

Following Ael's lead, the other puppet spiders run over to the hole as well.

Riel and Fiel jump in right away, followed by Sael after a moment's hesitation.

Sael is the total opposite of Ael, a timid sort who's treated like the youngest sister.

It's a little worrying that she seems afraid to attack the ants, despite being far stronger than they are.

With that, the slaughter begins.

I mean, the puppet spiders are actually terrifying monsters with stats over a thousand each.

The ants' stats barely reach three digits, so it's no wonder they don't stand a chance.

Sael keeps making frightened noises as she fights, but it's only because she's freaking out, not because she's having any trouble.

The puppet spiders' blades shred through the ants in no time flat.

As a result, while Mera managed to draw his sword, he didn't even get a chance to use it.

The four puppet-spider girls high-five on top of the pile of ant corpses. It's insanely surreal.

I feel a little bad for Mera and his unused sword.

At any rate, I head into the hole to collect the ant corpses.

As I put the bodies away in Spatial Storage, I use Detection to check things out farther belowground.

This ant hole is way bigger than I thought. It's practically the size of a small dungeon.

The puppet spiders wiped out all the ants in the immediate area, but there are still plenty more deeper inside the nest.

Incidentally, these ant monsters are called efejicotes.

After a moment's thought, I realize that sounds similar to the bee monsters in the Great Elroe Labyrinth. Those were called finjicotes, if I remember correctly.

Ants and bees... I guess they're not dissimilar, but still, isn't that kinda weird?

While I mull over some pointless things, I keep using Detection farther and farther down.

And then I stumble something a little bit intriguing.

"That was unfortunate. You all right?"

"Yes, I'm fine, thank you."

"Oh good. Wanna come back up, then?"

Mera grabs on to the Demon Lord's dangled thread and starts climbing.

But I start walking down the path toward the ants' nest instead.

"Huh? Whiiite? Where're you going?"

Ignoring the Demon Lord's call, I keep making my way down the tunnel.

I can sense through Detection that the rest of the party is exchanging confused glances behind me.

But when I don't stop, they hurriedly chase after me.

"Hey, paaal? Can you hear me, White? Why're you going that way, huuuh?"

Don't talk to me right now. I'm trying to focus here.

Hrm. I still can't reach.

I'm too far away to tell exactly what it is.

I'll have to go farther down.

I use Earth Magic to create a hole that goes straight down.

This shaft leads somewhere different than the ants' nest.

I jump right in.

When I land, I'm surrounded by dozens of ants.

I can't exactly read ants' expressions, but they seem kinda surprised to me.

Using Cursed Evil Eye, I instantly finish off the ants.

Then, after quickly shoving the corpses into Spatial Storage, I make another hole going downward with Earth Magic.

Rinse and repeat.

At the bottom floor, I kill the queen and her bodyguard ants, but they're so weak compared to me that they're barely any different from the regular ants.

"What are you doing, White? I don't know if you should be randomly destroying ecosystems like this." The Demon Lord catches up to me, masking her confusion with a wry comment.

It's not like I particularly wanted to kill a bunch of ants, okay?

They just happened to be in the way, so I took care of them, that's all.

"Come on. Let's go back."

The Demon Lord tries to lead me back up, but I'm not finished yet.

My goal is still farther belowground.

I make another hole with Earth Magic leading below the queen's area in the bottom of the ant nest.

"Whaaat?"

Realizing that I'm going even farther down, the Demon Lord lets out an irritated groan.

Everyone else seems less fed up with me and more concerned that I've lost my marbles.

Either way, I ignore all of them and keep digging farther down.

As she follows me, the Demon Lord's face gets more serious. I guess she figured it out.

"White, isn't this..." Her voice is more urgent than before.

Noticing her sudden change in attitude, the others get more serious, too, presumably realizing that I'm not doing this for shits and giggles.

All I do is keep digging deeper into the ground.

The Demon Lord follows me without further comment, with Mera, Vampy, and the puppet spiders close behind her.

Then, after digging for who knows how long, I finally reach it.

There, quite a bit deeper than even the lowest part of the ants' nest, my destination comes into view.

"Wha...?"

As soon as she sees it, Vampy mumbles in awe.

I gotta admit, I get how she feels.

Because this is something you'd never expect to see here.

I use my Earth Magic to clear away the dirt that obscures it.

In front of us is a door.

A metal door, unlike anything I've seen in this world.

It might be possible to find metal doors elsewhere but none will ever be as perfectly crafted as this one.

This world doesn't have the technology to produce something so advanced.

Much less to install it somewhere so deep underground.

So there we stand, in front of a door that shouldn't exist.

Out of step with the current level of technology in this world.

The only civilization that could have made this is the one that has long since collapsed.

We've stumbled upon the ruins of something made by the ancient civilization the Demon Lord told us about, one that destroyed itself long ago.

3 Ancient Ruins Discovered!

So we're standing in front of this metal door.

Um... Now what?

I was so focused on burrowing down and finding it that I didn't really think about what to do once we actually got here.

To be honest, I kinda just want to go back up and forget it.

I mean, this definitely can't be a good sign, right?

Come on—think about it. The ruins of a supposedly lost civilization? When does that ever end well?

What, are we just gonna waltz on in there in search of adventure and/or hidden treasure?

No, thank you! That sounds awful!

Plus, these ruins somehow evaded my Detection.

The only reason I was able to find them in the first place is because I sensed some weird spot underground where my Detection didn't reach.

For whatever reason, maybe the materials it's made out of or whatever, I can't sense anything in this area with Detection.

That's what piqued my curiosity in the first place.

This is sketchy. This is reeeal sketchy.

What're these ruins even doing so far down in the ground in the first place?

Especially underneath this dragon-ruled wasteland!

The very existence of this old civilization is taboo in this world. If the dragons knew about it, they'd probably destroy it or something.

Since they haven't, that means even the dragons haven't found this place.

So it's somehow stayed hidden right in the middle of dragon territory for who knows how long.

Either the dragons are morons or these ruins are that well hidden.

I hope it's the latter.

Actually, no, I guess it's bad either way.

If it's the former, I'd be worried about the fate of this world, and if it's the latter, then we're in danger just by being here.

CLANG! In case this wasn't dangerous enough yet, the Demon Lord literally forced the door right open!

Of course she did.

Knowing the Demon Lord, she can't ignore the existence of these highly suspicious ruins.

Ugh, guess there's no getting out of this one.

Especially because an alarm started blaring the moment the door broke!

A loud *BEEEEP! BEEEEP!* echoes from within, unmistakably the sound of an alarm.

Ignoring the annoying noise, the Demon Lord walks right inside.

Ugh, I guess there's no turning back.

"All of you, be ready for anything."

"Miss Ariel, is this...?"

"Yep. Ruins from that ancient civilization. I didn't think anything like this was still standing, so we'll have to investigate. There's no telling what might show up in here, so be on your guard."

The Demon Lord leads the way, followed by Vampy, Mera, and the puppet spiders.

Left with no other choice, I walk in after them, passing through the broken doors into the ruins.

Weirdly, the inside is a corridor so clean and uniform, it doesn't seem right to call it ruins.

It's a very calming design, or at least it would be if it wasn't for that super-annoying alarm.

Wow, that alarm is really starting to get on my nerves.

Since it's going off, that means these ruins are still active.

These super-ancient ruins, hidden deep underground, are still running smoothly.

Where's it getting the energy for that, huh?

Ooh, I've got a really bad feeling about this.

As if to confirm my suspicions, the walls suddenly crack open, revealing long, thin cylinders.

Yep, those are definitely gun muzzles. Great! Just great!

Several of these peek out from the walls, all pointing right toward us.

In the next instant, a roaring sound fills my ears.

The muzzles are shooting fire—wait, no, that was the sound of the Demon Lord destroying all of them.

She used thread stretching from each of her fingers, manipulating the strands like whips to break all the gun barrels.

Her speed with the thread was so fast, I doubt anyone but me could see it.

Sure enough, Vampy and Mera are gaping in confusion, clearly unaware of what just happened. Looks like not even the puppet spiders could follow her movements completely.

Quietly, I canceled the spell I'd been preparing.

I could've destroyed them all, too, okay?

I only hanged back and let the Demon Lord handle this one, since she's the oldest, okay?

I didn't miss my chance because I picked magic and it takes too long to activate, okay?

I'm not mad that she stole the spotlight, okay?

Okay? Okay? Okay.

…All right, I should probably stop getting all worked up over nothing.

The enthusiastic greeting we just received proves only that there's something here that intruders aren't supposed to see. That was way too excessive for ordinary defense measures.

Yeah, I'm pretty sure my instincts were right on the money.

But unfortunately, it looks like we're going to have to confirm that anyway.

Noticing a relatively intact gun among the wreckage, I pick it up to take a gander.

It's heavy and looks a lot like a machine gun.

Since it's not operated by people, there's no trigger anywhere.

BANG! A shock hits my forehead, whipping my head backward.

Apparently, my fiddling caused it to misfire.

Since I have Suffering Nullification, it doesn't particularly hurt, but I can't help feeling humiliated for doing something so stupid and angry at the gun for causing the trouble in the first place.

"What're you doing, White?"

The Demon Lord is staring at me, her eyebrows raised.

Dammit! She saw me do something so cringe!

At first, I was worried Vampy would laugh at me, but she's too preoccupied with staring at me, her mouth wide-open, shocked that I'm fine after getting shot.

Oh. Yeah, I guess that makes sense.

Last time, she saw Potimas turn me into Swiss cheese, so she must be wondering why I'm all right now.

But the bullets worked on me then only because Potimas's mysterious barrier had lowered my defense. Normally, my defense is high enough that they'd bounce right off me.

Sure enough, when I put a hand to my forehead, there isn't even a scratch there.

Although it might've turned a bit red.

But that doesn't matter right now!

The problem is that this is a gun, exactly like I thought.

Guns are an ancient technology that should be totally lost to this world.

Now we know for sure these ruins belong to an ancient civilization and that they're dangerous enough to kill intruders at the drop of a hat!

Good job, me! I was right! I was right, dammit!

To make matters worse, the bullets that gun fired weren't real, physical bullets.

They were made of some weird glowing energy, like the ones Potimas used.

These rounds certainly weren't as strong as Potimas's, but I have to assume they were made with similar technology.

Peering at the Demon Lord, I see that she's frowning, probably reaching the same conclusion as I am.

"Let's head inside."

I very reluctantly nod in agreement.

We continue walking down the corridor, which is way too modern to belong in this world.

We're keeping an eye out for any guns that might suddenly come out of the walls and whatever else might lurk in here, of course.

The Demon Lord is in the lead, followed by Vampy and Mera, who are flanked on either side by the puppet spiders, and I'm bringing up the rear.

This formation is set up to protect the baby bloodsucker and Mera, who aren't as battle-ready as the rest of the group.

That way, as long as nothing totally insane happens, we should be able to protect them.

As we proceed down the very long hallway, we reach a dead end.

But the wall here has strange gaps in the ceiling, the other walls to the side, and even the floor.

It's only touching the four corners of the hallway, and if you look closely, there seem to be rails of some kind there.

I poke around, wondering if there's a hidden door, but I can't find anything of the sort.

But there's no way this is the end. I bet the ruins continue behind this weird wall.

After a similar examination, the Demon Lord murmurs as if she's noticed something.

"Hmm? Maybe it's one of those?"

With that, she draws back her fist and punches the wall with all her might.

BOOM.

Her fist goes right through the wall, opening a huge hole.

Then she grabs the sides of the new hole, prying it open further.

You're outta control, Miss Demon Lord.

Well, this isn't a game, so it's probably fine to break the wall down and proceed, I guess.

Peering inside the hole, I see a small room on the other side.

There are no doors on any of the walls.

But for some reason, there is a door on the ceiling. Not only that, but it looks like an elevator door.

In fact, there are up and down buttons next to the door, so that's definitely what it is.

Huh? An elevator?

I turn around, looking back at the hallway we've been walking through.

Mentally, I compare its length to how deep underground these ruins are.

Yeah, it's about the same distance.

If you stood this hallway up vertically, you'd have an elevator to the surface.

That would explain why there's a door on the ceiling, too.

I'd been wondering how people ever got to these ruins from aboveground and back, but I guess they were probably able to use this elevator when needed.

Yep, yep, that makes sense... Wait, *WHAT*?

Is that seriously how this thing works? What about all the earth packed on top of it?

Did they use their ancient technology to dig through it somehow?

Every single time they wanted to enter or leave?

What kind of stupid gimmick is that?

If they could do that much, I feel like they should've been able to come up with a more effective method in the first place.

Although maybe there was a good reason for it at the time...

"Miss Ariel, is this an elevator?"

"Hmm, yeah, seems that way."

Looks like Vampy reached the same conclusion as I did, although judging by her face, she doesn't quite believe it.

Mera doesn't know what an elevator is, so he's just confused.

"This is a hidden elevator. They were rather popular when this civilization was around. They're normally buried deep underground, but they can be raised to connect to the surface when needed. They usually lead to a hidden subterranean base."

"What about all the dirt?"

"That's what's so crazy about these elevators. They can temporarily turn earth into mud. It's a stupid mechanism that wastes a ridiculous amount of energy, but...well, it is Potimas who came up with it, so that's more or less standard."

Potimas came up with these things...?

That explains a lot, but it also makes me even more convinced that these ruins are bad news.

A hidden base...? Is Potimas in here or something?

The Demon Lord goes inside the elevator and busts through the wall on the opposite side with the same method as before.

On the other side of the wall is a door—an exit to the elevator.

Once again, the Demon Lord pries it open with brute force.

At the same time, another alarm starts to blare.

Ugh, it's the same thing that happened before.

The Demon Lord ignores the alarm and steps through the door.

The rest of us follow her.

It's another corridor, similar to the one we just came down.

Unlike that one, though, it's kinda short; we reach the end quickly.

This time, instead of a wall, there's another door. This one is a double sliding door.

The Demon Lord walks toward it.

Then the door slides open on its own.

And here I was expecting the Demon Lord to force it open again.

The Demon Lord must have been thinking the exact same thing, 'cause she suddenly stops for a second.

Wait, no!

She didn't freeze because the door opened.

It's because there are countless inorganic eyes waiting on the other side of the door!

Tons of gun muzzles are pointed toward us.

This time, they're all being wielded by robots.

They're not humanoid cyborgs like Potimas's body double but simplistic robots that are more like basic weapons. There are more of them than I can count.

The only word I can think of to describe them is *weird*.

Each one has a single arm, which ends in a muzzle bigger than the ones we saw near the entrance. Then, there's a torso supporting the arm and continuous tracks that move it around. There's nowhere for a human to pilot it.

In fact, they're about the same size as a human, so the only way to "ride" one would be to wrap your arms around it and hope for the best.

Meaning they're self-propelled gun platforms, albeit not very large.

Anyway, these *hello, I am a weapon*–looking robots are lined up neatly in this huge room, all pointing their guns right at us.

Then, without warning, countless flashes of light erupt from their muzzles!

The shots streak toward us.

cause it's impossibly di
especially metal swords
one around with one ha
o, they use bamboo swo
body chooses to use two.
the puppet spiders, whos
ith one hand is no problem
te how cute they look, they'r
word style.

n't think any human swords
they trained. No waaay.

doesn't even look fazed as she t
This one's the efficient type, I thin
She's the kind who avoids pointless
Considering her shrewd personality
efficiency to make things as easy as po
Sael, on the other hand, is stressful t
Since she's so timid, she always freak
They're just dolls, so she doesn't real
I can already picture her shrieking *eek!*
Still, she's as strong as the other three
Now, Riel is nerve-racking to watch in
I mean, there's no telling what she'l
weirdo, so it's always hard to read her ne
Plus, sometimes she totally messes up.
I can't count the number of times I've
falling on nothing.
Generally, I catch her with my thread.
So even though it looks like she's figh
stressful to watch.
But Fiel is pretty scary herself.
Frankly, Fiel is totally reckless and const
She has a tendency to get carried away a
rying about the consequences. Even now, sh
the robots, leaving destruction in her wake.

Swinging her thread, the Demon Lord knocks them aw[ay]... least half the rounds.

…This demon lord's specs are kinda broken.

But even she can't completely block a constant stream of li[ght]... from dozens of robots, so a few stray shots come toward the[m]...

The puppet spiders take care of those with their swords, [...]

…This demon lord's underlings' specs are kinda broken, t[oo]...

Since the Demon Lord and the puppet spiders are blo[cking]... robots' attacks, I decide to go on the offensive.

But first, Vampy is flying into a panic because of all the [...] so I deliver a quick chop to her head to bring her back t[o]...

"Make an ice wall."

Figuring she can at least defend herself, I give her an order[.]... cade in front of her with magic.

The baby bloodsucker has the Water and Ice Magic skills,[...] a decent ice wall, it should be able to hold up against som[e]... attacks.

Luckily, she seems to understand what I'm saying, so she m[...] despite her tearful expression.

I have Mera take refuge behind the wall as well.

Both of them should be safe for the moment.

All right, now it's my time to shine!

The moment I think that to myself, the robots go flying all [...]

Looking back, I see that the Demon Lord is charging their f[...]

Whyyyy?!

Ahhh, maybe she decided to attack because the vampire d[...] secure.

She could've attacked at any time, I guess, but she was playi[ng]... so she wouldn't put the baby and Mera in danger.

Even as I process all this, the Demon Lord is already turni[ng]... into scrap metal.

Her thread is flying around like crazy, either smacking dow[n]... through the robots.

The Demon Lord's fighting style is very simple, but that on[ly]... even more powerful.

[...]nely high stats and maxed-out th[...]

[...]ong.

[...]etal robots are getting crushed and [...]

the first time I've actually watched the L[...]

[...]nishes everything in one blow.

[...]guess the best glimpse of her fighting style [...]

me?

[...]attle between Sariella and Ohts.

[...]e was using Gluttony to thwart all my attacks.

[...]ot using Gluttony right now, I guess she's [...]

[...]seriously overpowered.

[...]emon Lord crushes any robots within her reach, the p[...]

[...]ff any that escape her thread.

[...]sisters have deployed their hidden arms, so each of ther[...]

[...]ords.

[...]ff the robots' light bullets with their blades before cutti[ng]

[...]one smooth motion.

[...]ore robots fall to the floor, sliced neatly in half.

[...]ey cutting through these metal robots so easily?

[...]ppet spiders scatter in all four directions, beating down more

[...]Demon Lord is clearly dealing with the majority of the robots

[...]iders are still trashing a respectable amount.

[...]n Lord's strength is her sheer raw power; the puppet spide[rs]

[...]eir polished technique.

[...]all kinds of weapon skills at high levels, so while they're technic[al]

[...]look like master swordsmen as they slice the robots into ribb[ons]

[...]ntion that they're using six swords each.

[...]f "two-sword style" is cool in theory, but in practice it's prob[ably]

[...]elding two swords is actually allowed in kendo, but I'm a[...]

practically no one does it.

These robots are weak, so it's not a big deal right now, but I don't think it's smart to lose your head in battle like that.

Huh? Now that I think about it, do all of them except Ael have worrisome habits?

…Well, I'm sure it'll be fine. Maybe. Definitely. Probably.

Hmm. Thinking back on this journey, I have felt like I'm babysitting at times.

All of them, especially Fiel, like to climb on me and stuff.

Yes, my spider body is big enough to fit a child or two, but aren't these guys older than they look? Why do I have to babysit them like this?

Ael is the only one who doesn't try to ride me. Fiel just hops on whenever she wants, Riel climbs on me for no reason, and Sael shoots me puppy-dog looks like she's begging me to give her a ride!

Hmm? Hang on. Hasn't Ael ridden on me just once?

In fact, wasn't she the very first one to do it?

Huh?! Wait a second!

Did Ael deliberately give them the idea of climbing on me so I would have to deal with her sisters instead of her?!

I bet she did! That's exactly what that crafty little Ael would do!

Ooh, I can literally picture her saying *Just as planned!* with an evil look on her face!

Damn, Ael, you scary!

As I uncover a very alarming truth, the Demon Lord and company are making quick work of the robots.

Looks like I won't be getting a turn this time.

But it's only because these robots aren't worth the trouble, okay?

I'm letting the Demon Lord and her underlings take this one 'cause they're older, okay?

I didn't miss my chance because I waited too long for the right moment, okay?

I'm not mad that they stole the spotlight, okay?

Okay? Okay? Okay.

Listen, this place has gotta be some kind of armory.

Why else would so many stupid robots be in one place?

I glanced around again at the room full of robots.

It's about the size of a largish gymnasium, packed with robots from wall to wall.

The robots are moving now, since they're attacking us, but this must have originally been a storage room to keep the robots in a safe place, don't you think?

I mean, they were lined up very neatly at first. Obviously the Demon Lord has ruined that, but I think whoever put them here originally wanted to keep all the robots in one place.

In fact, I can see little pedestal mechanisms in the floor spaced out at regular intervals, the perfect size for holding a robot. Plus, there are cables sticking out of them that probably got unplugged when the robots moved.

These cables must have been providing the robots with power of some kind.

Let's just hope it isn't MA energy.

I realize that's probably exactly what it is.

Ancient ruins, connected to Potimas, with an armory full of robots.

With all of these unfortunate factors, I'd be more surprised if it *wasn't* MA energy at this point.

Guess I'll investigate those pedestals a bit.

But when I step forward to investigate, I immediately regret it.

As soon as I set foot from the hallway into the room, I hear a loud *CLANK* behind me.

Turning around, I see the walls on either side of the hallway opening up, and one robot emerges from each.

Hidden doors?!

The robots are right near Vampy and Mera.

They're protected in the front by the ice wall but totally unprotected in the rear.

Which means they're completely unprepared for a surprise robot attack from behind.

Finally, I get to be in the spotlight!

Since I've left the hallway, I'm a little far away, but at my speed, I can fix that in a matter of seconds.

I jump in between the robots and the vampire duo, ready to destroy the former.

Now I can really show off!

"Yaaaah!"

Oh. Looks like I spoke too soon.

Mera dashes forward with a shout, closing in on a robot.

Before it can fire its gun, he slashes at the muzzle with his sword, knocking it away.

The other robot aims its gun at Mera, but this one's muzzle freezes over.

It's Vampy's Ice Magic.

With the muzzle blocked, the energy inside has nowhere to go, and the frozen robot explodes.

Seeing this, Mera imitates the Vampy's moves and plugs up the first robot's muzzle, too.

He's naturally gifted with Water and Ice Magic, too, maybe because it's Vampy who turned him into a vampire.

His skill levels for those aren't quite as high as hers, but he makes up for that with his higher stats.

Frozen like the other one, the robot attempts to fire and explodes, too.

Nice. Very well done.

Mera used his quick thinking to aim the muzzle away in that first moment, and Vampy made a spot-on judgment to freeze the other robot.

On top of that, Mera realized he couldn't destroy the robots with his own strength, so he deliberately made it self-destruct.

Though it might be hard to tell from the way the Demon Lord and the puppet spiders are making quick work of them, these robots aren't actually all that weak.

In fact, from the perspective of a human from this world, they'd be damn strong.

If even one of those light bullets hit you, you'd end up with a breezy new air vent in your body just like that.

And since these robots can fire those powerful rounds in rapid succession, only an idiot would call them weak.

It's impressive that the bloodsucker duo managed to beat two of them without any help, even if they did get lucky by figuring out super fast how to make them self-destruct.

Really goes to show how much Vampy and Mera have grown.

Yep, yep. I believed in you guys!

I knew you could handle those robots without any help.

That's why I didn't get involved, okay?

I just wanted to give these two an opportunity to shine, okay?

I didn't miss my chance because I was too busy fantasizing about how cool I would look, okay?

I'm not mad that they stole the spotlight, okay?

Okay? Okay? Okay.

...Is it just me, or have I not done anything since we entered these stupid ruins?

The only thing I've accomplished is shooting myself in the face!

Uh-oh.

If I don't do something cool soon, my reputation will be down the drain!

Ugh, but at this point the Demon Lord and the puppet spiders have wiped out most of the robots.

If I jump in this late in the game, it'll probably be even more embarrassing.

I mean, I'm sure they're already wondering what the hell I'm doing, but that would just make it so much worse.

We can't have that, can we?

Yeah, it's better if I stay cool and don't do anything!

I'm the last line of defense.

I can't go wasting my time on every insignificant little enemy that shows up!

Panicking and leaping into action because the spotlight keeps getting stolen is waaay beneath me.

I'll be the bigger spider and let everyone else look cool for now.

Hmph! I won't swoop in until it's absolutely necessary.

It's the protagonist's job to come through in the most dramatic moment possible. Duh!

That's why I'm not gonna bother with these stupid little robots.

Heh-heh. Yeah. I'll just save my strength for a bigger, better fight.

Anyway, while I was standing around being a sore loser, it looks like the Demon Lord and company finished turning all the robots into a scrap heap.

A second later, one of the puppet spiders—Sael, the timid one—goes flying across the room with a loud *boom*.

Huh?

?! What the hell just happened?!

I turn my gaze to both Sael and whatever sent her flying. (Having lots of eyes sure is convenient at times like these.)

Sael is missing all three of her left arms and part of her torso.

That'd be a fatal wound for a normal person, but since the puppet spiders' real bodies are small spiders inside of dolls, it doesn't matter too much if the doll gets damaged.

It'll take a while to repair, but that's no big deal as long as the Sael herself is unharmed.

Although if the hit had been a little closer to the center, it's possible the spider body might've gotten hurt, too.

Sael must have dodged just in time, or else the culprit's aim was off.

Either way, I'm sure Sael was targeted only because she was the closest.

The attacker, emerging from a door on the other side of the room, can be described only as a tank.

It's covered in very strong-looking metal armor, has a giant gun that makes the robots look dinky by comparison, and its tank treads are crushing the ruins of the smaller robots beneath it as it slowly moves forward.

This thing looks strong.

In fact, it has to be strong to send one of the puppet spiders flying despite her high stats.

Look, I know I said I wanted the spotlight, but I never said I wanted a big, strong opponent.

file.20

TANK

HP

error / error

MP

error / error

SP

error / error

error / error

status

Average Offensive Ability : error
Average Defensive Ability : error
Average Magic Ability : error
Average Resistance Ability : error
Average Speed Ability : error

skill

error
error error error error error error error error error error
error error error error error error error error error error
error error error error error error error error error error

A weapon that was kept in the ancient ruins. Its official designation is the G-Tetra. It is equipped with a High-Powered Type-5 Light Cannon as its main gun and four High-Powered Type-3 Light Cannons as its secondary guns. Because its armor is constantly producing an anti-magic barrier, it is highly resistant to magical attacks. Most of its power is provided by MA energy, and since it can also extract that energy independently, it can function indefinitely as long as it is not destroyed. With a main gun that can destroy even thick ramparts and tank treads that can crush houses simply by advancing forward, it is essentially a moving fortress.

4 ANTI-TANK BATTLE!

The tank's giant muzzle points right at the fallen Sael.

It emits a flash of light.

If the robots were firing light bullets, this thing is firing light cannonballs.

The robots' bullets weren't too shabby in terms of speed and power, but this is way worse.

Even if the tank caught Sael by surprise, the fact that it was able to hit her and cause that much damage is concerning.

And now that she can't move, what happens if it hits her with another cannon shot?

Luckily, we don't have to find out.

By the time the tank's round hits the floor, Sael is gone, carried to safety by the Demon Lord.

She must have run over, picked her up, and carried her away faster than the missile could move.

The Demon Lord even took care to restrain her movement so Sael wouldn't be hurt. Otherwise, if she snatched her up while moving faster than a bullet, the aftershock alone might have rattled Sael to pieces.

How did she even prevent that from happening?

I guess it's another case of physical mastery going beyond even what stats can manage.

Unlike me, who got strong by fighting tons of battles over a short period of time, the Demon Lord has honed her strength over a very long period. That means she has that much more abilities and experience.

Strength that isn't reflected by stats and skills.

That's just one more way the Demon Lord outstrips me.

Hmph. Hmm. Hahhh.

Well, I guess the fact that she's stronger than me isn't exactly news.

What's most important here is that the Demon Lord saved Sael.

In that moment, she had several options.

For instance, she could have used Sael as a decoy and attacked the tank. With its sights fully on Sael, it was totally open to attack from anyone else.

If she'd given up on Sael, she could have easily gotten in a major attack on the tank.

But she didn't abandon Sael.

She chose to rescue her, even though it meant she risked getting hit by the light missile herself in the process.

That says a lot about the Demon Lord.

It also says a lot about the person who did decide to abandon Sael and focus on attacking the tank: me.

A single Black Spear closes in on the tank, produced by my Black Magic spell.

Right as the Demon Lord moved to rescue Sael, I focused on destroying the tank.

Using Sael as a decoy.

That's the difference between the Demon Lord and me.

She thinks of other people, while I worry only about keeping myself out of danger, even when it meant giving up on Sael.

But in this case, it meant we were able to do both, so maybe it worked out.

The Black Spear pierces the tank's side, which is utterly undefended after firing a shot.

Wait, no.

It disappeared as soon as it hit the tank's armor.

My Black Spear is gone so fast, it's like it was never there in the first place.

It only looked for a split second like the spear had pierced the tank because it disappeared so completely and naturally that I assumed it must've gone right through.

Is that the same mysterious barrier Potimas used?

As I'm about to launch another spear so I can find out, the tank turret turns toward me with a loud whir.

I retreat right away, and a light cannon round slams into the ground where I was standing mere moments ago.

Yikes, that was close.

It's so hard to read this tank's movements that I almost ate a direct hit to the face.

Uh-oh. I can't see what the tank's going to do next.

My Future Sight skill doesn't seem to work on it.

Since I'm used to being able to predict my enemy's next move with this skill, it takes me that much longer to react when I can't rely on it.

The only foe I've ever had this problem with was Potimas.

Which means this tank is definitely using the same kind of barrier as Potimas did.

Crap. This is gonna be an even bigger pain than I thought.

Having to deal with a bunch of robots at once already seemed annoying, but now there's this giant weapon on top of all that?

See, I told you ancient ruins were never good news!

Is this my divine punishment for stupidly wishing I could get a chance in the spotlight?

If so, whatever god is responsible has a nasty sense of humor.

Oh wait. I happen to know an evil god who matches that exact description.

Damn you, D! Is this your doing?!

As I pointlessly shout at that evil god in my mind, I shot another Black Spear at the tank.

As soon as it reaches its target and makes contact with the armor's surface, it disappears, just as I feared.

I can activate my magic perfectly fine. The barrier must not cover this whole space.

Potimas's mysterious barrier was crazy effective, rendering most skills and stats totally useless within a certain range.

Maybe the tank is using a similar kind of barrier, but it works only in very close proximity to the tank.

Otherwise, I wouldn't be able to use magic at all.

Still, since it's totally nullifying my Black Spears without a problem, it's probably safe to assume that most of my long-distance attack methods are useless here.

With its ease of use and high power, Black Spear is one of the most useful of my beloved Dark-type spells.

The only spells I have that are stronger than this are Abyss Magic and stuff like that.

Those spells take time, even with my Height of Occultism skill, and I don't even know if they would work.

It's probably best to assume they wouldn't and forget about magic for now.

Which means I have only one option: a physical beatdown.

Whether it's Potimas's magic barrier or whatever else, the best way to deal with these anti-magic-barrier jerks is to hit them with raw power.

As I dodge the third light shot, I produce my weapon from Spatial Storage: a white scythe with a very sinister aura.

I made this scythe when I decided I wanted some kind of weapon for close-quarters combat.

Believe it or not, it's actually crafted from part of my own body.

I used the scythes that make up the front legs of my spider half as the base, then used my other legs and thread to whip up this little number.

It feels like an extension of my body, probably because that's what it's made out of. And since my stats are so high, it's super-sturdy and cuts like a dream.

The only problem is that it's been letting off this weird aura for a while now.

Maybe it's just my imagination, but it definitely looks like the whole scythe is emitting some kind of black glowy effect.

By the way, the scythe's Appraisal results look something like this:

<White's Scythe
Attack: 14,899
Resistance: 99,999
Special Traits: [Automatic Growth] [Automatic Repair] [Rot Attribute] [Dark Attribute]>

Yeah. Is that weird or what?

Its attack obviously means how strong it is as a weapon.

That means this scythe alone is strong enough to cut right through the puppet spiders' defenses.

And resistance measures how strong an attack would have to be to damage it.

That means it won't break unless it's hit with an attack higher than that number.

In other words, the only way to break this scythe is by hitting it with the max amount of damage.

In other words, it's basically unbreakable.

However, that number will go down whenever it's hit with an attack, so I have to be careful... Or at least, I would with an ordinary weapon.

But this scythe also has a special trait called automatic repair. It's a useful trait that recovers its resistance over time, all on its own.

As long as it has this trait, I don't have to worry about the resistance going down.

And that resistance is so high that nothing short of a max-damage attack would break it.

It's the unbreakable scythe, dude.

I gotta admit, that's kinda weird.

I know I used my own body to make it, but even I don't have such crazy-high defense, y'know?

And that's not the only thing that's weird.

Since when does it have the Rot and Dark attributes?

It didn't have anything like that when I first made it.

These attributes must be what's causing the creepy aura.

Yeah, this is weird, all right.

And it even has this weird automatic-growth trait now.

In fact, that must be what's causing all the other strange stuff, huh?

When I first made it, its attack and resistance weren't this high, and it didn't have any of those weird traits.

But at some point, it gained this automatic-growth thing, and now the scythe's stats and traits have been increasing at random.

They say that when you use materials from a strong monster to make something, it sometimes ends up having a piece of that monster's power.

But it's supposed to be only a piece, like the faint remnants of the monster.

A weapon shouldn't randomly be growing on its own.

The only explanation I can think of is that maybe it's the effect of Pride.

Pride is a cheat-like growth-enhancement skill, after all.

If this weapon somehow inherited that…well, it would explain a lot.

There's something else that worries me, though.

It sure would be nice if this weapon was strong because I made it out of my own parts, but that seems almost too convenient, so I can't help but suspect that someone else was involved.

Namely, a certain someone who gave me the cheat skill called Wisdom.

Yeah. D would do that.

Knowing that self-proclaimed "evil god," I could just imagine D handing out an ultra-strong weapon just because it would be amusing.

That would certainly explain why it's so incredibly high-powered.

Still, it's not like I have any proof of that, and it hasn't caused any trouble for me so far.

But come on, this evil aura totally makes it seem like a cursed weapon!

Hrm.

Is this scythe actually going to work on that tank?

It's got the Rot attribute, but that's the attribute that controls death, and a tank isn't a living thing.

As I stand around contemplating this, the puppet spiders rush forward to attack the tank.

Aside from Sael, who's injured, the other three are charging from all sides.

And the tank's muzzle is still pointed at me.

Did they use me as a decoy?!

Well, I guess I can't blame them. I did the same thing to Sael earlier.

As the puppet spiders rapidly close in, the tank extends four arms to fend them off.

They're the same kind of gun arms I saw on the robots we wiped the floor with.

The guns start shooting light bullets.

Of the four, two fire at Ael, and the other two shoot at Riel and Fiel.

Though the tank couldn't have possibly known this, it was smart to focus its fire on Ael, who's basically the eldest sister of the puppet spiders.

Even Ael has no choice but to stop when two guns are shooting at her, fending off the shots with her blades.

It's still kinda impressive that she isn't taking a scratch, though.

While Ael is keeping those two arms occupied, Riel and Fiel work their way closer to the tank while blocking and dodging its shots.

Clearly one arm each isn't enough to stop them.

Next thing you know, their swords swing at the tank's armor.

There's an unpleasant metallic CLANG as the swords clash against the armor, sending sparks flying.

But that's it.

The swords cut through those robots easily, but they aren't working on the tank's outer defenses at all.

Forget slicing any part of the tank to ribbons. At most, they can leave only a tiny scratch.

Having thrown their full weight into the charge, Riel and Fiel are forced to pause for a second as their attacks are blocked.

The tank wastes no time in taking advantage of that opening.

With a loud grating noise, it rotates like a giant top, sending Riel and Fiel flying.

Luckily, they react quickly enough to push off the hull, adjusting themselves in midair and landing safely on their feet.

However, the tank isn't done.

It keeps spinning as it charges toward Ael, who's stopped in place.

Plus, its arms start firing off light bullets in all directions as it spins!

What an aggressive tank!

The indiscriminate barrage forces Riel and Fiel to fall back.

Ael retreats, too, but the tank stubbornly pursues her, so she can't put much distance between them.

Geez, that tank is a total stalker.

A stalker that sends bullets flying everywhere and rotates at high speed while it chases you?

Worst stalker ever!

Okay, this is no time for jokes.

While the three puppet spiders are keeping the tank occupied, the Demon Lord brings the injured Sael to a safe place.

Namely, the hallway we came through earlier, where Mera and Vampy are holed up.

But she'll be back on the front lines soon. Knowing the Demon Lord, she could topple that tank no problem.

As long as the puppet spiders buy some time for her, I'm sure the Demon Lord will destroy the tank without me having to lift a finger.

But we already know the tank's main gun can bust through the puppet spiders' defenses.

If something goes wrong, it's possible one of them might die.

…I guess I'll save them so the Demon Lord will owe me one.

As far as I can tell, I should be fine as long as I keep an eye on that main gun.

Scythe in hand, I break into a run.

Up the wall I go.

For a spider like me, wall running is a piece of cake.

In no time flat, I've climbed all the way up to the ceiling.

I run upside down along the ceiling until I'm directly above the tank.

Then I release my grip and free-fall.

As I'm getting ready to swing my scythe at it from above, the tank's turret whips toward me.

Whoa, so you've got anti-air capabilities, too, huh?

A light shot comes flying toward me, and I immediately fend it off with my scythe.

The scythe slides right through the shell with a sound that can be described only as *shiiiiing*, splitting it perfectly in two.

Whoa! I gotta admit, I'm as surprised as you are.

I didn't think that was gonna work, to be honest.

Not only that, but the two pieces of the shell suddenly lose their momentum and scatter into nothing.

The main gun that fired the cannonball is totally defenseless now, so I slice at it with my scythe.

The scythe cuts through the gun like butter, and it even keeps going, piercing into the body of the tank.

And since the tank is still spinning, it basically slices itself up on the scythe, turning into bits of scrap.

All that's left are lumps of metal that look like a toy that someone tossed into a blender.

On top of that, the chopped-up bits of tank silently fade into dust.

It's exactly like when I hit something with a Rot Attack.

Whaaaat? I thought the Rot attribute was all about death.

Why would it work on a nonliving thing?

And wait, what happened to the barrier that surrounded the tank's armor?! Why was I able to cut through it like that?!

Seriously, what is going on here…?

Well, uh, okay. I took care of the tank before the Demon Lord came back, and I got to have the spotlight for a bit, so I guess all's well that ends well.

Yeah. Let's not think too deeply about what just happened.

"Well, that was something…"

The Demon Lord looks at the pile of dust that was once the tank, her expression tense.

Even the puppet spiders look creeped out.

Come on—I just saved your asses. Do you really have to make that kind of face?

Wait a minute. The puppets' expressions don't change on their own. Does that mean they deliberately moved the thread around just to make these faces?

No waaay.

Behind the Demon Lord, Vampy peeks in from the hallway.

Glancing around, she confirms there's no immediate danger and steps inside.

Mera follows behind her, carrying Sael on his back.

Sael is still missing all three of her left arms, plus a decent chunk of her abdomen.

She can't seem to move her left leg, either.

Since the puppet spiders control their doll-like bodies with thread, they can't move their limbs if the thread attached to them is broken.

It's sort of like the motor nerves in humans. The thread Sael used to control her left leg must have snapped, so now she can't walk.

Otherwise Vampy probably wouldn't let Mera carry another girl like that.

I guess even she can put aside her jealousy in an emergency situation.

"Hmm. This place is worse than I thought. Since Sael's been injured and all, maybe Sophia and Merazophis should head back to the surface."

Not one person objects to the Demon Lord's statement.

Ah, not that any of us is a person to begin with.

Putting jokes aside, if there are any more weapons like that tank in here, Vampy and Mera would only hold us back.

Neither of them are weak by this world's standards, but it still took both of them to fight one or two robots.

They wouldn't stand a chance against a large group of robots, never mind another tank.

Even the puppet spiders were having trouble against that tank.

The ruins continue past this room, through the door the tank emerged from.

Since there's more to see, that means we have to keep investigating.

It would be best if Mera and Vampy went back to safety along with Sael.

But just as we all decide that, the earth shakes as if in protest to our decision.

This is one big quake.

The Demon Lord and I stay standing as if nothing happened, but the vampiric duo winds up falling to their hands and knees. Even the puppet spiders are wobbling as they try to stay balanced.

Then an alarm starts blaring.

The previous alarm had been going off this whole time, but with the addition of this new one, the noise is truly eardrum shattering.

If that wasn't ominous enough, red lights start flashing all over the place.

"Yikes. This can't be good, huh?"

Yeah, no kidding.

My danger senses are flying off the charts.

"Forget what I said before. Let's all get out of here!"

With that, the Demon Lord scoops up Vampy and Mera under each arm and makes a break for the hallway.

The puppet spiders take off after her, still a little shaky on their feet.

I bring up the rear.

We dash through the hall, through the hole in the elevator, and back into the long hallway.

The moment we get that far, there's a particularly large tremor and a loud *boom*.

The sound clearly came from behind us, so I look over my shoulder.

A wall of flame is rushing toward us at an alarming speed.

Uh-oh. This is bad.

Making a snap judgment, I charge right into the puppet spiders in front of me, wrapping my arms around them.

The impact lowers their HP a little, but there's no time to worry about that right now.

I race down the long hallway at full speed.

Faster than the flames closing in on us!

Speeding along the hallway, I burst through the busted door and start climbing the holes I made back to the surface.

In front of me, the Demon Lord is escaping even faster than I am, so maybe she's using her full speed, too.

Our bodies bump against the sides of the cramped tunnels, but that doesn't matter.

I sure wish I'd made these things bigger, though!

I keep climbing the tunnels I'd dug before until I reach the ants' nest, then keep speeding toward the surface.

All I'm thinking about is moving forward, trying not to focus on the heat licking at my back.

As I hear the ants' nest collapsing behind us, I finally see the light of the surface!

Aaaalmooooost theeeeere!

I jump out of the hole so fast, I can almost hear a popping sound effect.

Then I keep sailing up in the air.

Whew, we made it!

Before I can breathe a sigh of relief, the ground explodes.

A giant flame pillar shoots upward, barely missing my nose by an inch.

That was close!

If I'd been a second slower, we would've gotten roasted by that fire.

But my relief lasts for only a second.

Uh-oh.

In my arms, the puppet spiders are staring down in horror just like I am.

They're so surprised that they've forgotten to change their expressions.

And I can't say I blame them.

There's an even bigger flame pillar coming up below us, so huge it makes the previous one look like a joke.

The word "pillar" doesn't even seem like enough anymore. It's more like a solar flare.

It's like we're watching the end of the world.

The scene is so unbelievable that I almost don't even notice the heat pushing toward us.

Then I see something flying upward in the middle of the inferno, seemingly slowly but it must actually be flying into the sky at an astounding speed.

Once it's ascended, the flames settle down.

But that's not the end of it.

If anything, I get the feeling that our battle has just begun.

Something emerges from the remains of the flame.

I can describe it only as a gigantic UFO.

An enormous round flying machine, so huge that you would have to measure its length in miles.

That's what's calmly flying into the sky.

Close by, the Demon Lord mutters what we're all thinking.

"Unbelievable."

5 Unidentified Flying Objects Always Appear Out of Nowhere

Man, what the hell?

Seriously…just…what?

Hang on a minute.

Let me calm down a little.

How did things end up like this?

We randomly found some ancient ruins.

We explored them and got attacked by a robot army.

Then by a big, scary tank.

Things started getting sketchy, so we escaped from the ruins, then *boom!* Fire pillar.

And then, of course, this colossal UFO appeared.

Nope! Nope! Nope!

I still don't get it!

Seriously, what's going on?!

How? Why? What do we do?!

Help meeee!

As I fly into a total panic, I hear the sound of wings flapping closer.

"Hey, buddy! What's the big idea, you damn dirty spider chick?!"

A giant pteranodon-looking wind dragon flies up to the Demon Lord.

Of all the dragons that rule over this wasteland, this one's probably the strongest.

"We let you pass 'cause you said you wouldn't do nothin', but fat lot of good that did us! What's the deal?"

…Why is it talking like that?

Even through Telepathy, this guy totally sounds like a second-rate grunt.

C'mon—this is a dragon, though. I'm sure it's just putting on an act. Right?

"Better fess up, or things are gonna get ugly!"

"Oh? And what's a wind dragon possibly going to do to me?"

"I ain't stupid. I know I can't whoop you, spider! But if you lay a hand on me, the boss is gonna have a thing or two to say to you, got it?"

Ah. I see.

It really is just a lowly grunt.

As soon as the Demon Lord got a tiny bit threatening, its tail went between its legs.

Plus, it's totally hiding behind the authority of its so-called "boss."

Is that really okay with you, dragon?

I dunno, considering how Araba was and all, I thought dragons were proud, powerful beings as a rule.

This guy's totally ruining that image right now.

Ugh. I'm kinda getting bummed out by this.

"Oh yeah? All right, that's perfect. I have a feeling we might not be able to handle this thing alone. Go ahead and call Gülie, will you?"

"Wait, you for real, girlie? He could bump you off in one blow, y'know?"

"Yeah, yeah, just call him. Can't you see what we're up against?"

The Demon Lord points at the giant UFO.

Ah, so "boss" was referring to Güli-güli.

Right, I guess if a dragon was going to call for a superior, it'd obviously be Güli-güli.

"Of course I can, you palooka! What the hell is it anyway?!"

"That's what I'd like to know! You realize it was buried under this wasteland, right?! How could you not notice something like that was here?!"

"Huh?"

The wind dragon closes its mouth and looks down stupidly.

What are we gonna do?

This guy seems like a total moron.

I'm starting to wonder if the ruins were actually that well hidden or if it's just that the dragons here were too stupid to notice them.

"Listen up. I'm gonna explain really simply so that even your tiny little brain can understand. We happened to find some ruins hidden underground dating to an era before the system started operating, so we took a look around. And then that thing came out. Got it?"

Yeah, that was a brief summary, all right.

"I don't get it!"

And yet, the wind dragon is doing somersaults in the air to show how confused it is, or at least that it doesn't believe the story.

Honestly, it looks like a giant baby dinosaur throwing a tantrum.

This isn't gonna work.

"It doesn't matter! Just call Gülie already!"

Her patience running out, the Demon Lord gives the flailing wind dragon a light shove.

It looked fairly restrained, no more than a gentle prod, but due to the Demon Lord's crazy-high stats, it still sends the wind dragon plummeting downward.

"……"

The Demon Lord watches the wind dragon fall for a while, then turns back toward the UFO, utterly expressionless.

I guess she's just going to pretend that never happened.

No waaay.

That was ridiculous.

Okay, maybe she's right. We'd better get back to the problem at hand.

We'll just ignore the fallen wind dragon.

It's still got some HP left, so it's not dead, at least.

Right now, we have to figure out what to do about this UFO in front of us.

There's actually a decent distance between the weird floating craft and us.

But since the damn thing is so big, it messes with your sense of scale, so it feels like it's right under our noses.

That's how huge it is.

I can't help being impressed that something that big was somehow buried underground.

I guess that's what the heart of the ruins really was.

The robots and the tank were nothing but its defense force—this UFO is its ultimate weapon.

Frankly, the tank was enough of a pain for me, but this giant thing totally upstages it.

I kinda want to run away from reality, to be honest.

Quit busting out stuff that doesn't fit into a fantasy world!

Whose idea was this stupid giant UFO?!

It obviously doesn't work with this setting!

But complaining in my head won't change what's in front of me.

What are we going to do about this?

It almost seems like the kind of thing we can't do anything about to begin with.

"Erm, Miss Ariel? What are we going to do?"

Vampy voices my question for me, still in the Demon Lord's arms.

"Good question. I get the feeling even I would have trouble bringing that thing down. We might just have to wait for Gülie to get here."

That's a surprisingly meek statement from the Demon Lord.

But up against that thing, I guess even the Demon Lord falls short.

Something thuds against my chest.

Looking down, I see Ael struggling to get free of my arms.

Oh right. I guess I'm still holding them.

Riel and Fiel aren't moving, just staring at the UFO in shock.

This situation is so crazy, their minds might have frozen up entirely.

Of course Ael would be the one to come to her senses first, as the "eldest."

But I can't let go of her up here.

I tighten my grip, trying to send a message to her to keep still.

Ael tries to give me the puppy-dog eyes, but I ignore her.

There's no time for that now.

The UFO has sent something flying toward us.

At first, it looks like a swarm of insects. Like mosquitos or something.

But that's only because it's so far away. These things are actually way bigger than insects.

In fact, they're fighter planes that are around the same size as the tank from before, and they're zooming right toward us.

It looked like a swarm of insects because there are so many of them.

"Retreat!" the Demon Lord shouts.

Holding Vampy and Mera, who still has Sael on his back, the Demon Lord quickly dashes away in midair from the swarm of fighters.

I follow close behind her, of course.

I'm not fighting all those things!

And if they're the same size as that tank, does that mean they're about as strong, too?

We can't beat those!

No matter how strong the Demon Lord might be or how nearly immortal I am, none of that matters against this horrifying force.

Our only option is to run for our lives, without looking back.

The wind dragon?

Who cares!

Dragons should be able to take care of themselves!

Besides, I heard some kind of shriek behind me, then the panicked flapping of wings, so it's probably fine.

"Oh man, we're screwed."

"You said it. That thing's bad news, man. Real bad news."

Having shaken off the fighters that were tailing us, we finally catch our breath in a remote corner of the wasteland.

The wind dragon somehow managed to safely keep up with us, too.

Although its vocabulary has depleted so much that it's just saying "bad news" over and over.

"So? Did you call Gülie?"

"Oh."

The dragon looks away awkwardly.

It was probably so focused on fleeing that it forgot to call in its boss.

"Hurry up and call him already! This is exactly the kind of thing an administrator should take care of! Call him! Call him now!"

"All right already! Just quit wringing my neck, crazy lady!"

The Demon Lord is shaking the wind dragon back and forth by the neck.

I wish they'd drop the comedy act and just call him already.

As I shoot them a bland look, something tugs on my sleeve.

"Who is this 'Gülie' she's talking about?" Vampy asks, still with a slight lisp.

Normally she'd just ask the Demon Lord directly, but since the Demon Lord seems to be busy forming a comedy duo with the wind dragon right now, the baby's asking me instead.

Uhhh.

How do I explain this?

Gülie, who I call Güli-güli, the man in black.

If I try to explain who he is, I'm going to have to talk an awful lot.

I mean, he's an important figure.

Güli-güli is an administrator. In this world, that practically makes him a god.

He manages the system and makes sure the world is operating smoothly.

The UFO that just appeared is clearly an anomaly in said world.

In other words, it prevents this world from running smoothly, which means it's within an administrator's power to remove it.

A god like Güli-güli should be able to do something about this.

That's why the Demon Lord is demanding that the wind dragon summon Güli-güli.

Dragons are basically his underlings, after all.

They're like his on-site staff who keep things under control in various places.

So of course the wind dragon must have a way to contact its boss, Güli-güli.

We just need to get it to call in Güli-güli so he can take down the UFO lickety-split.

That pretty much sums up the information I have, but...can I actually explain all that?

I have absolutely no communication skills, so how am I supposed to get through that much talking?

Most of the time, I can barely manage a single word.

This is mission impossible here!

What am I gonna do? Huh?

I'm in trouble.

A different kind of trouble from our last situation.

I managed to run away from the UFO, but this time I have nowhere to run.

Vampy is gazing up at me with such pure eyes. I can't let her down... I can't... Or can I?

Wait, why should I have to explain such complicated stuff in the first place?

Can't I just push that responsibility off onto the Demon Lord?

I'm sure she'll explain things soon enough.

Explaining stuff like that is the Demon Lord's job. She's just busy with the wind dragon right now.

Yeah. That's it.

I don't need to take the most difficult pass through this.

All I have to say is, *Just ask the Demon Lord!*

But right as I'm working up the courage, somebody interrupts me.

"Could it be the black-clad gentleman who visited us one evening?"

Dammit, Mera! Why do you have to cut me off me like that?!

"What? When was that?"

"I believe it was shortly after we met the pontiff of the Word of God religion."

Thinking about it, Vampy nods slowly.

I'd forgotten. The bloodsucker duo actually met Güli-güli once.

It was after he showed up to tell me to stop my rampaging Parallel Minds.

"Oh, that's right. The person who just casually joined our group for an evening and then was mysteriously gone the next day?"

Looks like Vampy remembers him, too.

Güli-güli's a distinctive-looking dude, so it makes sense that he'd leave an impression.

And like the Vampy said, he just randomly started drinking with us that one time; then he was totally gone the next day.

"It seemed as though Lady White and Lady Ariel already knew him. May I ask who he is, Lady White?"

Oof! Now Mera's coming after me, too!

Why does everybody have so many damn questions for me today?!

I mean, I guess I can't blame them for being curious about who the Demon Lord would depend on for help in this situation, but still.

Ask her, not me!

"A god."

This was becoming more and more of a pain, so I gave the shortest, most arbitrary answer.

Of course, that only left the bloodsucker duo even more confused, but I don't feel like explaining any more than that.

"That doesn't tell— What?"

Vampy starts to press for more information, but Ael stops her, sensing that my irritation meter is getting high.

For whatever reason, the puppet spiders are better at gauging my feelings than the vampires in our party.

I don't know if it's because they're spiders like me or if it's simply their animal self-preservation instincts, but when my mood starts to sour, they tend to sense that and stop bothering me.

I guess they understand that I prefer being alone.

Ael must have put a stop to this conversation because she noticed my mood, but apparently Vampy isn't amused.

She gives Ael a pouty glare, but the puppet spider ignores her.

I can't blame her for not being scared of an angry baby.

Man, though, leave it to the eldest sister of the puppet taratects. She's great.

I guess I don't mind letting her sneakily steal the spotlight once in a while.

Leaving Ael to take care of Vampy, I go to check on Sael instead.

She's lying on the dusty ground, attended to by Riel and Fiel.

With her three arms and part of her torso still completely gone, it's painful just to look at her.

The left side of her abdomen has been blown away, so her left leg isn't working, either.

But while it might look bad, her actual spider body isn't injured at all.

The puppet spiders' outer bodies are just that, after all: puppets.

As long as the small spider within is unharmed, they can just fix their puppet bodies if they get broken.

But I put a lot of hard work into their puppet bodies.

Since I took such great pains to make sure they looked as close to humans as possible, I can't remake those limbs in a single night.

But in this situation, Sael not being able to fight is a problem, too.

We don't know what's going to happen next, so at the very least, she ought to be able to protect herself.

Just look at the fight against the tank. Since Sael was injured, we lost our biggest powerhouse, the Demon Lord, while she was bringing Sael to safety.

No opponent is going to miss an opportunity like that.

I don't want anybody dragging me down.

It's not like the puppet spiders are weak. Their stats are all over a thousand, making them obscenely strong monsters from any normal perspective.

But in this case, they aren't well suited to this particular battle.

I don't think the puppet spiders could have beaten the tank alone.

Their swords were getting deflected, and magic wouldn't work because of the mysterious barrier.

But the tank's main gun easily blew through the puppet spiders' defenses.

They couldn't have won that fight.

The tank was so strong that even the powerful puppet spiders were just holding us back.

If we have to fight something like that again, I'd like them to at least be able to stay out of my and the Demon Lord's way.

If nothing else, I need to get her back to a functional level.

It's not going to look pretty.

That bothers me aesthetically, since it's like slapping a half-assed touch-up over my delicate masterpiece, but this is an emergency measure.

I use Divine Thread Weaving to start working on Sael's missing parts.

As long as I don't get hung up on appearances, I can restore her functionality from before she was injured in just a few minutes.

As I'm working on fixing Sael up, I sense a warp in the air nearby.

It's a sign that someone is about to Teleport here.

But who?

Güli-güli? No, it's not him.

Güli-güli's teleportation is a lot cleaner than this. His runes are so precise, I can't help admiring them.

But the warp I'm sensing right now isn't clean at all.

Frankly, the runes are a lot cruder than mine, even.

It can't possibly be Güli-güli.

Who is it?

A certain mechanical elf appears in the back of my mind.

For now, I stop working on Sael and get ready for battle at a moment's notice.

Then two men arrive via Teleport.

…Who are these guys?

One is a very suspicious-looking fellow whose face is covered with a cloth, probably the one who did the Teleport spell.

The other is an old man wearing fancy-looking priestish robes.

This is shady.

The first guy seems suspicious because of his getup, but the second guy seems suspicious, too, because he's so out of place here.

I Appraise the two of them right away.

To very surprising results.

"Forgive us. I must apologize for appearing in front of you so suddenly, but this seems to be an emergency situation."

The old man smiles so gently, it practically calms down the whole wasteland.

He looks like such an affable geezer that it'd be easy to let my guard down, but I definitely can't do that.

Because the only result I got from this old man when I Appraised him was <Appraisal Blocked>.

That means this guy must be a ruler with at least one Seven Deadly Sins or Seven Heavenly Virtues skill.

And I have a feeling I might know which one.

"Dustin. What is the pontiff of the Word of God religion doing here now of all times?"

The Demon Lord confirms my suspicions: This guy is the leader of the biggest religion in this world.

The other guy must be a guard whose role is to transport the pontiff via Teleport and protect him.

The Demon Lord looks at the old man—the pontiff—with an intense glare.

"This busy time is exactly why I made haste to come here. You may not like this, but could we perhaps call a temporary truce in order to deal with this threat?"

As the pontiff makes this proposal, I notice him glancing briefly at Vampy and Mera.

I guess I have heard about this guy. The others ran into him while I was dealing with my rampaging Parallel Minds.

So the pontiff is this old man?

The Word of God religion stands in direct opposition to the Goddess religion, which is worshipped by the people of Sariella, the location of the bloodsucker duo's hometown.

Since this old man is the head of that religion, he's the guy who gave the order to destroy Vampy's town.

That means that, to the vampires, he's responsible for the deaths of their family and masters.

Since he appeared, Mera and Vampy haven't exactly looked thrilled, but they haven't said anything yet.

It seems like they're trusting the Demon Lord to take care of things.

The Demon Lord glances at them and appears to pick up on that decision.

She nods briefly, then turns back to the pontiff.

"Oh yeah? I won't deny that things look bad right now, but what exactly do you think you can do by waltzing in here now? Against *that* thing?"

She points at the UFO floating in the distance.

"Anything I can do, of course. Surely we cannot ignore it."

"Hmm? Aaaanything, you say?"

"Just so."

The Demon Lord sounds jokey, but the pontiff nods with a deadly serious expression.

Luckily, I don't think anyone but Vampy and me noticed that she was joking.

The Demon Lord continues as if nothing happened. "Okay, but is there anything you *can* do about this? Even I get the feeling I'm kinda out of my league here."

The Demon Lord glowers at the UFO.

She's extremely powerful, but she's still just one individual.

I guess a single person can only do so much against a giant weapon that's probably out to slaughter everybody.

"I hate to say it after you came all this way, but I'm fairly confident our only option is to have Gülie take care of it."

I agree with the Demon Lord.

That UFO isn't the kind of thing any single individual can go up against.

Unless that individual happens to be a god.

It would be insane for the humans of this world to try to fight that giant thing.

"That is correct. This is a situation for me to deal with alone, not any matter for you to worry yourselves about."

A voice echoes through the air.

Moments later, I sense another warp in space.

That means he sent his voice ahead in a way that I couldn't even sense? This guy really is amazing with runes.

Another man teleports among us.

Clad in black armor, with black skin, black from head to toe.

Administrator Güliedistodiez.

One of the strongest beings in this world has made his appearance.

"There you are, boss!"

The wind dragon bows its head to Güli-güli.

This just makes it seem even more like a small-time grunt.

Man, dragons are supposed to be majestic, y'know?

"Thank you for informing me. Ariel, I am afraid you have been inconvenienced due to my own oversight. Let me take care of things from here."

Ooooh.

Now, that's a dependable guy.

I mean, gallantly showing up to rescue his underling? Is this guy a hero or what?

This makes me feel a little better.

If Güli-güli's saying he'll take care of it, that means he can bring that UFO down, right?

Then the Demon Lord and I just have to sit back and watch.

Whew. Thank goodness.

But right as I'm relaxing, there's another warp in space.

The third time today.

I have a bad feeling about this one.

And I mean a really, reeeally bad feeling.

Two more men appear by way of Teleport.

"Oh good. The rest of you are all here."

As soon as the first man appears, everyone else turns a murderous gaze toward him.

"Now, now, don't be so quick to anger. I've come to help this time."

An ordinary person probably would've passed out from all the hate being directed toward him, but this man just lets it roll right off him.

"Unfortunately, Güliedistodiez alone cannot take down this foe. As much as it pains me, we have no choice but to combine our forces."

I'm sure everyone else had the same thought: *It pains us a lot more than you.*

The man known as the patriarch of the elves, Potimas Harrifenas, takes a single graceful step toward us.

FIGHTER PLANE

HP

error / error

MP

error / error

SP

error / error

status

Average Offensive Ability : error
Average Defensive Ability : error
Average Magic Ability : error
Average Resistance Ability : error
Average Speed Ability : error

skill

error
error error error error error error error error error error
error error error error error error error error error error
error error error error error error error error error error

A weapon that was kept in the ancient ruins. Its official designation is the G-Tri. It is equipped with two High-Powered Type-4 Light Cannons as its main guns and two High-Powered Type-3 Light Cannons as its secondary guns. Because its armor is constantly producing an anti-magic barrier, it is highly resistant to magical attacks. Most of its power is provided by MA energy, and since it can also extract that energy independently, it can function indefinitely as long as it is not destroyed. It specializes in using high-speed flight to lay down deadly barrages.

The Demon Lord, the original taratect and strongest monster in existence to my knowledge.

The pontiff of the Word of God religion, the biggest religion in the world, who also holds ruler authority.

Güli-güli, who as an administrator is essentially a god in this world.

And Potimas, the patriarch of the elves, who wields technology supposedly lost in ancient times.

It's an impressive lineup.

Four of the most prominent figures in this world, all gathered in one spot.

But the atmosphere isn't exactly pleasant.

You can feel tension crackling in the air.

Some of our number, like Vampy and the puppet spiders, have already pulled back far away to escape the intensity.

Although I gotta say, it's a little disappointing that the wind dragon who supposedly rules this place joined their retreat.

Come on—you're a dragon. Don't run away.

I feel a little bad for the pontiff's guard and Potimas's aide, though.

They're both Spatial Magic users, so they must be here for transportation and protection.

But they hardly have any other skills, maybe because Spatial Magic costs so many skill points.

I've only ever seen one other Spatial Magic user, the mage I've run into a few times, but these guys are way weaker than he is.

Frankly, I don't think they're qualified to be guarding these people.

It looks like they have no choice but to just stand here in this horribly awkward face-off. They must feel like their life spans are draining away.

I mean, they are guards, technically speaking.

So of course they can't run away.

Honestly, I'm starting to feel pity and even empathy for them.

Why, you ask?

Because the stupid Demon Lord isn't letting me run away, either!

I tried to leave with Vampy and company, but she said, "White, you're with me," and stopped me with a big smile on her face.

Why am I getting tossed into this meeting of the minds?

I don't get it.

As a compromise, I've got Sael with me.

C'mon—she's injured, so I *have* to fix her.

She can't do it without me, so I'm working on that while I listen in.

Besides, I have to do something or I'll go crazy from all the tension!

Since I dragged her into this, Sael's been sitting there stiffly with the expression of a dead fish.

Seriously, you've never seen a puppet with eyes this clouded.

"Well? What do you mean, Gülie can't do it alone? In fact, what are you even doing here? Did you finally decide to show your face so I can kill you or what?"

The Demon Lord tosses a match into the powder keg.

"Don't be so hard-hearted. I only happened to see something interesting while I was monitoring you people, so I decided to come by. I figured you'd need me to deal with this situation anyway."

Brushing off the Demon Lord's murderous glare, Potimas flicks his hair back with a melancholic expression.

Did he just casually admit that he's been spying on us?

Well, there are a few surveillance bots in my Detection range right now, so I guess that's not too surprising.

But has he been watching us from outside my Detection range somehow, too?

With Panoptic Vision, maybe?

But Panoptic Vision is a skill, so I feel like that would register on Detection, too.

Wait, was he using some physical means like a telescope or something?

Hrm. I guess I wouldn't be able to detect that.

There were times when he seemed to lose track of us, so I'd like to think he hasn't been watching us around the clock, but there's no way to be sure.

Besides, there's someone else here who's probably been monitoring us, too.

I steal a surreptitious glance at the pontiff.

He might look like a kind, harmless person, but considering the timing with which he arrived here, he was almost certainly keeping an eye on us.

Otherwise, how would he show up right after that UFO thing appeared?

The elves and the Word of God religion… I guess two major groups have been spying on us, then.

Maybe I can report them as stalkers to the police?

Oh, I guess there isn't any police in this world, huh? Riiight.

"Look at this."

Reaching into his breast pocket, Potimas produces a spherical, palm-size object.

There's a round hole in the center of the ball, which starts emitting light that projects a three-dimensional image into the empty air.

Ooooh! Now, that's pretty futuristic.

I get excited for a second, but that lasts only until I take a look at the image.

It's unmistakably a projection of that UFO.

"What is this?" Güli-güli asks, sounding perplexed.

"Can't you tell?" Potimas responds coolly. "It's the schematics of that floating weapon, code name 'G-Fleet.'"

Wait a second.

Why the hell do you have that?

"Why in the world do you have such a thing?"

The pontiff voices my question out loud.

"Do I really need to spell it out for you to understand?"

Potimas simply sneers mockingly at the pontiff and gives no further explanation.

I could swear I see a little vein popping on the pontiff's placid face.

You can practically hear the air crackling as the tension reaches a breaking point.

Hmm. So my guess was right, then?

This elf bastard must be the one who developed that UFO!

Otherwise, why would he have the schematics for a weapon that's clearly supposed to be top secret?

Why would you make something like this, man?!

"So this whole mess is your fault, then."

The Demon Lord takes a long, slow step toward Potimas.

"Do not rush to conclusions," Potimas responds calmly, practically rolling his eyes. "Yes, I created the plans for it, but I did not create it. In fact, I did not even know it had been made until now. Otherwise, why would I come all the way here?"

Somehow, his attitude seems to imply that anyone who would fail to understand such a basic fact and recklessly attack him is nothing but an annoying fool.

The Demon Lord seems to sense that he's mocking her, too; she's smiling like always, but it doesn't reach her eyes.

I imagine a grating noise as the air gets even heavier.

"Long ago, I gave the schematics to a certain nation in exchange for funding and supplies for my research. I thought they would simply use parts of the designs to create other weapons, but I never imagined they would actually build it to completion like this."

He heaves a deep, heartfelt sigh.

The rest of us stare at this uncharacteristic state in confusion.

"Who would develop a thing like that? It's simply not realistic. I wasn't even completely serious when I created those plans. Frankly, it's nothing short of shameful to see it take form like this."

Apparently, Potimas has his own unique standards.

To him, the existence of that UFO is...an embarrassment, I guess?

I don't get it.

But, well, I can see why he would say it's not realistic to actually make that UFO.

I mean, look how huge it is.

That must have made it crazy difficult to create.

Even on Earth, building something that colossal would take an unthinkable amount of time and money.

How many hours did it take to make that several-miles-long UFO?

Not to mention, when it was finally finished, they buried it deep underground without even using it, only to bust it out randomly so many years later? What a massive, confusing pain.

"So that is why you intend to assist us?" Güli-güli asks, but Potimas shakes his head.

"No. That is only my personal feeling on the matter. I have another reason to help: If we leave that thing to its own devices, it could very well destroy the planet. Obviously, even I wouldn't be thrilled about that."

Sorry, what?

Did he just casually say something about destroying the planet?

Seriously? Is this UFO really that dangerous?

"Is that true?" Güli-güli asks dubiously.

"Sadly, it is the truth. I would be much happier if it was a joke." Potimas almost looks meek. "The G-Fleet itself does not have that much destructive capability. The problem is the bomb that is most likely loaded on board."

Potimas touches the ball in his hand that's displaying the 3-D schematics.

The projected image changes into a new object: a sphere.

It's a small ball, not much different from the projection device Potimas is currently holding in his hands.

"The GMA bomb. The more MA energy it is filled with, the more powerful it becomes."

Potimas's explanation is short and simple.

Everyone reacts to the phrase "MA energy"—including me, of course.

"Hrm. And what is the difference between this bomb's minimum and maximum power?"

The pontiff looks at the image of the bomb thoughtfully.

"Hmph. Is there really any need to discuss its minimum power? That would mean its state when the bomb has no MA energy at all. It cannot run without fuel. In other words, it would not explode. Was that not quite obvious?"

Potimas's tone is obviously insulting.

Instantly, the pontiff's normally genial expression goes flat.

Crackle, crackle. There's serious electricity in the air now, and not in a good way.

"And its maximum power is as I just said. In the worst-case scenario, it could blow away this entire planet. However, that is only a theoretical maximum; it would be impossible to extract that much MA energy. According to my simulations, the damage would probably be limited to destroying this continent at the most. Although, that would really not be much different from the destruction of the planet."

Oh. Uhhh. Um.

Is this a joke?

No, Potimas isn't the type to make that kind of joke... So it's true, then? For real?

That UFO is carrying a bomb that could wreck this continent?

Well, shit!

This thing already seems like it could wipe out humanity without much trouble, but it's *also* got a bomb that could destroy this entire continent?!

Dude, this is even worse than I thought.

"Why do you believe it's equipped with this bomb?"

"That, too, is a schematic I gave to that nation. The plans for the G-Fleet, along with the plans for the GMA bomb. And the G-Fleet is designed to carry the GMA bomb. That way, if the G-Fleet has insufficient fuel, it can draw energy from the GMA bomb. Essentially, it is a backup fuel source. If these people went so far as to make the G-Fleet, I doubt they would leave out such a crucial component."

"I see."

In other words, the UFO is designed to work as a set with the bomb, so it's probably best to assume that it's got one on board.

"And according to my observations with a MA-energy measuring instrument, it is all but certain there is a GMA bomb on board."

Potimas looks at the UFO in the distance.

There's a way to measure MA energy?

And he's saying the results somehow confirm that the UFO has this bomb?

I guess it must have detected the MA energy being used by the bomb or something.

"Fortunately, it does not seem as if the G-Fleet is going to drop the GMA bomb right away. As you may imagine from the GMA bomb's power, the G-Fleet is only designed to drop the bomb from outer space, high enough that the G-Fleet will not be caught in the ensuing explosion. Since it has not ascending to that height, it is safe to assume that it is not actively attempting to drop the GMA bomb."

Well, if the designer of the damn thing says so, I guess he's probably right. Still, it's not exactly reassuring.

"However, it is possible that it will passively drop the GMA bomb."

Great. I knew I was right to still be nervous.

"There are several emergency situations in which the G-Fleet will eject the bomb. For instance, if the G-Fleet is shot down."

The damn thing self-destructs?!

I mean, I guess that's kinda poetic, but come onnn.

But now I can guess why Potimas came here so quickly.

If Güli-güli had unknowingly brought the UFO down, it would have dropped a bomb that might have destroyed the whole continent.

Bringing the UFO down apparently won't prevent the bomb from exploding, either.

So Güli-güli could have acted as an administrator to protect the world from danger, only to end up pulling the trigger that destroyed the world instead.

Yikes.

"You said 'several,' did you not? What are the other conditions?"

"If it enters a confrontation with a dragon."

Potimas's utterly casual response makes the rest of our expressions freeze.

"It was originally designed as a countermeasure against dragons, you see. Is that really so surprising?"

So if Güli-güli, the dragon boss, tries to attack it, it'll automatically drop the bomb?

We're screwed, then!

Hmm. Wait a minute, though.

Doesn't that seem a little too convenient?

"Is that really true, I wonder?"

The pontiff seems to have the same suspicions as I do.

He might look like a kindly old man, but the way he's glaring now, he could probably kill someone just by looking at them.

"If you doubt my words, why not find out for yourself?"

Potimas ignores the pontiff's glare, turning to stare at Güli-güli.

In response, Güli-güli closes his eyes, looking conflicted.

Is Potimas lying? It's entirely possible.

We definitely can't completely trust anything this guy says.

But even if some of the information he's given us is false, it would be impossible to tell which parts, and I don't know what he would gain by lying.

If any of what he's said so far isn't true, the only reason I could think of is that he doesn't want to let Güli-güli deal with the UFO, which doesn't make a lot of sense.

I don't know what he would want instead, and we don't even really know if he's lying.

"Well, whether you believe me or not, there is something I would like you to do if possible."

As all of us mull over our doubts about Potimas, the man himself throws us another curveball.

He manipulates the projector in his hands again, displaying a different schematic.

The new floating image is...an octopus?

Some kind of multi-legged machine anyway.

"This is another weapon schematic I gave those same people. It is a defective weapon, however—since it has no use except for the G-Fleet, I assumed it would not be made."

Potimas smiles at his own folly.

It's a very specific kind of pathos, like someone whose stupid drawings of "legendary weapons" from their nerdy past had been made into reality and shared with the world.

That might even be how Potimas feels right now.

"The G-Meteo. A disruptive weapon that is meant to pull in asteroids from among the moons and drop them onto this planet."

...Wait, what?

For a second, I don't understand what Potimas is saying, but you can't blame me.

Moons? Asteroids? I guess those aren't words you'd normally hear in this world.

I'm still learning the language around here, okay?

But once I understand the words, it makes even less sense.

Seriously, *what?*

Dropping asteroids on the planet?

"Ariel. Did you see anything get fired up toward space?"

Potimas looks at the Demon Lord.

She pauses for a moment, maybe searching her memories, then makes a face as she remembers.

I remember, too. I saw it.

The flare that spewed up from the ground before the UFO appeared.

And in that flare, the shadow of something flying up toward space.

The Demon Lord and I both saw it.

If what we saw was the octopus thing Potimas is talking about, then it's already well on its way into space.

"I did," the Demon Lord says, looking reluctant to admit it. "I don't know if it was this thing or not, but something definitely shot up there."

"I suspected as much. If they made the G-Fleet, then I feared they might have made this as well… So they really did, did they?"

Even Potimas looks pained now.

Guess I don't blame him.

The weapons he semi-jokingly designed have all been made into reality.

I mean, those octopus things are weapons designed to drop meteors, right?

How could that possibly be anything but a joke?

A meteor falling from the sky? That's the kind of thing you talk about as an apocalypse-level disaster, no matter what era you're from.

The kind of end you can't do anything about.

Good-bye, world. That's what a giant falling meteor means.

And you're telling me this guy intentionally designed a weapon to do just that?

How stupid can you get?!

Why would you *make* something like that?!

If you thought about it even a little bit, anyone would realize you could never use it!

"Ugh, what the hell were you thinking when you designed this thing?"

The Demon Lord shakes her head tiredly.

"It was so long ago that I've long forgotten, but I was probably just blowing off some steam after a long stretch of research."

Great. Now the entire world is in danger thanks to you "blowing off some steam."

"All right, first things first. I'm gonna kill you."

"Just so we're clear, I designed those weapons, but I did not actually make them. The blame lies with the people who actually built these things."

"So you're trying to say it's not your fault that the world is about to be destroyed? That's a bit of a stretch, don't you think?"

"I certainly do not. I simply provided the knowledge—what they decided to do with it is none of my business. I've done nothing wrong."

The Demon Lord and Potimas glare at each other.

The tension in the air is snap, crackle, and popping now.

"Enough. Debating where the blame lies is pointless."

Good thing Güli-güli's here to intervene.

The Demon Lord huffs anyway, looking even more irritated.

But she still drops her fighting stance because she's an adult... I guess?

"For now, let us summarize the situation. Firstly, that floating object is a weapon called a G-Fleet. It is equipped with a so-called GMA bomb, which has the capacity to destroy an entire continent. And the G-Meteo, a weapon that can catch asteroids and drop them onto this planet, is already flying into space. Does that sound right so far?"

We all nod at Güli-güli's simple summary.

"These weapons' goals are currently unknown. However, since they have been activated without purpose, it is possible they will begin destroying things indiscriminately. The G-Meteo, in particular, may already be trying to drop asteroids onto this planet. Is that correct?"

"It is." Potimas nods grimly.

So these weapons have activated their attack mechanisms solely to fend off intruders, then.

Hmm? Wait, does that mean we're also at fault for activating those things?

If we hadn't entered the ruins, the UFO might have stayed sleeping underground.

...Let's not bring that up.

Wouldn't want people to start blaming us.

"Whether they plan to begin wreaking havoc or simply stay on standby, we cannot leave them be. Now, let us begin our plan of attack for each weapon. Potimas, you want me to deal with the G-Meteo, correct?"

"I am glad you understand, Güliedistodiez. Now that the G-Meteo is in space, you are the only one who can destroy it."

Of the weapons we have to destroy, one of them is already flying into space.

And the only one of us who can do anything in outer space is Güli-güli, being a god and all.

We don't have any other choice.

"Then the role of dealing with the G-Fleet will fall to our remaining number, yes?"

Potimas looks at the Demon Lord, the pontiff, and finally, me.

Hey, don't include me in this!

And why is the Demon Lord nodding in agreement?!

"Is it not possible for me to assist with the G-Fleet before moving to deal with the G-Meteo?"

Ooh, good thinking, Güli-güli. But Potimas shakes his head.

"It would be best if you didn't. As I said before, that is an anti-dragon weapon. And one loaded with an extremely dangerous self-destruct feature, no less. What do you think will happen if a dragon like you approaches it?"

Güli-güli falls silent, unable to retort.

"Besides, either way, we cannot waste time waiting for you to return."

Potimas manipulates the projector device again, showing a new image.

It's live footage, probably taken by a remote recording device.

"Whoa," the Demon Lord murmurs.

The image shows the UFO, sending countless robots to the earth.

The UFO has dropped its altitude until it's floating just above the ground, its hatch open to dispatch robots down a long ramp. There are even some of the tanks we saw in the ruins.

I see at least a few thousand robots, maybe even tens of thousands.

And it still keeps producing more.

Once the robots reach the ground, they line up in formations and start moving forward.

"As you can see, the G-Fleet's forces have already begun their advance. Judging by their current speed and direction, they will reach human habitation within a half a day."

The pontiff turns pale at this.

Judging by his reaction, he must be thinking that these things can't be allowed to reach a human town at any cost.

"There is no time to spare, then."

"Indeed. We have no choice but to attack them simultaneously."

Güli-güli looks at Potimas intently, as if trying to gauge his true motives.

Potimas meets his gaze steadily.

From his attitude, it doesn't seem like he has anything to hide, but that in itself is kind of suspicious, which is a little amazing in a way.

What he's said so far has made sense, but I do get the feeling he might be deliberately trying to get Güli-güli away from this planet.

Maybe that sounds paranoid, but I know better than to trust this guy completely.

"May I see those schematics?"

"Go ahead."

Güli-güli asks Potimas to show him the schematics in more detail. He must have the same suspicions.

Potimas agrees right away and hands Güli-güli the projection device.

Güli-güli fiddles with it, pulling up the schematics to take a closer look.

I don't have any technical knowledge, so staring at these schematics doesn't really tell me anything. But everyone else is peering at them intently.

The UFO, the bomb, the octopus. He pulls up each schematic one by one.

"He does not appear to be lying."

Finally, determining that there are no contradictions in the plans, Güli-güli hands the device back to Potimas and sighs.

I mean, it would've been kinda hard to whip up fake plans in such a short span of time, so I think he's probably telling the truth.

But they say the best liars tell 90 percent of the truth with 10 percent lies mixed in, and based on this short conversation, I wouldn't be surprised if Potimas was exactly that type.

He's not lying, but he might be trying to use the situation to his advantage for some kind of scheme.

Like, it's true that Güli-güli has to be the one to deal with the octopus, but what if this is a *while the cat's away* type of situation where Potimas is going to get up to no good as soon as Güli-güli's gone?

Everyone else stares at Potimas suspiciously, just like I am.

"I am sure I cannot convince you to trust me completely, but I swear to you that I fully intend to focus on dealing with this situation with all my might. I would not want this planet to become devoid of life, after all."

The Demon Lord, Güli-güli, and the pontiff all exchange glances.

I can pretty much tell the silent conversation that's going on among them.

What should we do? This seems suspicious, but we have no choice.

Not much of a private conversation, guys. Well, I guess they're not really trying to hide it.

"Very well." Güli-güli nods reluctantly. "I will go deal with the G-Meteo while the rest of you contend with the G-Fleet."

That means this planet's strongest defense will temporarily be up in space, but at least there won't be any asteroids being dropped on us by that octopus.

I'm sure Güli-güli can deal with that octopus no problem.

The real issue is what the rest of the group is going to do.

How are they going to beat that UFO?

Ah, I guess I shouldn't be talking like this isn't my problem.

"So? What's our plan of attack here?" the Demon Lord drawls.

Her attitude says that she'll hear out Potimas's strategy, but if she doesn't like it, she's absolutely gonna disagree and do whatever she wants.

"Obviously, our top priority should be dealing with the GMA bomb. As such, we will have to infiltrate the G-Fleet. The infiltration team will disable the GMA bomb, while the rest will keep the G-Fleet occupied from the outside. Once the GMA bomb has been disabled, we can either entrust the rest to Güliedistodiez or bring it down with our own hands. Is that acceptable?"

Potimas's proposed plan is simple but effective. Honestly, I don't think we have any other option.

The Demon Lord and the pontiff both nod.

"Dustin." Potimas turns to the pontiff. "How many forces can you gather here?"

"Thirty thousand elite human soldiers."

Wow, that was a quick response.

You can really gather that many people so quickly?

"You can mobilize that many at the drop of a hat? How'd you manage to fail at invading Sariella and lose so many soldiers, then?" The Demon Lord snickers.

The pontiff did attempt to attack Sariella and failed.

Mainly because the Demon Lord and I had a huge face-off that decimated their forces in their first battle, and then my Parallel Minds went on a rampage that did even more damage.

In other words, it's basically all my fault!

But in the end, it meant I was able to protect Vampy's homeland, so I don't feel bad in the least.

In this case, however, it's kind of a negative, since it means the pontiff has less forces to put into action.

"No need to worry. The troops I intend to dispatch for this are my emergency defense forces, unrelated to the army that was sent to Sariella."

Ooh, gotcha.

"So that means if you bring 'em here, your homeland's totally defenseless, huh?"

Oof! The Demon Lord's being ruthless right now!

She's right, though. If what the pontiff says is true, that means he's bringing all the soldiers who would normally defend his nation over here.

In other words, he's leaving his homeland wide-open to attack. Should a leader really be doing that?"

"As I said, they are my emergency forces. And I have determined that this is indeed an emergency. My people will have nothing to fear," the pontiff replies flatly.

Well, if he says so, I see no reason to argue.

Not like I was really worried about some weird holy land I've never been to in the first place. That's none of my business, right?

"Well then, summon them at once. Have them move to intercept the route the G-Fleet's forces are taking."

"I do not take orders from you. I would have told them the same regardless."

Unlike the others, the pontiff blatantly rejects the Demon Lord's demand.

"Excuse me for a moment, then. I imagine it will take a bit of time to summon the troops, but I will attempt to return with the utmost haste."

With that, the pontiff teleports away with his Spatial Magic–using guard.

Damn, that guy acts fast.

Can he seriously gather thirty thousand people on such short notice, though?

And even if he can, are they gonna do the job right?

Honestly, no matter how many humans you gather, I dunno how much good they're gonna do against those robots and tanks and all that junk.

I'm a little worried, but the pontiff seemed raring to go, so I guess we'll just have to trust him.

"I will bring elven reinforcements as well. However, I myself intend to participate in the infiltration of the G-Fleet, as I am by far the most qualified to handle the GMA bomb. Ariel, and you there, you will enter the G-Fleet alongside me. That is acceptable, I assume."

Potimas is looking right at the Demon Lord and me.

Who, me? So I can't run away; I really have to do this, huh? Gotcha.

Plus, what with the "*I assume*" and all, he's not really even asking us if it's "*acceptable*" or not.

So I'm being forced to participate. Cool.

"We're sending in a small, elite team, then?"

"That is correct."

"Hrm. All right. But if you try anything funny, I'm gonna kill you, got it?"

"Certainly. If you think you can handle this without me, then go right ahead."

Potimas's prompt agreement sorta catches me off guard, but it just seems to make the Demon Lord even warier.

"Give me that."

The Demon Lord points at the projector in Potimas's hands; he nods and hands it to her.

Wow, he really is being cooperative.

That thing contains the plans for the UFO and the bomb and everything.

If we have that, the Demon Lord and I might be able to get by even without Potimas.

In a way, that means it was kind of his lifeline, but he handed it over without a second thought.

Huh. I guess he must be serious about taking down this UFO, too.

So maybe he'll actually be on his best behavior at least until we finish the job?

Obviously, I can't let my guard down, but I shouldn't be overly paranoid, either.

"Now then, I, too, shall depart for a moment. We will begin our operation once Dustin and I have returned."

Like the pontiff, Potimas and the Spatial Magic elf mage teleport away.

Now it's just the Demon Lord, Güli-güli, and me.

"I shall take action now, as well. Hyuvan!"

"Y-yes, *sir*!"

Güli-güli calls the wind dragon that'd retreated far away the second this little meeting began.

So this guy's name is Hyuvan, huh?

Not that I really plan on remembering that.

"Keep an eye on things here while I'm gone. Follow Ariel's orders and help in any way you can."

"*Heh-heh!*"

Did its personality change or something?

It still seems like an underling, but now it's a bit more like it's the aide of a corrupt feudal lord or something.

"Ariel. I shall return the moment I've taken care of things up there. Be sure not to do anything foolish before then."

"Sure thing. Although I might not have a choice if things get too crazy down here."

"Even then. You must not die before I come back."

Güli-güli pats the Demon Lord's head gently.

Ah! Finally, the adorable scene where the Demon Lord gets treated like a child!

But the Demon Lord politely removes his hand.

Come on. That's not what you're supposed to do!

You're supposed to blush a little and say *I'm not a kid, you know!* or something like that!

"I'll be off, then."

"Mm-hmm. You be careful, too."

After an exchange that makes them seem like a married power couple, Güli-güli teleports away, too.

I really hope he gets back before the pontiff and Potimas.

Then we wouldn't have to infiltrate the UFO or anything crazy like that.

But I have a hunch it won't be that easy.

And my bad feelings are usually right, as much as I wish they'd be wrong once in a while.

"*Whew. You guys goin' up against that thing or what? Hey, spider lady. It wouldn't hurt you or nothin' even if you gave us the day off, y'know?*"

"Oh, don't you worry. I'm gonna work you so hard, even the boss of a sweatshop would be horrified."

The wind dragon whimpers in response.

Oh boy. The Demon Lord and the wind dragon are doing their comedy routine again.

Is it just me, or do they actually put on a decent show?

And wait a second, does the wind dragon even know what a sweatshop is?

Maybe it doesn't, but it's imagining a terrible fate based on context?

Frankly, I'm pretty afraid myself of what my immediate future has in store for me.

In my arms, Sael has turned pale and practically passed out from the killer tension that was flying around throughout this meeting.

Yeah, I don't blame you. Sorry about that. Thanks for sticking with me through all this.

file.22

WIND DRAGON HYUVAN

LV.98

status

HP

12545 / 12545

MP

15494 / 15494

SP

32588 / 32588

31102 / 31102

Average Offensive Ability : 15176
Average Defensive Ability : 12490
Average Magic Ability : 15055
Average Resistance Ability : 12027
Average Speed Ability : 32776

skill

[Wind Dragon LV 10] [Divine Scales LV 10] [HP Rapid Recovery LV 1] [Magic Power Perception LV 10] [Precise Magic Power Operation LV 5] [MP Rapid Recovery LV 10] [MP Minimized Consumption LV 10] [Magic Divinity LV 4] [Magic Super-Attack LV 6] [SP Rapid Recovery LV 10] [SP Minimized Consumption LV 10] [Destruction Super-Enhancement LV 2] [Impact Super-Enhancement LV 4] [Cutting Enhancement LV 8] [Piercing Super-Enhancement LV 7] [Shock Super-Enhancement LV 6] [Flood Enhancement LV 10] [Gale Enhancement LV 10] [Bolt Enhancement LV 10] [Battle Divinity LV 10] [Energy Super-Attack LV 10] [Flood Attack LV 1] [Gale Attack LV 10] [Bolt Attack LV 2] [Dimensional Maneuvering LV 10] [High-Speed Flight LV 10] [Cooperation LV 10] [Leadership LV 7] [Kin Control LV 10] [Concentration LV 10] [Thought Super-Acceleration LV 10] [Future Sight LV 3] [Parallel Minds LV 3] [High-Speed Processing LV 10] [Hit LV 10] [Evasion LV 10] [Probability Super-Correction LV 10] [Stealth LV 10] [Concealment LV 10] [Silence LV 10] [Odorless LV 10] [Heatless LV 10] [Emperor] [Presence Perception LV 10] [Danger Perception LV 10] [Motion Perception LV 10] [Heat Perception LV 10] [Water Magic LV 10] [Flood Magic LV 10] [Tide Magic LV 3] [Ice Magic LV 3] [Wind Magic LV 10] [Gale Magic LV 10] [Tempest Magic LV 10] [Lightning Magic LV 10] [Bolt Magic LV 10] [Thunder Magic LV 5] [Shadow Magic LV 10] [Dark Magic LV 3] [Destruction Resistance LV 8] [Impact Resistance LV 8] [Cutting Resistance LV 6] [Piercing Resistance LV 7] [Shock Nullification] [Fire Resistance LV 4] [Flood Resistance LV 8] [Ice Resistance LV 7] [Gale Nullification] [Earth Resistance LV 6] [Bolt Nullification] [Light Resistance LV 3] [Black Resistance LV 1] [Heavy Super-Resistance LV 4] [Status Condition Super-Resistance LV 3] [Acid Resistance LV 1] [Faint Resistance LV 9] [Fear Super-Resistance LV 2] [Heresy Resistance LV 1] [Pain Nullification] [Pain Super-Mitigation LV 3] [Night Vision LV 10] [Panoptic Vision LV 3] [Five Senses Super-Enhancement LV 10] [Perception Expansion LV 10] [Ultimate Life LV 10] [Ultimate Magic LV 10] [Ultimate Movement LV 10] [Fortune LV 10] [Fortitude LV 10] [Stronghold LV 10] [Deva LV 10] [Sanctum LV 10] [Skanda LV 10]

The leader of the wind dragons, who reigns over the wasteland within the borders of the coalition of minor countries. One of the eldest and strongest of the already powerful dragons. Specializing in incredibly high-speed flight, this dragon boasts unrivaled power in the skies. It can even control the weather, blowing away enemies with violent storms. As such, the surrounding nations view it with both fear and reverence, and their people will sometimes pray to this dragon as a rain-making god during times of drought. It is a legendary-class monster, assumed untouchable by humans.

7 ANTI-UFO BATTLE STRATEGY

It's been three hours since the soul-crushing awkwardness of that meeting.

In that time, I've taken care of Sael's repairs and evacuated Vampy and Mera.

I figured it was too dangerous to let them participate in this battle, so I popped them into the Great Elroe Labyrinth.

Why the Great Elroe Labyrinth, you ask?

Well, if I left them in a village or town somewhere, Potimas might take a shot at them.

He really is serious about dealing with the UFO, I think, but that doesn't mean I can trust him without any doubts.

For all I know, he might try to pull some shady crap behind the scenes while we're working on the UFO.

That's why I put them in the labyrinth, which even Potimas can't stroll into so easily.

Incidentally, I left them in the care of the spider army my Parallel Minds created.

Since they were created by a part of myself, I can use my Kin Control skill to give them orders.

And my Parallel Minds must have done a good job training them, because they're crazy strong.

They wouldn't lose to any of the monsters that inhabit the Great Elroe Labyrinth, and even if Potimas did attack, I think they'd be able to defend themselves to a certain extent.

That means the bloodsucker duo is safe for now.

The baby didn't look too thrilled about being surrounded by a huge spider army, but Mera's with her, so I'm sure she'll be fine.

So yeah, she and Mera are finally out of the line of fire.

The problem now is the puppet spiders.

I've finished repairing Sael. Unlike the rest of her humanlike body, the new parts are unmistakably puppetlike, but they work just as well.

Now she can fight again.

The question is whether the puppet spiders have high enough specs for this fight in the first place.

The puppet spiders could take on any number of those robots without a problem. They proved that in the underground ruins.

But the tanks were a problem for them.

A single tank destroyed almost half of Sael's body, and the other three's attacks didn't work on it.

I don't think it's impossible for them to win in a similar fight, but they lack both the offense and the defense.

The tank's main gun can tear through the puppet spiders' defenses, but their attacks don't work on it at all.

Their only option for defense is to dodge.

But that still leaves the issue of offense.

Riel and Fiel's attacks definitely hit the tank, so if they had some way of breaking through its armor, they should be able to win.

But that's easier said than done.

The tank's armor is covered in the same mysterious barrier Potimas used, which renders magic totally useless.

It would probably negate any buff effects, too, so destroying the armor requires brute physical strength.

For some reason, my scythe was able to rip right through it without a problem, but that doesn't help much, since I still have no idea what's going on with this thing.

It does point me in the right direction, though.

They'd need better weapons.

That's the only way.

There's no point trying to raise the puppet spiders' own attack power at this stage, so our only hope is to give them stronger weapons.

But even that isn't so simple.

The puppet spiders' current weapons are incredibly sharp swords.

They're strong and sturdy enough that they don't break even when whipped around by the puppet spiders' powerful arms.

It wouldn't be easy to find weapons that outclass those.

But if we can't find them, we'll just have to make 'em!

That's how I got my scythe, so this can totally work!

As far as the kind of weapon, I don't think blades are a good option.

Trying to break through that armor with a blade is kinda stupid to begin with.

When you're trying to break through crazy-strong armor, the obvious choice is always gonna be blunt weapons. It's better to try to punch through than to try to slice it up.

That way, even if you don't break the armor, you have a chance of busting up the mechanisms inside with an attack.

For the materials, I'm using ancient metal.

It's high-quality stuff, at least as strong or even stronger than the metal used to make the tank's armor.

Huh? Where did I get that stuff, you ask?

From the underground ruins, duh.

I went back down into the ruins via the former ant nest.

Then I tore off the metal that was used for the walls of the actual ruins and went on my merry way.

I mean, that stuff kept its original shape even after those crazy flames ran through it.

All I had to do was a little tampering with Repellent Evil Eye and Warped Evil Eye to compress it.

Then I squished it together and made a handle, and voilà, a simple blunt weapon.

I made six of these for each of the four puppet spiders, for a total of twenty-four.

They're a little haphazard, but they should still do more damage than the puppet spiders' usual swords.

Since they're new weapons, the puppet spiders are waving them experimentally, getting used to their weight.

Hopefully they'll get the hang of it by the time the battle begins.

Now the puppet spiders should be all prepared.

Meanwhile, the Demon Lord was...summoning queen taratects.

Four of them, no less.

I couldn't believe my eyes at first.

These are queen taratects we're talking about, y'know?

They're the same species as Mother. Can you imagine how I felt seeing four of them right before my eyes?

I was so shocked, I couldn't even react!

I guess Mother wasn't the only queen taratect serving the Demon Lord.

Four crazy-strong beasts like Mother? The Demon Lord's scary when she gets serious.

"I figured this isn't the time to be stingy. I'm pulling out all the stops."

The four queens form an imposing line.

And then there's the dragon-wyrm army, led by the wind dragons.

Looks like all the dragons and wyrms in this wasteland have gathered here.

What's up with this monster army? I kinda feel like they could easily destroy the world by themselves.

Shoot. I did think about bringing the spider army from the Great Elroe Labyrinth, but I figured it was better to leave them there to guard the bloodsucker duo and all.

Giant spider monsters, dragons, and wyrms, oh my.

"Pardon the wait. I have returned with the Word of God army of thirty thousand."

The pontiff shows up to add his army to the mix.

The mage who undertook this huge Large-Scale Teleport to bring the army all this way died in the process.

Several of them, in fact.

I didn't actually see the bodies, but I heard the pontiff mention it in his speech to the Word of God army after they appeared in the wasteland.

"Give thanks for the sacrifice of the brave men who gave their lives to create a gate to this place for the holy war!"

Large-Scale Teleport is so tough that even I have trouble with it.

If you tried to do it with a human body, I can see how that would mean literally putting your life on the line.

This method sacrificed the lives of several valuable Spatial Magic mages.

That's how determined the pontiff was to bring his forces here.

To be honest, I'm not sure how much help they're going to be. They might have big numbers, but they're still human.

To the Demon Lord or me, they just look like an army of weaklings.

But they seem determined to join the fight.

I can sense that they're willing to lay down their lives with a fervor that borders on madness.

I don't know what the pontiff told them before we got here, but they seem perfectly willing to team up with us, and it looks like they understand what kind of enemy we're facing.

They even seem to realize that most of them won't be coming back alive.

And yet, none of them seems to be afraid, and their morale only keeps getting higher. I guess they've been trained well.

That's what's so scary about religion.

There's nothing stronger than that kind of faith.

"It appears I am the last to arrive."

Finally, Potimas shows up with his mechanical army.

There aren't that many, probably only about two thousand soldiers.

But instead of humans, these are machine soldiers.

They're over fifteen feet tall, clad in tough-looking armor and wielding several weapons each.

The machines are sorta freaky to look at, too: It's like if you shoved a humanoid upper body onto a multi-legged lower body.

But as freaky as it is, they look efficient, too.

The upper body seems like it was designed to wield weapons as effectively as possible and only happened to come out resembling a human.

It's sorta like the product of a design focused purely on making a functional, elegant weapon, not a cool-looking robot like you'd see in a mecha anime.

Not exactly romantic but definitely promising as a fighting force.

I just hope I'm never up against these things instead of with them.

"Looks like we're all ready," the Demon Lord remarks.

Yeah, unfortunately.

Güli-güli didn't make it back in time after all.

If only he'd gotten here sooner, I wouldn't have to deal with this stupid UFO.

"So White here, I guess Potimas, and I are gonna assault that thing, okay?"

"Right."

It's not really okay with me, but I can't run away at this point—and even if I did, it might mean the end of the world.

So I just nod, albeit very reluctantly.

"So? How do we get inside?"

"We'll use this to make a hole in the outer wall."

Potimas indicates some kind of massive tube thing.

Hmm? Is that like a giant bazooka or something?

"It's a single-use gun, but it's extremely powerful. It should be able to make a hole in the G-Fleet's exterior without a problem."

Hey, I was right. It's a bazooka.

Still, the term "infiltration" had me picturing us entering through some secret air vent or something, not just busting our way through.

I guess it's more like breaking and entering, huh?

"So? Who's going to bring it?"

"I'll have you or that 'White' creature carry it. This body can probably lift it, but it isn't quite powerful enough to take aim properly."

"All right. Here you go, White."

What? Why?

Looks like I'm the one stuck carrying this bazooka.

Why do I have to take such an important role, huh?

I glower at the Demon Lord in protest.

"You can use Spatial Magic to put it away and take it out whenever you want. Besides, you've got a better physique for it than I do anyway."

Dammit. She's right.

I can put it away in Spatial Storage until I need to fire it, and the Demon Lord's childlike body is hardly suited to operating a bazooka.

And Potimas says he can't do it, although I don't know if that's true or not, so that leaves only me by process of elimination.

But I reeeally don't wanna be given such an important task.

If I miss or something, we won't be able to get inside anymore, right? He said this was one use only.

I can't afford to mess up.

Rationally, I know it'd probably be harder to miss that giant thing than to hit it, but that doesn't stop me from being nervous.

Should I get as close as I can and shoot it from point-blank range?

That would involve flying, then.

Of course, since I have Dimensional Maneuvering, that's not a problem for me.

Dimensional Maneuvering uses magic power to create footholds in empty space, allowing me to run through the air or whatever like I'm on the ground. That means I can move through the air without a problem.

But isn't that UFO gonna have the mysterious barrier?

If it activates that barrier while I'm using Dimensional Maneuvering, it'll cancel out the skill and I'll fall.

I don't like that one bit.

Since the tank used that barrier, there's no guarantee the UFO won't use it.

I have to come up with a way to fly without using skills.

Just then, I make eye contact with a certain someone who's been listening with a meek yet relaxed attitude, as if none of this has anything to do with it.

Aha. That'll do.

I beckon to the wind dragon.

Making a "?" face, the wind dragon putters over.

I quickly move around to its side, jumping onto its back.

"What the—?!"

Great. The size is perfect.

My upper body is the same size as a normal human, but my lower body takes the shape of a gigantic spider. Luckily, the wind dragon is just big enough to fly with me on its back. .

Without further ado, I wrap my spider legs around the wind dragon's body.

There, that feels nice and secure.

This is perfect!

"The hell are you doing?!"

"Ooh, I get it. Good idea."

"Agreed. Perhaps Ariel and I should ride some dragons, as well."

"You said it."

While the wind dragon throws a fit, the Demon Lord and Potimas figure out my logic and actually agree with me.

"You heard him, wind dragon. You guys are gonna transport us up there."

"'You heard him,' my ass!"

The wind dragon keeps complaining and trying to throw me off, but it's already been decided.

"Shall I take charge of matters on the ground, then?"

It's already starting to get chaotic down here, so the pontiff offers to rein things in.

"Might as well, right? Although I do kinda feel like our forces should just do our own thing."

"I concur. Their methods and abilities are simply too different."

Oh, I guess they have a point.

It'd probably be harder to control this mixed-up army than to just let them run wild.

In fact, these guys would normally be fighting one another, so it's a miracle that they're even on the same side in the first place.

And now you want to say, *All right, let's all work together and win this thing?* Forget it.

"I'll tell the queens and the puppets to listen to your orders, but don't get your hopes up too much."

"Seconded. I shall grant you the authority to give orders, but my soldiers will be the ones to decide whether to listen."

Huh?

Does that mean there are people inside those machines?

It doesn't look like there's enough space in there, so I just assumed they were preprogrammed on autopilot.

…Maybe it's best not to delve too deep into this.

I'm afraid I'll learn something I'm better off not knowing.

"Very well. I only intend to provide minor adjustments. No doubt it is better to let each force act at their own discretion."

I guess the pontiff wasn't looking to take direct control of this crazy army anyway.

Maybe he suggested this only to get their consent in case of an emergency?

If you don't establish the chain of command early on, it can lead to disputes down the line, after all.

"The G-Fleet is slowly making its way toward us. It has deployed a force of approximately a hundred thousand on the ground."

Silence follows that number.

A hundred thousand.

Our forces number about forty thousand in total.

And thirty thousand of those are humans, who are weaker than the robots that make up most of the opposing army.

The queens, the puppet spiders, the dragons, and most likely the machine soldiers are all considerably stronger than the robots, but this will probably still be a difficult battle.

"Well, our main goal is getting rid of this bomb anyway. As long as we can do that, we've basically won, even if we can't wipe out their forces. Then we'll just let Gülie take care of the rest."

The Demon Lord's unconcerned comment lightens the mood a little.

She's right.

If we take care of the bomb that could very well destroy the world, the rest of the problems are a whole lot less urgent.

Then we only have to wait for Güli-güli to get back and finish the job for us.

"Dustin." The Demon Lord turns to give orders to the pontiff. "Please focus on slowing the enemy down and buying as much time as possible on the ground. Try to avoid any unnecessary sacrifices, okay?"

"Understood. I shall handle matters as carefully as I can."

"Wind dragon. We're gonna have you carry White, but have the rest of the dragons fight in the skies. It might be the toughest job, but don't let them steal control of the air. Otherwise, we're all doomed. Prepare to risk everything if you have to."

"Huh? Why do we gotta work twice as hard as the goons on the ground, eh, spider lady?"

"There's no way around it. If you don't give it your all, we have no hope of winning."

"Argh! What the hell?! Fine, we'll do it!"

The wind dragon complains some more, but it seems to understand her reasoning.

The dragons are our only ally who can move freely through the air, so they're very important.

They're the only ones who can put up a fight against the UFO's fighter aircraft.

Giving the enemy air superiority would have a devastating effect on the fight on the ground, so we really need the dragons to put their backs into this.

"And Potimas… Don't betray us, got it?"

"Hmph."

It's hard to tell whether the Demon Lord is joking, but Potimas only responds with a snort.

Uh, are we sure this is gonna be okay?

He won't betray us, right? Right?!

At any rate, this means our anti-UFO strategy has been decided.

The Demon Lord, Potimas, and I are going to infiltrate the UFO.

The dragons, led by the wind dragon, will carry us to the UFO, then fight in the air to keep our escape route open.

There are about eight thousand of them. Most of them are wyrms, though, with only twenty-four dragons.

Normally, twenty-four dragons would be a huge number, but in this situation, it doesn't feel like nearly enough.

Our ground forces include the pontiff's Word of God army of thirty thousand, Potimas's two thousand machine soldiers, four queen taratects, and the four puppet spiders.

The UFO's army, on the other hand, has about a hundred thousand robots.

A thousand tanks.

I see about five thousand fighters in the sky.

And then, there's the supreme commander, the UFO itself.

There might even be more forces inside the UFO, so their total could be even larger.

Our forces are made up of some of the strongest troops in this world.

But even then, we don't know for sure if we'll win.

The fate of the world hangs in the balance.

If we lose, everything might be destroyed, so we have no choice but to win.

The curtain has violently opened on a battle against relics of the past.

Interlude

THE VAMPIRE MISTRESS AND HER SERVANT DISCUSS MACHINERY

"Young miss, may I ask you a question?"

"Yes?"

"Could you tell me more about these 'machines'?"

"Machines?"

"Indeed. I cannot quite grasp what exactly a 'machine' might be. And so I was hoping you could impart your wisdom unto me."

"Okay. I don't know the finer details, though."

"That is quite all right. If you can share what knowledge you do have, I would be very grateful."

"Very well. But it might take a while. Do you mind if I use Telepathy?"

"No, please go ahead."

"*Thank you. You want to know about the kinds of machines that were in those ruins, right, Merazophis?*"

"Yes and no. I have very little understanding of machines in general. Please share anything that comes to mind, young miss."

"*All right. I'll talk about the machines from my old world, then.*"

"By all means."

"*To put it simply, a machine is something that exists to make life easier.*"

"Is that right?"

"*As far as I'm concerned anyway. Of course, there are weapons like the ones we saw in those ruins, but you could say that those, too, are meant to make life easier in a broad sense, right? By protecting people from enemy attacks.*"

"Ah, I see."

"So machines make life easier. Since you were in charge of a mansion, you know how taxing even everyday life can be, right? Cleaning, cooking, laundry. It's a lot of work."

"Quite."

"Machines are supposed to help with that. In my world, for example, we had a machine called a vacuum cleaner, which gathered up dirt and garbage much more easily than a broom."

"More than a broom?"

"Yes. I don't quite understand the principles behind it, but you could say a vacuum cleaner was like an evolved form of a broom. Machines are basically evolved tools—more convenient, often able to do their work automatically. I think that's a decent way of looking at it."

"So the machines in those ruins were the same?"

"Yes, even those. Swords and such are weapons for fighting, yes? It's just like if those evolved. Weapons that can move and fight on their own. That's what a mechanical weapon is."

8 SKY BATTLE! FANTASY VS SCI-FI

NYOOOOOM! The sound of something tearing through the air zips right past my ears.

You know, the kind of sound that an F1 or whatever would make.

I'd only ever heard that noise on TV before, but it turns out it's really freakin' loud when you hear it up close!

I feel like my eardrums are gonna burst!

In fact, it wouldn't be that unusual if they really did burst in this situation!

I mean, we've gotta be a good ten thousand feet up in the air.

That's at least as high as the peak of Mount Fuji, maybe even higher.

If you're doing acrobatic maneuvers that high up, you might bust an eardrum or two!

Although I don't think mine have actually burst just yet.

That's right. I'm flying in the sky right now.

Clinging to the back of a wind dragon, locked in the middle of a not-very-fun dance with a giant swarm of fighters.

"Whooee! Now, that one made my blood run cold for a second!"

The sound I just heard was the aircraft I shot down, hurtling right past us on its way to the ground.

The wind dragon's Telepathic message is so lighthearted, I even heard it whistle, but that's just its tone—in reality, it's deadly serious.

This dragon is doing some insane high-speed evasive maneuvers to dodge the fighter jets' attacks while firing back at them with Wind Magic.

It can't let its guard down for a second or we'll both be shot full of holes.

That's how intense the battle against these fighters is.

While the dragons have taken off, the ground troops are still staying in place.

Their main job is to keep the UFO and its army occupied, so instead of charging forward, it makes more sense to wait and intercept the enemy instead.

The dragons are our air forces, though, and they have the job of bringing the infiltration team up to the UFO.

That means they have to break through the UFO's defensive line of five thousand fighter planes, so they have no choice but to go on the offensive.

We've got to detach that bomb from the UFO as soon as we possibly can.

Since the UFO activated with no clear purpose, we have no way of knowing when it might drop the bomb.

According to Potimas, it's not supposed to drop the bomb unless certain conditions are met, but we don't know if it's actually going to follow those rules.

I mean, this UFO is a relic from waaay back.

How do we know if it's even functioning properly?

As it is, it's already half on a rampage here, so it wouldn't be that surprising if it decided to drop the bomb while it's at it.

And another weapon, the octopus thing, is already on its way to space to try and drop a meteor on this planet.

So we can't leave just this one hanging around with a literal ticking time bomb.

We were right to start the charge once our preparations were complete.

But we underestimated the fighters' power.

I don't think we were making light of them, but whatever the reason, we still assumed we could get past them easily enough.

But that illusion is about to be blown to pieces.

So the battle ten thousand feet above the ground is unfolding explosively.

Dragons versus fighter aircraft.

Fantasy versus sci-fi.

It's a surreal scene.

I mean, should this really be happening outside of a superhero show?

However, my five senses are all screaming at me that this insane battle is quite real.

The aircraft's automatic weapons are spraying light bullets all over the place.

Looks like they have the same kind of guns as the robots and the tanks.

One of the wyrms fails to dodge the barrage of light completely, and the bullets pierce right through its scales, cutting into the flesh and spraying blood everywhere.

The wyrm lets out a shriek of pain and plummets toward the ground.

I don't think I need to tell you what happens after that.

But the wyrms are fighting back, too.

They dodge around the trajectory of the incoming fire, zooming toward the planes as they do so.

Then they damage the wings or the engine, sending the fighter crashing to the ground.

Compared to the fighters, which move in simple straight lines, the wyrms can maneuver around freely and organically, sneaking into the fighters' blind spots.

And then there are the dragons, assaulting other aircraft with magic.

Like the tank, these fighters have the mystery barrier around their armor, so normal magic would just bounce right off.

Luckily, these dragons have the right kind of magic for the job.

As wind dragons, they obviously use Wind Magic.

And Wind Magic basically moves the air.

When this magic hits the aircraft's exterior, it does indeed dissipate—but the air keeps on moving.

Spells like my Dark Magic use magic that didn't have any physical form before, so of course they become useless once the effect is destroyed by the barrier. But since Wind Magic moves something that's already there, it doesn't really make a difference if the magic is canceled out after the fact.

They just lose control of the wind after it hits the barrier.

Violent airflow created by magic speeds toward the fighters, which spin out of control, plummeting to the ground.

The dragons can't control the wind after that because of the barrier, but since they're still wind dragons, a little turbulence isn't going to affect them.

In fact, they use that to their advantage and keep going after the aircraft.

It's a midair melee, with neither side budging an inch.

Unfortunately, if it drags on like this, we're the ones who are gonna suffer.

Even the leader of the wind dragons is under so much pressure in this fight that it can't let its guard down for a second.

The fighters can fight indefinitely, but we're living creatures.

Even dragons get tired eventually.

And that's especially true in this world, where our energy is strictly controlled by SP.

Most stats tend to work in our favor, but that's not always the case with SP.

If you run out of yellow SP, which indicates immediate energy, then it gets hard to breathe. Worse, if you run out of the red SP that indicates your overall stamina, you'll die on the spot.

We have to get through this situation on the limited SP we have.

And yet, even the head wind dragon has to put all of its strength into this battle.

The fighters have no such disadvantage.

I'm sure they can run out of energy, too, but their performance won't suffer from exhaustion or anything like that.

They can display their best fighting abilities right up until the second their energy runs out.

So we're getting more and more tired, but they can keep fighting at max power without rest.

The more time passes, the bigger our disadvantage gets.

That's all too clear from the way that the number of wyrms shot down by the fighter planes is steadily increasing.

The weakest wyrms that couldn't keep up with the aircraft's speed to begin with dropped out of the fight pretty quickly.

The ones that are getting shot down now are the wyrms that are too tired to maintain their top speed, and therefore unable to dodge the aircraft's aim any longer.

The dragons are all still intact.

But who knows how long that's going to last?

Because the biggest problem is that the number of aircraft isn't getting any smaller.

We've brought down a whole bunch of them already, yet it doesn't look like their numbers have decreased in the slightest.

If anything, it seems like there are even more of them flying around than before.

That might actually be the case. Because more aircraft keep coming out of the UFO.

The UFO must be some kind of flying base.

It's carrying tons of aircraft inside.

No matter how many we destroy, more reinforcements just keep pouring into the sky.

It's like an endless bullet hell game out here.

We're definitely damaging them, but since it doesn't feel that way at all, the wyrms are clearly starting to panic.

I can't blame them. We're getting more exhausted by the minute, yet our enemies' numbers don't seem to be going down at all.

There must be a limit to their numbers, of course.

But we have no idea what that limit might be.

Their mother ship, the UFO, is huge, so it's impossible to tell how many aircraft might be inside.

The only silver lining is that they're coming out steadily to replace the fighters we destroy, instead of all swarming out at the same time.

That seems like a stupid strategy to me, but I'm guessing it must be some kind of control issue that prevents the UFO from sending them out all at once.

These things don't have pilots. They're totally controlled by a computer.

So I suspect there's probably a limit to how many the computer can control at the same time.

There must be, or it wouldn't make any sense.

If the UFO did unleash all the aircraft it has in one big push, we'd be doomed.

We're barely holding them off to begin with.

This guy I'm riding on and the other dragons can still fight, but even the middle-range wyrms are starting to show warning signs at this point.

They're the ones making up our front line right now, so if they go down, the upper wyrms and even dragons might start taking damage, too.

I'm providing backup with Wind Magic of my own, but the situation doesn't look good.

Besides, if I use my Wind Magic to its maximum power, the wyrms will get caught in my attacks, too.

In this jumbled-up battle with allies and enemies on all sides, my wide-range magic would hit both friend and foe.

The wyrms have the Wind Nullification skill, so they wouldn't die from my magic. But that technically just protects them from the magic itself, not the aftereffects of the spell.

Just like the fighters, they'd get caught up in the resulting wind and fall to their deaths.

And with the power of my magic, that's the only outcome I can possibly imagine.

So instead of using any big spells, I have to shoot down each aircraft one at a time.

Between my power and the Demon Lord's, we could probably wipe all of them out with magic.

Maybe we should have the wyrms and dragons withdraw for now so we can hit the aircraft with one giant blast?

"Damn these chumps! They stay on my ass no matter what I do!"

The wind dragon lets out an aggravated yell.

Ah, I guess not.

The wind dragons are able to avoid the fighter attacks because they specialize in speed, but the enemy is still locked on to us.

They're staying hot on our tails, literally.

At this point, there's no way the dragons could retreat.

"Hang on tight, girlie! I'll show ya speed you've never even imagined!"

Despite the situation, the wind dragon is boisterously picking up speed.

It shakes off the aircraft chasing us, then spins around and knocks it out of the sky on its way past without even slowing down.

Whoa, cool.

That was flashy and all, but...sorry, pal.

My speed stat's actually higher than yours.

I have experienced speed higher than this.

I know you were trying to show off, but…yeah, sorry.

Still, I guess it's only natural that a wind dragon would be so acrobatic in the sky.

It's carrying me on its back, but it still keeps pulling these amazing moves as it dodges the fighter attacks.

Guess its thirty-thousand-plus speed stat isn't just for show.

And its other stats are all at least ten thousand, too, which isn't too shabby.

Despite the fact that this guy acts like a lackey, its stats are pretty impressive.

Even the puppet spiders wouldn't be able to take it one-on-one.

Four-on-one, maybe, but even then, it's hard to say.

If anything, I'm left questioning why this guy talks the way it does when it's so crazy strong.

Shouldn't you be a little more dignified, dude?

What, me? Pshhh, I'm the heroine. I don't need to have a personality like that.

Okay, fine, sorry. That was over the line.

Anyway, having a personality or not doesn't make a damn difference against our current opponent.

They're emotionless machines.

They don't have feelings or even thoughts.

Just programming that's optimized to destroy the enemy.

More dangerous still, their programming seems to be capable of learning.

They're taking very precise strategies against these crazy fantasy creatures, after all.

They turned this into a chaotic melee so we can't just blow them all away with magic.

They raised their altitude as well, reducing the amount of air available to weaken the effects of Wind Magic.

We're higher than ten thousand feet right now, but this battle started a lot lower.

And yet, they've been gradually leading us higher without us even knowing.

Deliberately leading us into thinner air, where we're at a disadvantage.

With less oxygen, the wyrms and dragons won't be able to perform as well.

On top of that, Wind Magic moves the air around, so it's obviously weaker if there's less air to move.

They led us onto a field advantageous to them.

The only way they could do such a thing is if they are able to analyze their opponents.

At first, I stupidly assumed they were just machines that could move only in designated ways.

But the more of them I destroy, the less effective those same methods become.

They're learning and adapting.

This is bad.

At this rate, it's only a matter of time until the wyrms get wiped out.

I've got to come up with some kind of plan, and fast.

"Hey, White lady."

As I start to panic, the wind dragon sends a telepathic message in a strangely calm voice.

"Take out that thing from before."

That thing? You mean the giant bazooka Potimas gave me?

"Things aren't lookin' good here, sweet cheeks. I gotta get you onto that ship, at the very least. If we move on our own, I can shake off these suckers long enough to get you over to the big guy there, no problemo."

…What is this guy saying?

If the wind dragon and I leave now, the front lines will seriously buckle.

Even if the wind dragon puts me on the UFO and turns around right away, it won't change the losses we'll incur in the meantime, not to mention that I won't be there to help anymore.

Is this guy so stupid that it doesn't even realize that?

"I know what you're thinkin', lady. But at this rate, we're all goin' down. The least I can do's carry out the mission I was given in the first place, see?"

For a second, the wind dragon flashes me a grin.

I mean, I can't read a dragon's expression, but for some reason I could definitely tell it was smiling.

A cheerful smile totally unsuited to the situation we're in right now.

Come on—you're just a grunt, so why would you pull such obvious foreshadowing?

Are you planning on dying or what?

"See, you oughtta know something about dragons like me. We're all here because we got some kinda job to do."

Hey, cut it out, stupid.

Don't you know that suddenly talking about yourself is like one of the top ten signs that you're about to die?!

Seriously, is this guy getting ready for a suicide mission or what?

"My job was cleanin' up this here wasteland. Around the same time this big fella was made, the whole area was hit with a nasty bomb that sprayed a cloud of poison all over the place. It was my job to get rid of that poison. And damn, did that take a long time. I had to chase all that damn poison up into space, bit by bit, see?"

A bomb that produces a toxic cloud?

…No way. Could he mean a nuclear weapon?

In that case, was the poison radioactive or what?

I mean, I don't know for sure, but that could be the case.

That explains why wind dragons are here, though.

I'd been wondering that for a while. Since it's a wasteland, earth dragons seem more natural, right?

But if they wanted to make sure the poison didn't seep into any other areas and wanted to send it out into space, it makes sense that wind dragons would be the right ones for the job.

"The poison made it so's not a single blade of grass grows in this here wasteland, but it was our job, so we watched over it right."

I see. I see…

Hoo boy. I feel like I might've realized something I probably shouldn't have.

Was this so-called poison bomb dropped here on purpose?

To hide the ruins where that UFO was?

Or maybe the bomb was even supposed to destroy the underground ruins?

The truth is lost to time now, but either way, I don't think that bomb was used for any wholesome reason.

"So we finished getting rid of all that poison. Give it a whole lotta years, and plants should even start growin' in this here ground again. But we don't gotta be the ones to see that happen. Our job here was done as soon as the poison was all chased out."

The wind dragon's tone sounds pensive.

"When ya think about it, ain't this the perfect place for us to kick the bucket? Our roles are complete, and now we get to die on the battlefield with the fate of this whole damn world hanging in the balance! Ain't that just about the best thing you ever heard?!"

Uh-oh. This dude really is planning to die.

Since when are lowly grunts supposed to die in the coolest way possible?

But its determination is coming through way too clearly.

"All right! Hang on tight, girlie! I'll show ya the fastest flying around!"

The wind dragon puts even more speed into its flight.

We're heading straight for the giant UFO up ahead.

It's planning to use up the last of its strength to charge through and get me there.

Countless aircraft stand between the UFO and us.

The wind dragon is going to scatter them, leaving behind even our wyrm allies, to clear a path to the UFO.

Then, as if in deference to its powerful determination—

—the fighters around us start to explode.

The huge number of aircraft suddenly starts decreasing.

Some of them explode, while others simply nose-dive to the ground.

Looking closely, I can see a tiny black shadow jumping from one aircraft to the next.

Not flying. Jumping.

Some wingless being is destroying the fighters right here in the air.

It's the Demon Lord.

She's jumping on one aircraft, neutralizing their ability to fly, then using it as a foothold to jump onto the next one.

And since she's doing it at a crazy speed, it looks from my angle like the fighters are just dropping like flies.

If I didn't have such good eyesight, I might not even be able to tell that it's the Demon Lord.

She was riding on a dragon before, but I don't see it anywhere now.

Checking around, I spot the dragon far in the distance.

She must have left it behind.

I guess to the Demon Lord, even a dragon is just one more thing holding her back.

So she shook it off and started jumping around, defeating fighters ten thousand feet above the ground. No big deal, right?

Ha-ha. Boy, this just shows all over again how crazy overpowered the Demon Lord is.

Maybe we should just let her deal with the rest?

"......"

"......"

The wind dragon, who was all ready to make a cool, dramatic sacrifice, is stunned into silence.

It's kinda awkward, to be honest.

I guess a grunt is just a grunt in the end.

Characters like that aren't allowed to have cool deaths.

See? The universe is telling you you're not supposed to die here.

"All right, then! Looks like the way's all clear! I'll carry ya there nice and safe!"

Okay. I guess we're just gonna pretend you weren't being all *"I'm gonna die for my duty!"* just a second ago.

Pretty anticlimactic, but is that really such a bad thing?

It'd be a waste for this guy to die here.

I gotta make sure it lives a good long life.

Grunt or not, it's got guts.

Guess I better put in a little effort myself so that Hyuvan the wind dragon lives to see another day.

The UFO produces more aircraft, but we ignore that and keep moving forward.

Phase two of our air battle has just begun.

Interlude

THE VAMPIRE MISTRESS AND HER SERVANT DISCUSS MA ENERGY

"Did the machines in your world run on MA energy, too, young miss?"

"Of course not. Most machines in my old world used electricity. You know, like lightning? The energy from that, basically."

"You were able to manipulate the power of lightning?"

"Mm, not exactly. The energy that forms the basis of lightning, I guess? I'm sorry—I can't explain it very well myself."

"Oh, no, it's fine. Whatever you know will be more than enough, young miss."

"All right. But explaining it to someone else makes me realize I actually didn't know much about how these things worked, even though I used them all the time in my old world. I really didn't study enough."

"I'm certain you had far more to learn in your old world, so much that you couldn't possibly remember all of it. The more you tell me, young miss, the more painfully aware I am of my own ignorance. If you say you did not study enough, then residents of this world like myself have not studied at all."

"Thank you for comforting me. But I don't think being truly wise is based on the amount of knowledge you have."

"How do you mean?"

"I think it's all about whether you can make the right decisions or not. That shows how wise you are. Of course, there's certainly no harm in having more knowledge on which to base your decisions. But if you ask me, wisdom is about what you come up with on your own, not how much you've learned."

"To have pride and confidence in what you feel is right…"

"*Hmm? That's a nice phrase.*"

"Indeed. A certain someone once said it to me while admonishing me."

"*I see. If you have pride and confidence in your beliefs, maybe that does make you wise.*"

"I certainly hope so."

"*I wonder what in the world those people were thinking when they decided to harness MA energy all those years ago.*"

"Nothing at all, most likely. They probably just set out to take whatever the world would give them, never thinking any further than that. Otherwise, I doubt they could have gotten their hands on MA energy in the first place."

"*I don't think you need to be that hard on them. They didn't know what MA energy really is, after all.*"

"Perhaps, but they must have at least felt that something was strange about it. Yet, they ignored that intuition, fell prey to the allure of MA energy, and went on using it."

"*True. I mean, it's a boundless source of energy that never runs out no matter how much you use it. I understand why they would want to keep using such a dreamlike source of energy.*"

"Even though limitless energy is the stuff of dreams alone."

"*Well, that's why they were woken up from the dream eventually. And when they did wake up, reality was waiting with the truth of the energy they'd been using.*"

"That must be when they found out. That MA energy is the life force of the planet, and the more you use it, the closer the planet comes to destruction."

9 The Enemy Is Everywhere!

The second phase of our air battle against the fighters is proceeding so smoothly that the first phase feels like a distant nightmare.

There are several reasons for this, but the biggest is that we opened with a preemptive attack.

Along with the dragons, the Demon Lord and I helped unleash an enormous Wind Magic attack on them.

Before, the wyrms and aircraft were so mixed together that this would've been impossible, but once the Demon Lord eradicated a whole bunch of fighters, it became a lot easier to separate friend from foe.

And we'd have to be morons not to jump at that chance.

So we smashed a giant mass of air right into the swarm of fighters that were flying toward us.

A "mass of air" might not sound all that impressive, but trust me, it was crazy.

Picture the big hurricanes you sometimes see on the news and stuff.

If you've seen trees getting uprooted and whole houses blown away, you'll understand just how destructive wind can be.

We controlled that wild force with magic and even compressed it to make it stronger and stronger before hitting the planes with it.

Wind Magic might make you picture sharp, cutting whirlwind attacks or whatever, but in reality, it's a lot bigger and blunter than that.

I mean, we were hoping it might even damage the UFO while we were at it, that's how big it was. Those stupid little fighters didn't stand a chance.

As a result, more than half of the second swarm of aircraft was brought down by that one blast.

Wary of being rounded up again, the aircraft started spreading out quite a bit after that, so we didn't get to use the same move again.

Kind of frustrating, since we probably could've really wiped all of them out in one go if they stayed close together.

Still, it was extremely effective.

With the momentum of that preemptive attack behind them, the wyrms have been taking down the remaining aircraft one by one.

Although unfortunately, even that giant spell didn't damage the UFO one bit.

The barrier protecting the UFO is so damn strong that even though the magic definitely hit it, it didn't budge an inch.

Will the bazooka Potimas gave me really be able to bust through that thing?

I'm definitely worried.

Still, things seem to be going in our favor for now.

The amount of fighters is finally getting sparse. Either the UFO figured that we'll just blow them away again if it sends out the rest of the aircraft all at once or it's finally running out of spares.

Since they've got the advantage in numbers now, the wyrms are dealing with the aircraft no problem.

The aircraft seem especially cautious of the Demon Lord, who was wreaking havoc on them not too long ago.

Wherever she goes, they're giving her a wide berth.

They know if they get too close, she'll jump on them and destroy them.

So for now, the Demon Lord is staying on top of her dragon, firing off little spells from time to time.

Although each time she does so, another aircraft goes down, so I guess they're not really "little."

Still, it's not nearly as flashy as the way she was jumping from plane to plane before, so we'll stick with "little" for now.

"Heh-heh! Outta my way! Wind dragon Hyuvan coming through!"

And then, of course, there's a certain someone who's getting super carried away.

I don't need to tell you who, I'm sure. Especially since it just said its name itself.

Cut it out, will ya, Hyuvan?

If you keep doing stupid stuff, it'll make me look stupid, too, since I'm riding on your back.

I can see how it'd want to get carried away, though.

Not long ago, things were going so badly that it was fully prepared to die, but now the tide has thoroughly turned in our favor.

Yep. It probably has to get this amped up if it wants to forget all the corny lines it was saying before.

I get it. I really do, bud!

Sometimes you say something that seems appropriate in the moment, but when you look back later when you're in your right mind, it seems really embarrassing in retrospect!

That happens to me all the time!

I mean, like, *all* the time!

That's why you always gotta keep yourself in check, or you'll say something in the moment that you might regret!

But then something hits me.

Aren't things going a little *too* well?

I mean, there are plenty of factors as to why it's going this well.

There's a good reason that we're pushing forward like this.

But if I step back and look calmly at this forward-moving situation, I can't help but feel like something's wrong.

Things were going so poorly for us before, so how did the tables turn so fast in our favor?

It's almost like we're being guided this way on purpose.

For just a second, I get goose bumps.

I check the wyrms' current state with Detection again.

The fighters and the UFO, too.

Those guys exist outside of the system, so skills like Analyze don't work on them.

That means I can't find out their exact strength and abilities, but there's an even worse effect: My Future Sight doesn't work on them.

I don't know what they're going to do next.

In this case, however, I think I can take a good guess.

The UFO is preparing something big.

"Take evasive action—now!"

I send a warning to all the wyrms via Telepathy.

If I tried to shout, it would only come out as a garbled shriek.

That's why I used Telepathy, although I'm not sure if it helped at all.

Since my panicked warning startled a good amount of the wyrms into obeying, I'd like to think it did some good.

But there were still significant losses.

For just a moment, the sky is completely filled with light.

The UFO just fired a huge laser beam.

It swallows up anything it touches, aircraft and wyrms alike.

When it dissipates, there's nothing left in its path.

It's all been evaporated into nothing.

Dammit!

We've been had!

The reason there were fewer fighters was so that they wouldn't get caught in the sights of the UFO's main gun!

It was trying to catch the wyrms off guard, too.

So that it could wipe them all out!

We were aiming to take down the fighters in one big blow, so it's only natural that our opponent would try to do the same thing.

Why didn't I notice?!

The fighters are just one of the UFO's weapons.

No matter how many of them we take down, it doesn't really solve anything.

I should've realized that. Our real enemy is the UFO, not those stupid planes.

The UFO, the one that withstood that giant wind spell without a scratch, is our opponent, and the aircraft are just extras.

But I forgot about that and assumed things were going well just because we had the fighters under control.

And this is the price we pay for that: half of the wyrms' numbers.

We even lost a few dragons, too.

Looks like they got even for the hit we landed before.

The UFO is a giant superweapon, so of course it would have powerful equipment.

Especially since it's also carrying a bomb powerful enough to blow up an entire continent.

"Ahhh, dammit! They got us good. We really screwed the pooch!"

The wind dragon Hyuvan howls with rage.

"Gotta thank you, though. Any later, and we would've been up in smoke, too."

I make a gesture at it not to worry about it.

Since I'm riding on its back, I don't know whether it can see me or whether it'd understand even if it could, but whatever.

It's the one who responded promptly to my warning and took evasive action.

Thanks to it, we didn't get blown away.

If Hyuvan had gotten hit, then obviously I would've eaten it, too, since I'm on its back. It doesn't need to thank me for saving both our lives.

Although I do have the Immortality skill, so I probably would've survived even if we did get blown to smithereens.

But I've got bigger fish to fry than thanking each other right now.

We have to get the wyrms back in line, or the UFO will come after us.

If I were the UFO, I know I wouldn't miss a chance like this.

Sure enough, the UFO deploys a whole bunch of fighters.

I guess it still had plenty of them in store after all.

If all those fighters attack our side right now, the wyrms will scatter and get picked off one by one.

I've got to get them back into formation to take on the aircraft.

As I look around in a panic, I see an even less welcome sight.

The UFO's main gun, the one that just fired on the wyrms, is slowly changing its angle.

Now it's turning toward our troops on the ground.

Damn that UFO. It figured out that the wyrms were too quick a target, so it decided to go after something easier.

Since the dragons are all scattered, it knows it can do more damage by firing on the tightly packed troops below.

Clearly, this UFO is equipped with some top-notch AI.

Seriously, enough already.

Aircraft coming after our guys in the sky, the UFO's main gun pointing at the ones on the ground.

We're in danger on all sides.

If we don't do something fast, we're seriously screwed.

"White!"

As I try to come up with a plan, someone sends me a telepathic message.

It's the Demon Lord.

"I'll take care of the fighters, so you do something about that flying saucer's main gun!"

Do something?

I mean, I'll try my best, but is that really the kind of thing I can do *anything* about?

"White one."

Another voice enters the telepathic conversation. This one must be Potimas.

"Use the weapon I gave you against the enemy's main gun. That should be enough to destroy it."

Oh yeah, now that he mentions it, I do have that thing.

The bazooka, the thing Potimas gave me so we could break into the UFO.

The idea was to use it to bust through the UFO's exterior so we could get inside, so I guess it can probably destroy the UFO's main gun, too.

I mean, if it can get through the exterior, why not?

But then I'd be using up the bazooka's only shot on the gun. How are we supposed to get inside?

"But we won't be able to break in if she does that."

The Demon Lord raises the same concerns I had.

"Fear not. It is more than powerful enough to destroy the main gun. It will destroy the outer wall along with the emplacement."

Ahhh.

So it's gonna blow away the main gun along with the wall behind it, and then we'll get in through there?

Hrmmm. Is that really gonna work?

Well, I guess I have no choice but to trust him on that right now.

"'Kay." I answer shortly.

"'Kay?"

"She means 'okay, no problem.'"

Potimas doesn't understand my shortened response, so the Demon Lord explains for me.

Yeah, it's kinda convenient to have her around at times like these, since she usually gets what I'm thinking.

"Gotcha. So we gotta fly on up to that big ol' gun, right?"

Hyuvan, who was listening to our conversation, confirms our course of action.

I nod.

"You got it, boss! Hang on tight!"

With that, it speeds toward the main gun.

As if guessing our intentions, a bunch of fighters start swarming us.

"Tch!"

"Ignore them—keep going."

Hyuvan seems concerned about the planes, so I try to tell it to just focus on moving forward.

As the fighters come toward us, I ward them off with Wind Magic.

They've got the same barrier as the tank, so my beloved Dark Magic won't work on them.

Which means I have to use Wind Magic, whether I like it or not.

Seriously, you never know what's going to come in handy someday.

I figured I might need Fire, Water, and Earth Magic, and I really do use them in everyday life from time to time, but I never imagined I'd need to use any other kinds of magic.

I mean, Dark Magic is more than adequate for attacking.

It's stronger and faster, since my skill level and experience with it are higher, so it doesn't make sense to use other kinds of magic that I'm not as used to.

Man, it's a good thing I still leveled up my other magic skills, though.

This just goes to show that you can never have too many skills.

Even my other totally useless skills might turn out to be my saving grace one day, maybe! At least I hope so.

Seriously, when am I supposed to use Shieldsmanship and junk like that?

Is there even any shield out there that's stronger than my body?

All right, yeah, I'm getting off topic here. Back to fighting the aircraft.

They must sense something about Hyuvan and me, 'cause they're coming after us like nobody's business.

I guess that might be for the best, since it buys the other dragons time to recover, but since I've got to destroy the main gun over here, I don't have time to mess around with these damn planes.

That's why I told Hyuvan to keep moving forward.

As I knock the pursuing aircraft out of the sky with Wind Magic, we keep heading toward the UFO.

Luckily, the main gun doesn't seem capable of firing in rapid succession. It appears to still be charging, so there's no sign that it's about to fire or anything.

Still, that doesn't mean we've got time to mess around.

If I don't destroy that main gun before it fires again, our forces on the ground will be wiped out.

That gun was strong enough to blow away a dragon without leaving a trace, so even the strongest part of our ground troops, the queen taratects, would be far from safe.

I can't afford to miss.

Ugh, if it wasn't for this UFO's stupid barrier, I could just teleport right in front of the UFO's main gun and blow it away with the bazooka, easy as pie.

Normally, I can use Short-Range Teleport to get to anything within eyeshot, but apparently, it doesn't work like that when that damn mystery barrier is in play.

I guess it's because Spatial Magic can't do anything until you've designated a point in space for it to work on.

But it's impossible to designate any space within the barrier. If I try, I'm just wasting energy.

And even if it's not touching the barrier directly, any space that's too close to the barrier is still hard to target properly.

The mystery barrier seems to act on space itself, so maybe that's why.

Dammit, these barriers are a pain in my ass!

Who the hell developed such a dangerous thing?!

It was Potimas, obviously!

I wish that guy would just drop dead already.

Preferably in the past, before he has a chance to develop this damn barrier.

Does anyone have a time machine I could borrow?

I just wanna pop in to whenever Potimas was born and kill him on the spot.

Then the past would get rewritten, so the barrier would stop existing in the present.

Whew. Okay. Time to stop thinking about stupid things and focus on my job.

I can ward off the fighters without a problem, and the Demon Lord is bringing them down left and right while protecting the wyrms, so I should be able to destroy the main gun before it fires its second shot.

If I miss with the bazooka, then we're totally screwed, so we have to get as close to the UFO as possible so I can fire from a distance where I can't possibly miss.

…Huh? Wait a second.

Get close to the UFO?

Q: Where am I keeping the bazooka again?

A: In Spatial Storage.

But if I'm near the mystery barrier, I can't use Spatial Magic.

Well, shit!

I won't be able to take out the bazooka if I'm too close to the UFO!

And since Hyuvan is a speed-centric dragon, we're getting closer to the UFO by the second.

It's practically right under our noses already.

Uh-oh. I gotta take the bazooka out fast!

Panicking, I hurriedly try to pull the bazooka out of Spatial Storage.

It's stupidly big and long, practically the size of a telephone pole.

Dammit! This thing is huge! How am I supposed to get it out?!

And *of course* you choose this exact moment to show what you're made of, you damn grunt!

How are you speeding so close to the UFO without losing a second?

C'mon! Slow it down a little!

I won't be able to pull out the bazooka!

This is a stupid yet serious predicament I've found myself in here.

But somehow, I barely make it in time!

Just as I manage to pull the bazooka out entirely, the effects of the barrier make the entrance to my Spatial Storage disappear.

Geez, that was close.

If that had happened while I was still taking out the bazooka, it might've gotten broken in half.

Or, like, gotten split between two dimensions or whatever.

"Nice! You ready, girlie?! Here goes nothin'!"

Seeing that I've got the bazooka out, Hyuvan charges right toward the main gun.

Pretending that our plan never came *this* close to being totally ruined, I put on a blank expression and ready the bazooka.

Seriously, nobody needs to know that the ground troops almost got blown away because of my stupid miscalculation.

Whew. Good thing I made it in time.

Seriously.

I steady the bazooka on my shoulder.

There's no complicated mechanism involved in firing this thing. All you have to do is pull the trigger.

Although you need to be crazy strong just to be able to hold up this giant thing.

The UFO's gun is right in front of us.

Even a total noob wouldn't be able to miss from this distance.

Perfect!

With that decided, I pull the trigger.

Bad move, as it turns out.

Between the stress of what just happened and the relief of making it in time before the second shot could be fired, I guess I was a little too careless.

I stupidly forgot exactly who made the bazooka in my hands.

Light blasts out of the bazooka.

This bazooka is apparently a similar weapon to the UFO and the aircraft, since it shoots a beam of light instead of physical ammo.

Now, that's all well and good.

The problem is, the light also blasts out of the other end, right toward me.

Uh-oh.

As soon as that thought crosses my mind, I relinquish my tight hold on Hyuvan's body, shoving off as far away from it as I can.

It's not like I did that with any real forethought, but it would've gotten caught up in it if I stayed there, so I think that was the right move.

Caught up in what, you ask?

The exploding bazooka, that's what!

The light from the bazooka hits the UFO's main gun head-on.

True to Potimas's guarantee, it busts right through the gun and blows through the wall beyond it.

That's also good.

But the light from the bazooka also blows away the hands I was holding it with.

Not only that, but the shoulder that was supporting it and even my human head.

In fact, my whole damn human half goes flying off, and half my spider body gets blown up right with it.

Luckily, I'm able to avoid any more damage thanks to the fact that I'm now free-falling away from the light.

That also distances me from the barrier's range enough that I can use magic again.

Forcing myself to stay conscious, I desperately cast Healing Magic on myself.

Thank goodness I learned Miracle Magic, the advanced form of Recovery Magic.

Otherwise, I could never have recovered from half my brain being blown away.

I probably still wouldn't have died, thanks to my Immortality skill, but I wouldn't be able to think with my whole head missing.

Even half my brain being gone is a huge problem. It takes time to heal that kind of injury, so I'm not gonna be able to fight for a while.

Obviously, normal Healing Magic takes a lot of time to restore a missing body part.

Especially a complicated organ like the brain.

In fact, if I didn't have both Immortality and Miracle Magic, I'd be dead right now, wouldn't I?!

Yeah, I know, that must have been exactly what Potimas was trying to do!

Yes, that bazooka did exactly what he said it would.

It destroyed the main gun and made a hole for us to enter the UFO.

The fact that it's one use only was true, too.

I mean, obviously you can't use it a second time if this is what happens!

How are you gonna fire it again when it blows itself up, not to mention takes the person who fired it down with it!

Which means Potimas intended to kill whoever used it—either the Demon Lord or me.

I knew that guy was our enemy!

How evil do you have to be to go after our lives while we're trying to save the world here?!

Gravity carries me toward the ground.

Most of my power is focused on healing my brain right now, so I can't reposition myself in midair.

I gotta finish healing my brain before I crash into the ground!

Luckily, it turns out I'm worrying for nothing.

Something catches my body from below.

"You okay, lady?!"

Hyuvan scoops me onto its back right in midair.

Ooh, nice catch, buddy.

I know I called you a grunt and all, but you're my favorite person in the world right now.

Dashing gallantly to the rescue when I'm in danger? You just gained a massive opinion modifier with me.

I can't use Telepathy properly just yet, so I tap its back to let it know I'm all right.

"You're alive! You had me sweatin' it out that you was dead, you stinkin' idiot!"

Hey, I'm not an idiot, and I don't stink.

Ahhh, my spider brain is finally intact again.

Boy, Miracle Magic is crazy, restoring half my brain in such a short time after it was blown away like that.

Guess they don't call it "Miracle" for nothin'.

"Hang in there! I'll find someone in a jiff who can use Healing Magic!"

Hyuvan's all worked up now. Sorry, pal, but I'm already on it.

It seems like it's about to turn around and leave, so I stop it with a telepathic message.

"It's okay. I can heal myself."

We can't turn back now.

I've gotta bust into that UFO right away.

"What? You sure?"

"I'm sure. Please bring me there."

I point at the UFO with a spider leg.

I should be able to finish healing by the time we get back up there, so it's no problem.

Right, I've got a job to do.

I've gotta get my revenge on the dirty bastard who's on his way into the UFO right now!

Heh-heh. Just you wait, Potimas!

I'll make you pay for trying to kill me!

The Vampire Mistress and Her Servant Discuss Potimas

"The more MA energy you use, the shorter the planet's life span gets. People didn't know that back then, so they mistook it for an unknown source of limitless energy and used it to their little hearts' content. That's what put their civilization on the path to destruction."

"Such grave foolishness. They must not have held a speck of the wisdom you described, young miss."

"I told you, we can't blame them. A certain bastard deliberately set them up, remember?"

"Young miss, you must not use such crass language. Even if he is a bastard."

"What else am I supposed to call him?"

"You have a point, but still…"

"That bastard killed my parents and tried to kill both of us, too."

"Yes, that's true."

"And Ariel told us that he's always been a bastard, even in ancient times when that civilization still existed. If that's not a bona fide bastard, then what is?"

"I understand your feelings, but I do not think it befits a lady to say 'bastard' so many times."

"Oh? Me, a lady? Goodness…"

(The young miss is embarrassed.)

"…Do you think they're all right up there?"

"We need not worry about Lady Ariel and Lady White, I am sure. Although I am a bit concerned for Miss Ael and company."

"But they're with Potimas, remember? I wouldn't be surprised if that bastard tries to stab them in the back."

"That certainly is possible. However, I am sure that Lady Ariel and Lady White will be prepared for such an eventuality."

"Right. You're right, of course."

"Besides, even that man would surely not attempt such foolishness when the world is at stake, no?"

"Yeah right. Potimas is a bona fide bastard, remember? Whether the world's in danger or not, he'd gladly betray someone if given the chance."

"My apologies. I confess I thought the same thing, but I did not wish to say so."

"Right? This is the same guy who discovered MA energy and convinced humans to use it even though he knew that could destroy everything. Why would he care if the world's in danger or not?"

"Indeed. I suppose there is no reason he would be concerned for the fate of the world now when he is the very same man who endangered it in the past."

"Not to mention, isn't he the one who developed that UFO in the first place? How many times does he have to put the world in danger of destruction before he's satisfied?"

"I suspect he will continue to do so until he dies."

"What a scary thought. But the scariest thing is that you're probably right."

10 RESTRAINT

"Hrmph. So you survived, eh?"

When I reach the UFO, I receive this brazen greeting from Potimas.

We're currently entering the UFO through the hole where the main gun used to be.

Amid the whirling dust and debris, Potimas looks completely calm.

"Hey, what's the big idea, punk? If you was behind that kablooey, you ain't gettin' off scot-free!"

Hyuvan glares at Potimas menacingly, but the elf is defiant.

"Do you really need me to explain it to you?"

Potimas's attitude only makes Hyuvan's rage even more intense.

It could've easily gotten caught up in the explosion of the bazooka if I hadn't jumped away, so I can understand why it's so angry.

The dragon that carried Potimas here joins Hyuvan in directing powerful anger toward Potimas.

And of course, I'm plenty pissed off myself.

Yet, despite the furious gazes focused on him, Potimas's lax attitude doesn't change.

"So what yer sayin' is, you went and did that on purpose. That right?"

Hyuvan's Telepathy carries the weight of a final warning.

Potimas snorts. "And what if I did?"

Clearly, he's not about to apologize.

The only response he gets is an attack.

Hyuvan's claws rake through the air where Potimas was standing just seconds ago.

However, the dragon's roar of frustration tells me that didn't go the way it hoped.

"Oh dear. That was close."

Potimas is now standing a short distance away from Hyuvan.

He dodged the attack of a dragon specialized in speed.

And judging by the way he's brushing the dust off his clothes, it didn't take a lot of effort.

...This guy's totally a narcissist.

Every damn move he makes comes off as smug somehow.

"Tch. Lucky break. I won't miss next time."

Hyuvan gets ready to attack again, but Potimas holds up a hand to stop it.

"Are you sure about that? If you were to dispose of me now, it would make dealing with the GMA bomb far more difficult."

"But not impossible, pal."

"However, no one but I will be able to do it quickly. Who's to say that the bomb won't be dropped while someone else is trying to figure it out? Or that they won't accidentally set it off in the process? Is it really in your best interest to harm the only person guaranteed not to run such risks?"

Hyuvan growls unhappily.

Potimas is basically using himself as a hostage. And unfortunately, it's working.

The Demon Lord does have the plans for the UFO and the bomb, so it wouldn't be impossible to disable the bomb with those as a guide.

But I have to admit that none of us will be able to do it as quickly as the man who developed these weapons in the first place.

If we want to be absolutely sure this will go smoothly, this guy is our best bet.

Even if he's not the safest or most optimal choice.

"What is your role, you so-called dragons? You exist to keep this world running smoothly, do you not? Think about it, then. Is destroying me right now in a fit of anger really what's best for this world or not?"

Potimas spreads his hands melodramatically.

As soon as it hears the words "so-called dragons," Hyuvan reluctantly backs down.

Hyuvan's grunt-like attitude makes it seem stupid, and I'm pretty sure it is, but it does understand its place.

If it puts its emotions aside, it can easily conclude that it wouldn't make sense to kill Potimas now.

Although I'm not sure if letting him live is necessarily a wise move, either...

But considering its role and responsibilities, Hyuvan can't kill Potimas.

And Potimas knows that, which is why he's being a huge asshole about it.

"How will your precious boss feel if you doom the world to destruction simply because you threw a tantrum over being nearly killed?"

Since Hyuvan can't respond, Potimas just keeps fanning the flames.

"It's not myself I'm mad about, pal. But you owe the white one an apology, if you ask me."

Oh my gosh. Hyuvan's not mad on its own behalf; it's mad because *I* almost died?

This is one hunky dragon! Pretty cool for a lowly grunt.

If I were a dragon myself, I'd probably fall for it.

I'm not, though, so we're safe.

"Ridiculous. We have been enemies from the start. What is wrong with attempting to get a leg up on your enemies?"

"You trash! Stickin' to your guns, huh?!"

Hyuvan bares its fangs at the unapologetic elf.

However, because of its position, Hyuvan can't lay a hand on him.

That's got nothing to do with me, though.

And if the man himself says there's nothing wrong with trying to get a leg up on your enemy, that goes for me, too, right?

"Hnnngh?!"

Since Potimas is totally focused on Hyuvan, I swing my giant scythe at him.

My body's already been restored to full power thanks to my Miracle Magic.

On top of that, the UFO's mystery barrier seems to affect only its exterior, not the interior.

In other words, I can use my skills in here no problem.

I should be able to fight to my full capabilities.

Which means I can catch Potimas off guard with a surprise attack and finish him before he has a chance to activate that barrier!

Potimas barely dodges the first attack.

But after that, he has no chance to dodge the second swing.

Gotcha!

But my confidence turns out to be in vain.

My scythe freezes in the air mid-swing.

The scythe and my body have been stopped by thread so thin, it's nearly invisible.

There's only one person who can pull that off.

"White, I get how you feel and all, but could you hold off for now?"

The Demon Lord is walking up behind me.

It's not a surprise, though. Thanks to Detection, I already knew the Demon Lord was inside the UFO.

But I wanted to see what she was going to do, so I'd been ignoring her.

Looks like she's planning on keeping Potimas alive until this whole affair is dealt with.

Hmm. If that's what she wants, I guess I'll go along with it for now.

I use Short-Range Teleport to free myself from the thread.

That might seem like an excessive use of Teleport, but honestly, that's the only way I can escape from the Demon Lord's thread.

For a moment after I free myself, the Demon Lord looks panicked, but she calms down when she sees I'm not going to do anything else.

"Honestly. You ought to at least discipline your spawn properly."

Potimas grumbles as he brushes some dusts his clothes.

That attitude pisses me off. If the Demon Lord hadn't stopped me, I would've had his head.

But then the cocky elf suddenly sinks to the floor.

That's not a metaphor or a joke. Literally, his body just sinks to the floor.

"You're the one who needs to be disciplined, don't you think?"

The culprit who sank Potimas to the floor, the Demon Lord herself, stands on his back.

In the blink of an eye, she used a move sort of like a judo throw to smash him onto the floor, then pinned him down so hard that he actually made an indent in the floor.

What an incredible, almost pointlessly polished move.

It might be even more impressive that Potimas didn't take any damage, despite being slammed to the ground.

However, that's only physical damage we're talking about.

Considering how enormous his ego seems to be, I'm sure being put in such a position must be humiliating to him.

"If you try to pull any more funny business, I'm going to kill you on the spot. Got it?"

"Hmph. If you think you can get by without me, go right ahead."

"So that means you *are* planning on more funny business?"

"If you let your guard down, certainly."

This guy just casually stated that he plans to betray us if he gets the chance.

No, I guess counting him as an ally was a mistake in the first place.

Are we sure we shouldn't just kill him right now?

"Oh yeah? Go ahead and try it, then."

The Demon Lord's voice is low and threatening.

She must have put more weight on her foot, too; the floor starts cracking underneath him.

But Potimas's expression is as cool as ever, as if he doesn't even feel pain.

Well, I guess a cyborg body doesn't need a sense of pain, so it makes sense that he wouldn't include such a feature, but I would've liked to see him struggle and suffer.

I guess seeing him crushed to the ground like this does help a little, but not enough to satisfy me, y'know?

There's definitely still a lot of anger pent up in my chest.

My body's fixed now, but my clothes got destroyed, for one thing.

I'm wearing a spare outfit, but the one I had on before was one of my favorites, I'll have you know!

"Hey, White. You wanna step on him, too?"

You better believe I do!

Leave it to the Demon Lord. She really gets me!

The Demon Lord removes her foot from Potimas's back, so I stomp on him instead.

He tries to get away, of course, but that's not gonna happen!

I pin down his back with one leg, then step on his head with the other.

Can't forget to grind my foot into his face, too, of course.

"Rrrgh!"

Potimas emits a groan, possibly from humiliation.

He's trying to squirm out from under me, but my feet have him pinned firmly to the ground.

It's convenient having so many legs at times like these.

The only problem is that my feet actually end in pretty sharp claws, so I have to be careful not to stab right into him.

Wait. Is it really a problem if I do stab him?

"Oh whoopsie, I jabbed you a little by mistake, sorry~" I can totally get away with that right now!

Let's get down to it, then!

Just then, my eyes suddenly fall on Potimas's lower half.

And a divine revelation descends on me!

Hang on, though. This might be too evil even for me!

But now that I've had the idea, I can't help it!

I've just gotta do it!

My third leg stabs right into you-know-what!

"Wha—?! Why, you!"

"Pffft!"

Potimas lets out a particularly dramatic reaction to that, causing the Demon Lord to snicker.

I did it. Oh, I did it, all right!

Aaaah!

What did I do, you ask? I stabbed his butt, that's what.

Since he's a cyborg, Potimas didn't have a butthole, so I figured why not make one for him?

So I did! You're welcome.

Potimas quakes uncontrollably with indignation, while the Demon Lord bursts out laughing.

Hyuvan and the rest of the dragons, on the other hand, look pretty freaked out.

"*Yikes. This chick's crazy.*"

"*Big bro, are we gonna have to start calling this lady Ms. White from now on or what?*"

"*We can't ever get on her bad side, that's for sure. She's a demon, a white demon!*"

Hyuvan, the dragon that was carrying Potimas, and the one that was carrying the Demon Lord all make their own comments.

They're using Telepathy for a private exchange that only they're supposed to be able to hear, but that stuff doesn't escape my Detection, you know!

Come on—even I don't do stuff like this normally.

"Bwa-ha-ha! Ah-ha-ha-ha-ha! Whew... Aaah-ha-ha-ha-ha!"

The Demon Lord is smacking the floor and wheezing with laughter.

At this rate, she might actually bust right through the floor.

Well, I'm pretty satisfied that I got my sweet revenge, so I'll take my feet off him now.

When I pull up the one that was jabbed into his butt, Potimas's body twitches, making my victory all the sweeter. It causes the Demon Lord to burst out laughing all over again, but it's worth it.

As soon as I remove my feet, Potimas scrambles away like a bat out of hell.

"It has been many an age since... No, this may even be the first time that I have been treated so disgracefully."

Potimas's normally composed expression is contorted with rage.

"I shall kill you. This I swear. And in the most gruesome manner I can imagine at that."

Aw, shucks. A vow of violence for little old me?

Thanks, ol' chap.

"Unfortunately, now is not that time. As I said before, I shall gladly make an attempt on your lives if given the chance, but right now, resolving this situation takes precedence."

Potimas closes his eyes and takes a deep breath, calming himself.

"Until said situation is resolved, I shall let this incident slide. Consider yourself fortunate."

Potimas's dramatic statement makes the Demon Lord start snickering again.

I can't blame her. Lines like that are pretty in character for this guy, but in this particular situation, it's just hilarious.

Like, he's clearly trying to hang on to his last shred of dignity.

That only makes it even funnier, especially to the Demon Lord, apparently.

"And you. How long do you intend to roll around laughing like an imbecile? Consider our situation."

He's not wrong, but since he's saying that with such a sour look on his face, it clearly just sounds like he's taking out his anger on the Demon Lord.

Amazing! Potimas's credibility as a big shot is going down by the second!

At this rate, his stock's gonna plummet so fast that they'll have to stop selling shares!

"Ahhh…ha-ha…whew. Heh. That was hilarious all right."

The Demon Lord wheezes as she tries to recover.

She's definitely still smirking, to the point where it looks like she might bust a gut again at any second, but somehow she manages to pull herself together.

"Ha… Okay, where were we? If we let our guards down, you'll kill us or whatever? I guess we'll just have to rip you another new butthole whenever that happens. Pffft!"

The Demon Lord starts laughing all over again at her own joke.

"Enough already."

I guess I can't blame Potimas for losing his patience.

We're not getting anywhere at this rate.

Although I'm the one who caused it in the first place (and I can't say I regret it).

But considering the current situation and all, we should probably move on already.

"All right, all right. Let's get down to business."

The Demon Lord suppresses her smile, nodding seriously.

I can still see the corners of her lips twitching, but I'll let it slide.

"We'll just call it even for now, okay? We're not gonna be able to work together as a team, but we can at least pool our resources here. You've got the know-how to deal with these machines, and we've got our serious firepower. So we'll just use each other. Instead of trying to play nice, we'll just assume we're going to stab each other in the back. Any objections?"

"None."

None? Really?!

Are we seriously okay with this?

The fate of the world is at stake—you know that, right?

But I guess it's not like we can just start trusting Potimas now.

Huh? Wait a sec.

Depending on how you look at it, isn't this kind of a three-way battle?

The Demon Lord and I are basically in a cold war right now.

And Potimas is obviously an enemy to both of us.

Since he called me "the Demon Lord's spawn" earlier, he must not realize that the Demon Lord and I are actually enemies with a shaky truce.

Depending on how this goes, couldn't I use Potimas to get rid of the Demon Lord once and for all?

But that also means that if I'm not careful, she could do the same thing to me.

And Potimas's aggro is totally concentrated on me right now…

Oh geez.

I guess I have to be even more careful than I thought.

Oh, I know! I can have Hyuvan run interference for me.

"Dragons, you guys can go back and make sure we keep control of the skies, 'kay? You don't need to do anything crazy, just help our troops on the ground keep the advantage."

"You got it, boss. You gonna be okay, though?"

"Yeah, we're fine."

We are certainly not fine!

"If you say so. Be careful in there!"

With that, Hyuvan and the other dragons take off into the skies.

Now it's just the Demon Lord, Potimas, and me.

Not exactly my ideal situation.

"Okay, let's get moving. Looks like there's a welcome party waiting for us first, though."

The Demon Lord scowls into the UFO.

A small army of robots is approaching from within.

Looks like they kept plenty of troops on board to deal with any intruders.

Special Chapter THE STRUGGLE OF THE PONTIFF'S GROUND FORCES

In the distance, I see a great number of machines approaching, creating an enormous cloud of dust.

I swallow my spit in an attempt to soothe my parched throat, but it has little effect in the dry air of this wasteland.

It appears I am more nervous than I realized.

As the pontiff of the Word of God religion, there is no reason I should be part of this battle.

As I stand under the pressure of the battlefield, I realize all too clearly that I am a politician, not a commander.

Or perhaps I should say *remember*, not *realize*.

Long ago, before the Word of God religion became such a large organization, I commanded an army once.

However, I soon learned that I had no talent for war.

As it is a role that uses one's mind, I thought I should at least be able to feign it adequately. Yet, when it came time to enter the battlefield, I found I was nothing more than a scarecrow.

There are times, such as this one, when I have no other choice but to participate, but otherwise I prefer to leave it to my more talented subordinates.

The right person, the right place, the right time.

This should not be my battlefield.

But this time, there is meaning behind my presence here.

Before me stand the knights of the Word of God.

There are thirty thousand of them, all told.

Normally, they are meant to stay at the Word of God's focal point, the Holy Kingdom of Alleius, as the strongest line of defense.

But these are the only men I could mobilize on such short notice.

As a result, the Holy Kingdom has been left virtually defenseless.

Furthermore, it is very likely that many knights will make the ultimate sacrifice in the coming battle, meaning that Alleius's military might will be vastly depleted.

Coupled with our recent failed attempt at invading Sariella, we are suffering so many losses that the kingdom itself could crumble.

However, we are in no position to hold back.

The fate of the world hangs in the balance.

I, of all people, cannot bring anything short of my full forces to such a battle.

Even if others might forgive it, I myself would not.

This is all so I can keep my vow to do anything it takes for the sake of humanity.

Even if I must sacrifice my "power" in the form of the Word of God organization, I will gladly do so if it means humanity is protected.

And if it will raise my knights' morale, then I cannot hesitate to be present at this battlefield, either.

Even if I am a subpar commander, my presence gives these knights strength.

If I am to send these people to their deaths, the least I can do is offer them that small comfort.

I cannot simply sit around when the world is in peril.

"Thank you for gathering here today, all of you."

My amplified voice reaches every knight.

"The forces you are about to fight are far stronger than any monsters you have faced; this battle will likely be the fiercest you have ever encountered."

The knights listen intently, hanging on to my every word.

"Your opponents are the vanguard of evil creatures who once felled our god. The surviving creatures have returned to attempt to destroy the world once more. Know that the very survival of our world depends on the outcome of this battle!"

When I finish my speech, the knights raise a battle cry so loud, it almost seems to shake the earth itself.

These knights are devout believers in the Word of God.

Normally, this situation would make no sense to most people, but they have absolute trust in the words of their pontiff.

This is my "power."

I know all too well that I am exploiting these people, in a way.

But the time when I felt guilt for such a thing has long since passed.

I have no hesitation about sending them to near-certain death.

"Charge!"

On my order, the knights raise another yell and rush forward.

But then an explosive roar drowns out their cries.

The wind blows so violently that I'm forced to shut my eyes.

When I attempt to open them again, another gale blows into my face.

But in the moment that my eyes are open, I see the mechanical soldiers' formation falling apart.

The machines are being crushed and annihilated along with the very ground.

And more attacks mercilessly follow.

This brutal assault is the work of the queen taratects: the legendary-class monsters Lady Ariel summoned.

The queen taratects' breath attacks are what's currently decimating the machine soldiers.

Few monsters are categorized as legendary class.

It's a level considered beyond the ability of any humans to fight—essentially a living natural disaster.

Most of them are beings that were made to manage this world, working under the supervision of Lord Black Dragon.

But the queen taratects, which Lady Ariel created, are a notable exception.

Unlike the other legendary-class monsters, which were designed to be such from the beginning, these are base monsters that have evolved to incredible heights.

It's said that a single one of these powerful beings can ruin an entire nation.

That is the queen taratect: a distinctive monster even among the rare legendary class.

And there are four of them here.

How many human kingdoms could these four monsters destroy?

It's said that an entire army led by a hero once managed to defeat a single queen taratect.

The hero and most of the army were lost in the process.

Even then, it was a miracle they were able to defeat it at all.

And now four of these almighty monsters are fighting on our side.

I cannot think of a more powerful ally.

The queen taratects take turns mowing down the enemy's mechanical soldiers with breath attacks.

This causes an unimaginable amount of destruction that stops the charging knights in their tracks.

They have no other choice.

If they kept advancing, they would be caught up in the queen taratects' destructive rampage.

There is nothing humans such as them can do in the face of such destruction.

Still, I would not complain if the queen taratects alone were to wipe out all our enemies.

Unfortunately, it looks as though we won't be so lucky.

Large balls of light hurtle toward the queen taratects.

It's a counterattack from the large "tank" machines, which are advancing right in the face of the queen taratects' breath attacks.

According to Lady Ariel, these tanks have a magic-inhibiting barrier.

The queen taratects' breath attack is a magic art, so the barrier renders it useless.

It cannot protect the tanks from collateral damage, like the shock waves knocking them into the air, but a direct attack from Breath has no effect.

And worse, there is little that any humans can do to break through these tanks' defenses.

The anti-magic barrier is troublesome, but worse yet, the tanks' armor is simply so sturdy that no human attack could hope to scratch it.

Our only choice is to entrust the tanks to forces other than the knights, like Lady Ariel's kin or Potimas's machine weapons.

Indeed, even the smaller machines are a great challenge for the knights.

It takes several of them to even stand a chance at destroying one machine.

These are elite soldiers who have undergone rigorous training, yet there is a limit to their individual strength.

The human race, you see, is terribly weak.

So what is their role in this battle?

Essentially: meat shields.

They are a living wall meant to slow the machine army's progress.

These knights are not here to defeat the machines but simply to buy time and nothing more.

It is for that small purpose that they die.

The tanks' attacks force the queen taratects to pause their breath attacks, and the machine soldiers use this chance to resume their advance.

Their numbers have been considerably thinned out by the breath attacks, but because there were so many to begin with, one cannot say that there are few of them remaining now.

These mechanical soldiers now begin to attack the knights.

Their light bullets pierce right through them, fatally injuring most of those in the front ranks.

And yet, the elite knights continue their advance until their very last breath.

When they fall, they fall forward, not one of them retreating.

And the fallen knights are quickly trodden over by the knights who were marching behind them.

Even as corpses begin to cover the ground, my soldiers continue to advance.

If our opponents were living things, perhaps they would feel fear or hesitation at the alarming determination of the knights' onslaught.

But on this day, we are fighting emotionless machines.

They calmly press forward, firing more light bullets at the knights.

Finally, the two sides clash directly.

The knights charge the machines and eat into their ranks, striking out with sword and shield.

They succeed in destroying a few of the machines this way, but many more of the knights are defeated instead.

It is a natural outcome, since the machines possess greater strength and numbers than the human knights.

No matter how hard they might fight, they cannot make up for this discrepancy.

However, their actions can still buy enough time to allow others to succeed.

One of the tanks, crushing the knights beneath it, is suddenly hit in the side by a powerful attack.

The giant hunk of metal flies through the air and crashes hard into the ground.

Then it continues to roll, destroying any mechanical soldiers in its path.

When it finally stops, there is a dent in its hull so deep, it's as if it took a direct hit from a cannon.

Another attack hits that same tank, sending it flying even farther away.

In its place stands a young girl, still swinging an indelicate blunt weapon that appears to be a hunk of metal with a handle.

Though she looks out of place on the battlefield, she is actually not a human but a puppet taratect, another of Lady Ariel's kin.

Despite her innocuous appearance, her kind is one of the strongest of Lady Ariel's spawn, second only to the queen taratects.

While her face may look cute, each of her six arms is brandishing one of these blunt metal weapons, so I doubt anyone would be foolish enough to misjudge her.

Lady Ariel told me before that even the puppet taratects were unable to match the tanks, but it appears there will be no such concern this time.

The other tanks nearby have already stopped moving, perhaps out of caution toward this new threat, but she strikes all of them anyway.

…Is that entirely necessary?

I would prefer her to focus on the tanks that are currently causing problems, not the ones that are sitting still.

As if hearing my thoughts, another one of the puppet taratects approaches the one still wailing on the stopped tanks and smacks her on the head.

Then the second puppet taratect points at a still-moving tank.

The first puppet taratect hesitates, though she seems to understand the second one's meaning, but then a third one comes and deals her a swift kick.

Were it not for our current circumstance, this would simply be a charming scene of some young girls play fighting.

But these girls represent a powerful fighting force.

They should be battling seriously, not messing around.

More of my knights are losing their lives while these girls jest.

As if to ease my frustration, a queen taratect's breath attack blasts through the machine soldiers' rear lines.

It wreaks destruction on the mechanical soldiers, whose advance my knights laid down their lives to halt.

A flying machine speeds toward the queen taratect, but a wyrm knocks it out of the sky before it can attack.

Even now, the wyrms and flying machines are engaging in a fierce battle in the air.

They've accomplished their task of delivering Lady Ariel and company onto the enemy flagship, but the wyrms and dragons have no time to rest.

If they were not there to keep the flying machines occupied, no doubt our ground forces would be destroyed from above.

Thanks to the clean sweep of the queen taratects' breath attacks, things on the ground are going more smoothly than expected.

However, that advantage is a delicate thing indeed.

The knights are currently holding back the machine soldiers' advances enough that the queen taratects can attack as they wish, but if the machines break through, victory will be far less certain.

I doubt the queen taratects will go down easily, but the machines do have the advantage in numbers, and even a queen taratect is not completely invulnerable.

If the tanks all concentrated their fire on one, even a queen taratect would not escape unharmed.

Right now, the knights must buy time as human shields, allowing the queen and puppet taratects to whittle down the enemy's numbers.

It will not be easy for the knights, but they must hold fast somehow.

However, the machines Potimas brought also concern me.

Thus far, they have not taken any assertive action.

They simply stay passive, as if waiting for the right moment, only occasionally intercepting enemy machines.

Instead of attacking independently, they primarily provide cover fire to maintain the front lines.

Considering their maker, surely they are capable of more than just this.

In this situation, I am certain that man would have brought more powerful machines.

Especially considering how the times have changed.

Our current enemies may have been created by a scientific culture at the height of its development, but they are now no more than relics that have been stored in underground ruins for countless years.

Yet, Potimas, the same man who designed them, has brought weapons to oppose them that he created a great deal of time later.

Since these machines share the same creator, it stands to reason that the newer ones should be far more powerful.

As long as he did not deliberately bring an inferior model, I cannot imagine that the weapons he chose would lose to these ancient machines.

And yet, they do not take any action of note. Could it be that he is plotting something?

It certainly could.

Knowing that man, I would not doubt it for a second.

The same is true of what happened earlier.

With my Panoptic Vision, I saw that strange creature with the upper body of a human atop that of a spider, the one they call "White," use the weapon Potimas gave her to destroy the enemy flagship's main gun. And I saw that same weapon attempt to destroy her, too.

That it injured its wielder so severely was no accident.

It was intended from the start to kill the one who fired it.

Yes, he was after Lady Ariel and Miss White.

He gave them that gun thinking it would be in his best interest to destroy at least one of them.

This was an assassination attempt. Potimas would surely do such a thing.

Even in an emergency as dire as this one.

Fortunately, it appears that Miss White was able to survive, but considering that the blast was powerful enough to destroy that enormous flagship's cannon, I would not have been surprised if she didn't.

In fact, it's likely that Miss White was able to survive only because she has Healing Magic strong enough to quickly recover from even a major loss of body parts.

If Lady Ariel had been the one to use that gun, the worst might have even come to pass.

Lady Ariel is the most powerful being in this world after Lord Black Dragon, but like the queen taratect, she is not entirely invulnerable.

Even she may die.

Which is exactly what Potimas must have been thinking when he set that trap.

This is Potimas, after all. I have no doubt he chose that gun with the confidence that it would be able to kill Lady Ariel.

It is even possible that Lady Ariel handed it off to Miss White because she suspected something was amiss.

Whether that was because she trusted that Miss White would not die in such an event or simply because she did not care whether Miss White died or not, I have no way of knowing.

A white spider.

Healing Magic that can restore even a lost limb or organ.

And enough strength to hold her own in battle even alongside Lady Ariel and the dragons.

With all these hints, it is quite simple to deduce her identity.

The Nightmare of the Labyrinth.

The mysterious spider monster that appeared from the Great Elroe Labyrinth and took up residence in Sariella.

Perhaps she has evolved since then, or perhaps this is simply her true form, but Lady White and the Nightmare of the Labyrinth are almost certainly one and the same.

I doubt there can be more than one such creature in existence.

Even if Lady Ariel did have more of such powerful beings hidden away, I cannot imagine she would not bring them forth for a situation such as this one.

Besides, Lady Ariel herself stated that the Nightmare of the Labyrinth was not her subordinate.

In other words, the Nightmare was never under her control—and could very well have even been her enemy.

At the battle between Ohts and Sariella, the Nightmare was said to be engaged in an intense battle with another being.

Who could hold their own against the Nightmare and happened to be in the area at the time?

I can think of none but Lady Ariel.

To me, that is a sure sign that Lady Ariel and the Nightmare are, or at least were, at odds with each other.

Shortly thereafter, when I encountered Lady Ariel and asked her about the matter, she stated that she "had things under control."

I took that to mean that either she had succeeded in defeating the Nightmare or recruited it onto her side, although I could not say which. But since my surveillance later witnessed Miss White traveling with Lady Ariel, I assumed that she successfully won her over.

However, as I continued my surveillance, I noticed something strange.

Lady Ariel was not treating Miss White as a lesser being.

According to my spy, she appeared to be treating Miss White as an equal.

My spies undergo special training to excel at lipreading.

With one as powerful as Lady Ariel, spying by way of skills is impossible, as she would undoubtedly detect it.

And primitive long-distance viewing devices could provide only an incomplete view of the situation, hardly enough to acquire all the information.

But even this highly inadequate manner of spying showed that the relationship between Lady Ariel and Miss White was most unusual.

Upon receiving this information from my spy, I realized I could not accept Lady Ariel's claim of "having things under control" at face value.

In other words, Lady Ariel and Miss White have not entirely made their peace just yet.

An outsider such as myself cannot possibly know the exact nature of their relationship, but even I can tell that they do not trust each other completely.

It is even possible that Lady Ariel deliberately used Potimas to try to dispose of Miss White in the midst of this situation.

However, considering Lady Ariel's personality, I have my doubts about that possibility.

Besides, it seems strange that one as strong as Lady Ariel would treat Miss White as an equal.

With her power, she should be able to force just about anyone to bend to her will.

If they were enemies before, surely Lady Ariel would have simply beaten her into submission.

But at a glance, it seems as though Lady Ariel and Miss White really do treat each other as equals.

Even seeing them up close with my own eyes, I never got the impression that one of them was serving the other.

In that case, there must be some reason that even Lady Ariel cannot force Miss White to do her bidding.

But what in the world could that be?

Even if Miss White really is the Nightmare, I find it hard to believe that her power would rival Lady Ariel's.

What conditions could prevent Lady Ariel from defeating one who is inferior to her in power?

One could technically say the same of Potimas, but his ability to deal with the bomb makes him a unique situation. It brings me no closer to discerning the reasons for Miss White.

No, I suppose she, too, could be using something as a shield to prevent Lady Ariel from harming her.

Then, could that shield be Sophia Keren?

No, that doesn't quite add up.

The puppet taratects, then?

But the puppet taratects are Lady Ariel's own summoned kin.

If she wished to keep them out of danger, she could simply undo the summons.

It doesn't make sense.

Then, does Miss White, like Potimas, have some kind of special capability that Lady Ariel would be reluctant to lose?

I suppose that would make sense.

But I cannot conceive of what ability Miss White might have that Lady Ariel would want.

In the back of my mind, I remember the last time I encountered Lady Ariel.

That's right. She did ask me about immortality back then.

It was an abrupt question, unrelated to the topics we were discussing at the time.

After that, she started acting even more strangely and took her leave, so I remember the encounter quite distinctly.

Immortality. Could that be related?

Is it possible that Miss White has the Immortality skill?

But no, that still doesn't make sense.

Immortality is certainly a rare skill, but even if Miss White does have it, that wouldn't explain why Lady Ariel has such pressing interest in her.

An undying fighter is certainly a powerful ally, but that would be far too risky a reason to invite a former enemy to join forces.

Besides, the Immortality skill has several shortcomings.

There are multiple ways to kill someone with the Immortality skill, like Abyss Magic, for one. Lady Ariel knows this, of course, so surely she could still slay an immortal enemy.

In that case, perhaps Miss White does not have the Immortality skill, but something still seems off.

Lady Ariel was definitely acting strangely when she asked about it.

"Do you know of any skills besides Immortality and your Temperance that might basically make someone immortal?"

What was the true meaning behind that question?

A skill aside from Immortality that would make someone immortal.

Even if such a skill exists, what would it have to do with Lady Ariel?

Does she want such a skill for herself?

Surely not. Now that she has resolved to become the Demon Lord, it would make no sense for Lady Ariel to seek such a thing as immortality.

Then, was it about Miss White?

Incredible. Could it be?

Did Lady Ariel try to kill Miss White only to discover that she could not?

If she was unable to kill Miss White, of course she would have no choice but to call a truce.

That line of reasoning would explain everything.

If Miss White also had no choice but to reach an agreement with Lady Ariel, since the latter is still stronger, then it would be no wonder that they have such a strange relationship.

Assuming they had no other option than to join forces, rather than working together of their own choice, it makes sense that they would still harbor animosity toward each other.

In that case, everyone who is currently on board the enemy flagship views one another as an enemy.

Potimas goes without saying, but Lady Ariel and Miss White are potential enemies as well.

And now the fate of this entire world rests on such a precarious trio's shoulders?

It is concerning, but powerless as I am, I have no choice but to entrust things to them.

This is a painful reminder: Compared to the likes of Lady Ariel and Potimas, everything I have built up is terribly weak.

So weak that it amounts to nothing more than a human shield to buy time.

And yet, I have done everything within my power to protect that weakness.

I have no regrets about the path I've chosen.

I cannot regret it.

An explosive sound different from the rest puts an end to my wandering thoughts.

Oh dear. My bad habit of getting lost in thought has reared its head again. This is hardly the time to be thinking about such things.

Looking around at the battlefield, I see that the situation is as tempestuous as ever.

The knights are still doggedly holding back the machine soldiers' advance.

The battle between the wyrms and the flying mechanical soldiers is still unfolding.

The queen taratects are still wiping out the machines' rear ranks with breath attacks, too.

However, there is one significant change: Potimas's weapons are now furiously fighting against the tanks.

The knights and even the queen taratects' breath attacks couldn't lay a scratch on the tanks, so of course most of them are still intact.

But now they're all under attack by Potimas's machines.

In fact, they all seem strangely concentrated in one place.

Looking more closely, I realize that another force is guiding all the tank machines into one area.

It's the puppet taratects.

They're skillfully shepherding the tank machines forward, directly into the ranks of Potimas's machines.

Perhaps the puppet taratects had similar suspicions to my own and decided to nip the problem in the bud before Potimas's machines could do anything suspicious.

These machines are now far too busy fighting off the enemy tanks to pull any sort of betrayal.

I must admire the puppet taratects: Not only have they prevented any suspicious movements from Potimas's machines, they've even forced the machines to deal with their most formidable foes.

The four puppet taratects couldn't deal with all the tank machines, so they're enlisting the help of Potimas's machines, which weren't contributing much.

That alone was a brilliant tactical decision, but the fact that it also quashes any potential revolt from Potimas's machines is true genius.

And at the same time, they've drastically reduced their own workload.

There were too many tanks for the four of them to take on, but now that they've found an alternative way to deal with them, that frees up the puppet taratects to move as they please.

Essentially, this one tactical decision has killed three birds with one stone.

They do say that the best tacticians are brilliant yet lazy.

The puppet taratects' leader, especially, seems to have the makings of an excellent commander.

Ah, but they're currently running all over the battlefield to carry out these tasks, so I suppose it was rude to call them lazy.

At any rate, I am little more than a figurehead commander myself, so I am glad to see there are some real leaders here on the battlefield.

Perhaps we will meet as enemies someday, but since the world is currently in danger, it would be foolish to bare our fangs at each other.

Although I wish we could be sure that Potimas's machines felt the same way.

Those machines are now too occupied to do anything else, so we will never know whether they intended to betray us.

However, I must say I would be more surprised if that was not the case.

Yet, as long as their guns are not pointed our way, I will be glad to have them demonstrate their full strength.

Just as I predicted, Potimas's machines are more powerful than the enemy tanks.

Though not without effort, even one of them can take on a tank.

While they could doubtless win such a one-on-one battle, Potimas's machines are fighting each tank with larger numbers.

There are around two thousand of them, so it's unlikely that Potimas's machines will be crushed. However, they are suffering a few losses.

Superior though they might be, both are still machines designed by Potimas. No matter how long ago he developed it, no weapon made by that man would go down easily.

As reluctant as I am to admit it, that man is extremely capable.

I have no choice but to acknowledge him as such.

And there is one more thing I must acknowledge: He is a bastard.

This combination of being both extremely capable and utter scum is what makes him Potimas.

Which is why, when I look out at the battlefield again, I am not as shocked as I could be.

Still, I cannot stop a choice word or two from slipping out.

"Bastard."

The attendant priest next to me gasps.

I'm sure he's never seen the look on my face before.

Most people get the wrong impression, since I always take great pains to keep a gentle smile on my face at all times, but the truth is that I am quick to anger by nature.

It is simply that I take care not to let it show on my face.

But this time, I cannot keep up my usual appearances.

"Truly, you still have a horrible tendency to toy with life itself."

I know that Potimas cannot hear me, yet I cannot help myself.

For my eyes have fallen on one of Potimas's broken machines.

Within the remains, I can see something slimy and raw.

A strange thing to find among the wreckage of a machine but unmistakable.

A person's brain.

Instead of artificial intelligence, these machines use brains.

The brain and nothing else.

I have no way of knowing whether these brains still possess the will of the people they came from.

It's entirely possible they are only equipment for controlling the machines, no longer capable of thought.

Even so, that does not change the fact that these machines are abominations, flouting of the very laws of nature.

Only Potimas could make such a horrific machine.

As long as it helps him reach his goals, he will gladly cast aside morality.

And he will gladly tread on the backs of others.

I tear my gaze away from Potimas's horrible machines.

I cannot bear to look any longer at the poor beings who have been used for that man's foul purposes.

But when my eyes fall instead on the knights being trampled by the enemy machines, I realize my own hypocrisy.

Having sent these knights knowingly to their deaths, how am I any different from Potimas?

If he is a heretic, then so, too, am I.

Just another monster who toys with life itself.

And yet, I have no choice but to continue along this path of heresy.

For it is the path I have sworn to follow.

Even if I have fallen from grace, I cannot stop moving forward.

I am sorry.

No matter how many times I apologize in my heart, I cannot say the words out loud.

I have no right to do so.

But even if it is heresy, I shall hold on to my conviction of protecting humanity.

"Hey, Potimaaas. Isn't anything going to come out of that new hole of yours? C'mon, like fire or something? Maybe you can cast magic out of your butt! Pfffft!"

Heresy.

There's a heretic here.

Not that I can talk, since I'm the one who started all this in the first place.

Our latest battle is getting rave reviews from the critics.

And yet, this slacker is still messing around.

Sure, we're absolutely owning this swarm of robots. These little ones are so weak, I'm practically falling asleep here.

That's why the Demon Lord has decided to start poking fun at Potimas while we're fighting.

And then busting out laughing in the middle of her own damn jokes.

Cut it out. Magic's not gonna come out of his butt.

Actually, maybe it could if he really tried?

Hey, wait a second. The Demon Lord and I are both spider-type creatures, so aren't *we* the ones who make magic thread come out of our butts?

Having realized this horrifying truth, I decide to keep quiet.

I guess this is what they call putting your foot in your mouth. Or your butt, in this case.

Anyway, since the Demon Lord seems to be having a grand old time, she's mowing down the robots like crazy.

Potimas, on the other hand, is silent. He's completely ignoring the Demon Lord and focusing on fighting the robots.

I thought he was going to turn his arm into a gun or whatever like he did before, but this time he's just holding a gun and firing it like a normal person.

He's holding it up with both hands, aiming at the robots, and firing light bullets—but these aren't like the ones the robots use.

Potimas's light bullets can pulverize several robots in a single shot.

Is it my imagination, or is this gun just as powerful as those tanks' main gun?

It might be big, but the tank's gun was obviously way bigger. Maybe he found a way to shrink that down with technology or something?

Either way, it's scary.

And yet, the Demon Lord is picking a fight with this guy and his giant gun.

I'm stuck in the middle of them, but of course I'm destroying my share of robots, too.

You know, firing magic, using my Evil Eyes, tying thread to my scythe, and playing with it like a sickle and chain, that kind of thing.

Oh, uh, did I say "playing"? I'm not playing. Of course I'm not.

I'm taking this robot fight very seriously, I swear.

But no matter how many of them we break, more robots just keep coming.

Can you really blame me for wanting to experiment a little and try something new?

By the way, my "giant scythe and chain" is working out great.

Since I have Thread Control, I can move it around however I want.

And my giant scythe cuts through these robots like butter.

It's not exactly like a real sickle and chain, but I think it'll be a great close-to midrange-attack method.

Magic and Evil Eyes for long-range.

Thread for midrange.

And my scythe for close-range.

Heh-heh. I've got a pretty good strategy, if I do say so myself.

And since I have both a spider brain and a human brain, I can even use both of them at once.

Normally, I could even use my Parallel Minds with both brains to get a double-galaxy brain effect going on, but right now I've got Parallel Minds turned off.

I mean, what if I turn it on and they go crazy again?

I don't really have a choice here.

Still, I've gotten pretty strong, if you ask me.

I used to be so weak that any single hit would kill me, but now I'm an all-rounder who can handle close combat and long-distance alike!

There's hardly anyone who could beat me now!

Although the top two contenders are right here next to me.

The number one threat, also known as the Demon Lord, is cackling away as she destroys more and more robots.

Watching her fight certainly is instructive.

After all, the Demon Lord is an all-rounder who excels at any distance, too.

She can use magic to fire at long distances, attack with thread for middle distances, and any brave soldier who gets through those first two will find Gluttony waiting for them.

Seriously, there's not a single gap in her defenses.

That last one, Gluttony, is particularly scary.

Whether it's light bullets or the robots themselves, she can swallow them whole.

All she has to do is open and close her mouth, and the predation is complete.

That's broken even for one of the Seven Deadly Sins skills.

Even though the robots are giant hunks of metal that would clearly never fit into the Demon Lord's mouth, all she has to do is one big chomp and they're gone without a trace.

There must be some kind of spatial shenanigans going on here.

Can you imagine somehow getting past the Demon Lord's magic attacks and crazy thread moves only to find out that she's most dangerous of all at close range?

She only has to open and close her mouth, and bam, you're in her belly!

That's crazy, man.

Even a close-combat master wouldn't stand a chance in hell.

I guess that means the Demon Lord *is* a close-combat master.

How are you supposed to tackle that?

Just fire at her from afar, you say?

Well, bad news. She can swallow those attacks with one bite, too.

There's really no way around it.

Sounds like cheating to me, don't you think?

Supposedly, I have cheat skills that are just as good, but they don't really seem that way, do they?

Pride is a growth cheat that has no effect on actual battle.

Perseverance is a defensive cheat that lets me use MP if I run out of HP.

Sloth is an attack cheat that increases all my damage to my opponents.

Hero is a support cheat that lets my allies heal automatically.

Yep. Gluttony is definitely the best out of all of them, dammit!

Considering how much stronger I've gotten because of it, I guess Pride is at least as good or maybe even better, but the other ones, not so much.

Okay, I'll admit they've all helped me in the past, but still!

Yes, there were times when I would've died if I didn't have Perseverance, and without Pride, I wouldn't have been able to defeat Araba.

And I guess without Hero, I would've died in that explosion earlier.

Well, technically, that wasn't Hero; it was the Miracle Magic skill I got along with Hero.

So I guess I still have Hero to thank, huh.

But Pride doesn't have any direct effect on battle, and Perseverance is a little irrelevant now that I have Immortality, and Sloth is no help right now because my enemies are machines that don't have HP.

Huh?

Is it just me, or are my cheat skills not really helping me cheat at all?

Th-that's not true.

It can't be true.

I'm telling you, it's not!

Let's just say it's not, okay?!

Ugh, this is all the stupid Demon Lord's Gluttony skill's fault!

Gluttony is way too useful!

What the hell kind of skill lets you eat literally anything and turn it into energy?

She can eat your attacks, eat right through your defenses, and it takes only an instant to activate.

It works as offense *and* defense and even recovers her SP.

That's way too broken of a cheat.

How could anyone beat this monster?

Is a surprise attack from behind the only way or what?

And even that would be pretty damn near impossible.

Yeah. The more I think about it, the less likely it seems one could kill her, even if her guard was down.

How in the world does Potimas plan to do it?

I glance over at Potimas, who's silently shooting down the robots.

Considering all that big talk he was doing, does that mean he actually has some kind of method to kill the Demon Lord?

Hrmmm.

What should I do?

I don't think the Demon Lord's going to let her guard down in the first place, but if Potimas did try to kill her, what would the right reaction be?

The Demon Lord is a regular pain in my butt—I know that much.

If you think about it, we've been clashing ever since I first started fighting against Mother.

She's the one enemy I never found a way to defeat.

Instead I just kept running away from her, antagonizing her as I went, which finally led to this current cease-fire situation.

And I came up with a system that makes it pretty difficult to kill me and, more importantly, makes the Demon Lord think it's impossible.

It took all that just to get to a truce.

Actually, beating her would be way beyond my abilities.

That's the Demon Lord in a nutshell.

She's like a thorn in my side that I can't get rid of.

So if I could actually kill the Demon Lord...what would I do?

To be honest, I don't know what the best answer is anymore.

If I'd found a way to kill her before our truce, I probably would've done it without hesitation.

But now, it's been about two years since we agreed to stop fighting.

We've been traveling together all this time, so I've gotten a pretty solid grasp of her personality.

And from what I can tell, the Demon Lord is super-freaking-nice!

Seriously, it's like, the Hero skill would suit her waaay better than me! She's practically a saint!

Why is she even a demon lord in the first place? It really makes you wonder.

She's such a good person that Vampy and Mera obviously adore her.

Honestly, I'm starting to feel like I should just accept her already.

The only reason we were enemies in the first place was that I was fighting Mother, her kin.

Now that Mother is gone, there's no real reason for me to want to fight the Demon Lord.

Sure, she's still kind of a threat, but I think even the Demon Lord would have a hard time killing me at this point.

When I was fighting Mother, I was struggling just to survive, but now, I don't need to be so scared of every little thing.

I'm starting to wonder if maybe giving up on that animosity is for the best.

The Demon Lord's an angel.

If we can just let bygones be bygones, I have a feeling we could actually get along really well.

Except I don't think that would be so easy.

I mean, the Demon Lord really values her friends and family.

The way she rushed to Sael's rescue in the ruins just shows how much she cares about protecting the people close to her.

And I'm the one who murdered one of her children—Mother.

I'm sure she doesn't exactly look fondly on me because of that.

So even if I'm willing to forget the past, would the Demon Lord really feel the same way?

She suggested the truce, since she can't kill me, but doesn't that mean she would still want to kill me if she could?

And now that I've gone and pissed off Potimas, he's way more likely to come after me than the Demon Lord.

If he uses his mystery barrier, I don't know whether my immortality method would work or not.

And if the Demon Lord decided to side with Potimas then?

Ha-ha-ha.

Yikes...

Yeah, I'd totally be dead, probably.

The secret to my ability to never die is the Immortality skill and my egg-revival technique.

As the name implies, the Immortality skill means that you can't be killed.

Thanks to this skill, I wouldn't die even if my body was blown to bits.

Although I would certainly be rendered unconscious while my body rebuilt itself with HP Auto-Recovery.

Without HP Auto-Recovery, you'd just be stuck in a state of eternal unconsciousness, which is probably a fate worse than death. So Immortality's already a pretty defective skill.

Not to mention, there are other ways around this so-called Immortality.

So that makes it an even more defective skill.

The countermeasure I developed for this is something I call "egg revival."

I use the Egg-Laying skill to make eggs, and then the moment I die, I can transfer my soul into one of those eggs like a pseudo-reincarnation.

The reason this crazy stunt works is because the Egg-Laying skill essentially creates inferior clones of me.

I can even use my Parallel Minds to do other crazy soul stuff, too. Specifically, I sent my Parallel Minds to attack Mother's soul directly and stuff like that.

Skills are the power of the soul.

Mother was trying to use one of those skills, Kin Control, to manipulate me.

So I used it in reverse and managed to eat away at her soul instead.

It's thanks to that soul-related know-how that I figured out a way to transfer my own soul into another body.

Since there aren't any skills for messing with souls like that, I think this is a technique that works outside of the constraints of the system.

So there's a lot even I don't know about how it works.

Like whether I can still do it inside Potimas's barrier or not, for instance.

I definitely don't want to try it, but if it turns out I can't do egg revival inside Potimas's barrier, I really would die.

If Potimas was my only opponent, I might have a chance.

After last time, I made my giant scythe so I'd be prepared.

Since Potimas's barrier renders most skills ineffective, the best way to combat it is with my own physical strength in a close-combat battle.

That and Warped Evil Eye, the only Evil Eye that works in the barrier.

But Potimas has already seen Warped Evil Eye, so there's a good chance he's come up with a way to counter it by now.

That's what I would do, if I were him.

In which case, close combat using my scythe is the best way to deal with him.

The scythe has surpassed my expectations in the best way possible, becoming crazy strong.

And it was able to slice right through that tank, which used the same kind of defenses, so I think it would work even within Potimas's barrier.

Potimas doesn't know that, and even if he did, I seriously doubt he could come up with some way to deal with it in such a short time.

In other words, I do have a method for fighting back against Potimas.

It's possible that Potimas has also prepared some new weapon or something since our battle, but I still think I'd have the advantage, or at least I hope so.

Honestly, there's no way of knowing unless we actually come to blows.

But I do think I'd have a chance of winning, even if that's partially just wishful thinking.

But if the Demon Lord was teaming up against me, too?

Then I'd be totally doomed.

Potimas would be hard enough to fight on his own, so if you add the Demon Lord on top of that—forget it.

Even if I unleashed my Parallel Minds, which I've currently got shut off, I wouldn't stand a chance.

Hrmmm?

We're still just having a friendly little robot cleanup here, so why do I suddenly feel like my life is in pressing danger?

Q: What am I gonna do, seriously?

A: I'll just have to make sure I don't let my guard down.

Uh-huh. Potimas said himself that he'd try to kill us only if we let down our guard, which means if we don't give him the chance, he won't make a move.

For the sake of my sanity, let's just go with that.

Other than that, all I can do is hope that egg revival would work inside that mystery barrier.

If there's someone out there who can make that wish come true, I'll happily pray to them, even if it's a certain self-proclaimed evil god.

Ughhh, now my stomach hurts for some reason.

Guess I'll just have to take this stress out on the robots!

Keeping an eye on Potimas's movements, I continue wiping the floor with the machines.

But there are still way too many of them!

No matter how many robots I break, they just keep coming.

Seriously, how many of you are there?

Well, given the nature of this UFO, I guess maybe that's to be expected.

I mean, it's basically a flying military base.

The UFO itself isn't equipped with *that* many weapons. The main gun was the worst of it, and I destroyed that.

But that's because its role isn't attacking; it's deploying troops.

Yeah. The whole point of its existence is to carry those tanks and fighters and stuff.

Which means there are plenty of spare robots inside the UFO to back up the ones it's already sent down to the ground.

And we have no way of knowing just how many reserve robots there are.

I'd like to think that there's less than the number that's already on the ground, but it's entirely possible it's around the same amount.

If it wasn't sending out too many aircraft at once because of a control issue, then maybe there's even more robots on here than there are down below.

But that can't be the case, I'm sure.

Right?

As the waves of robots show no end in sight, I'm starting to get a little worried.

I mean, no matter how many there are, they're not really a threat to us, but still…

Just as that thought crosses my mind, I see a tank coming up behind the robots.

Yay! Just as I was thinking that these robots are no big deal, this big shot suddenly comes rolling in!

Great timing. You should be an actor!

While I'm distracted by these stupid thoughts, a ball of light fires from the tank's main gun—headed directly for the Demon Lord.

CHOMP! You can practically see the sound effect as the shot disappears into her mouth.

I've heard of omnivores, but this is ridiculous.

The Demon Lord promptly grabs the nearest robot and flings it at the tank with all her might.

As soon as the two collide, they're both reduced to scrap metal.

Geez. The tank looks like a car that's been totaled in a nasty traffic accident, and the remains of the robot are just stuck to the front.

Talk about an unholy fusion.

Yep. Not only are the robots no match for us, even a tank doesn't stand a chance!

As long as we have the Demon Lord on our side, we've got nothing to fear! Bring it on!

Then, as if on cue, a whole bunch of tanks come out at once.

...Seriously, are you guys waiting for the right time to show up or what?

Are you? Huh?

Ughhh, enough already, for real.

If these guys were monsters, that'd be one thing.

I get experience for killing those, and I can eat the bodies.

But since robots are machines and not living things, you don't get any experience for killing them, and they're metal, so you can't eat them, either.

I know I have the title Foul Feeder and all, but even I have my limits.

That's not exactly the kind of iron that's good for your body!

The Demon Lord has Gluttony, so she can eat them just fine, but she's the exception to end all exceptions.

In other words, I have absolutely nothing to gain from this battle.

We have to win or the world's in big trouble, so obviously I'm gonna make sure we don't lose, but it feels more like work than anything.

Just thinking about that sorta drains my motivation.

The Demon Lord can probably handle it by herself, so why do I even need to be here?

C'mon—didn't I already fulfill my role by busting the UFO's main gun and making a hole for us to enter through?

Why do I have to hang around and fight alongside some crazy elf who's after my life?

Seriously, how did things end up like this?

It's all this stupid UFO's fault!

Ugh, just thinking about it is pissing me off.

As if in response to my anger, the ominous aura around the scythe in my hands gets even more intense.

In fact, it's sorta starting to look like the white blade is letting off a visible black haze.

Uh, what's going on here?

I'm not sure, but I get the feeling it's not anything good.

Right away, I swing my scythe around as if to shake off the black haze.

Just like that, the haze dispels.

However, it has some unexpected consequences.

The black cloud spreads, enveloping all the nearby robots and tanks, and destroys every last one of them.

"......"

Silence falls.

The Demon Lord and I, and even Potimas, are at a loss for words.

It's like, the robots are one thing.

They don't have the mystery barrier, so any reasonably powerful wide-range magic could probably have done the same thing.

But that's not true of the tanks.

Since they're protected by the mystery barrier, magic doesn't work on them, so you're supposed to be able to beat them only with physical attacks.

And yet, the black haze my scythe produced just melted them down to nothing.

Despite the fact that you definitely couldn't call that a physical attack.

I guess the light bullets used by Potimas and the enemy robots aren't affected by the barrier, so maybe it's not *that* strange, but this is still different.

Because the robots and tanks that were destroyed by the black haze turned into dust.

That's the telltale sign of the Rot attribute at work.

The power of attributes is connected to the system and therefore shouldn't work within the barrier.

But that black haze went right through the mystery barrier like it was nothing.

And it was produced by my scythe, which even I don't really understand.

Potimas and the Demon Lord stare at me with their mouths open.

Uh-oh.

If I let them see that I'm just as shaken as they are, I have no idea what they'll do.

That's right. I knew this would happen.

My goal all along was to show Potimas what would happen to him if he messes with me!

Yeah, let's go with that!

Keeping a straight face, I lower the scythe to its original position.

My heart is pounding, but they don't need to know that.

Hey, wait a second. My MP went way down.

Um, *excuse* me?! Why does the scythe I made have so many features I don't know about?!

It's pretty useful, but still!

Come on! Can't I get a user's manual or something?!

All of this shock is gonna ruin my poker face!

Just as my composure is about to hit its limit, more robots and tanks start showing up.

The Demon Lord and Potimas turn their attention toward them.

Nice timing!

Seriously, these machines always know right when to show up!

"Well, if White's going to take this so seriously, I guess I'd better do the same."

A shudder runs across my skin.

The Demon Lord, who was right next to me moments ago, disappears.

Technically, she just moved so fast that it looked like she disappeared into thin air, but it was so sudden that it might have well been magic.

Even I couldn't follow her movements with my eyes.

The sound and shock waves follow a few seconds later.

My High-Speed Processing skill means that things seem to move more slowly around me, but even then, I can barely follow what's happening.

The new wave of robots and tanks is turned to scrap in an instant.

Talk about cheating.

Yeah. I knew something seemed off.

The robots and tanks are annoying, but the Demon Lord is obviously way stronger.

She should be able to crush them all easily, no matter how countless they might seem.

The reason the battle was dragging on so much is that the Demon Lord wasn't going all out.

I suppose I wasn't going all out, either, but can you blame me?

Both of us were saving our energy in case Potimas tried anything, obviously.

We were both trying to stay on our guard so we could deal with it if Potimas tried anything strange.

That might sound bad in an emergency situation like this, but what was I supposed to do?!

I couldn't help it, even if it was less than ideal.

But if we keep dragging things out, we won't be able to resolve this situation.

The longer we take, the more likely it is that the UFO will drop the bomb.

I'm still not sure what exactly would cause that to happen, but obviously it's safer to take care of things as quickly as possible.

So when I made my move, the Demon Lord took that as a sign to start taking this battle more seriously, too, even if it meant neglecting our caution toward Potimas to focus on destroying these robots and tanks.

What actually happened was that my scythe acted of its own accord, but nobody else needs to know that.

And it seemed to intimidate Potimas a little, so maybe it was for the best?

At any rate, the Demon Lord's serious battle mode is so intense that this'll all be over before Potimas can even lift a finger.

Was there really any point in being so cautious in the first place?

Uh… Hmm.

W-well, that's just because Potimas is the kind of guy you have to be careful around at all times!

In fact, having Potimas nearby is clearly doing far more harm than help, so should we really even be letting him live in the first place?

"That seems to be the last of them. Let's go."

As if suspecting my thoughts, Potimas briskly strides forward.

Feeling like I missed my chance, I give up on that line of thinking for now and follow after him.

Special Chapter   THE BLACK DRAGON'S SPACE BATTLE

As I proceed through empty space and pass a certain boundary, I feel an ever-present magic-runelike link weaken: the rune that connects me to the system.

The connection hasn't been cut, but I know from experience that I cannot interact with the system from this distance.

From here on out, I will have to fight with my own power alone, not the power provided by the system.

Of course, I have never fought using the power of the system, so it makes no difference to me. I can function perfectly well without it.

As a true dragon, no mere weapon made by human hands is a threat to me.

However, that takes only my own self into account.

When I consider the possible harm toward others it could cause, the difficulty level rises considerably.

A man-made weapon could never kill me, of course.

No matter how advanced it might be, it cannot possibly defeat a true dragon, a god.

If only humans understood that, then this current strife could have been avoided, but I suppose there was no use trying to tell them as much.

Even if they had known that, I doubt the people of the past would have given up on developing these weapons.

To know something and to understand it are two very different things.

If you don't accept a fact as reality, you cannot really say that you understand it.

And even if you do understand it, accepting it is yet another story.

A difficult conundrum.

Instead of judging what they can or cannot do, humans make their conclusions based on what they *want* to do.

Their desires, their noble intentions, and their feelings toward others.

They all have different reasons, but ultimately, that is the primitive drive that moves humans to act.

If you probe deeply enough, it all comes down to the simple question of whether they want to do something or not.

Their motives are all the same; it is only the resulting directions that differ.

Although it is these differing directions that cause such problems.

Their different desires are exactly what cause humans to fight among themselves.

Since they always prioritize what they want to do individually, it leads them to clash with one another.

And if they cannot reach an agreement, it comes to blows and eventually to war.

Arguments. Violence. Military might.

In order to accomplish their personal desires, humans will use any means to push through all obstacles.

In which case, the machine I am about to destroy was likely made with such a purpose in mind.

Even if the meaning of that purpose may be long lost to the past.

We cannot possibly know what its purpose might have been.

Of course, if I look into the past, I would be able to see what was happening at that time.

But in the end, that is nothing more than reading memories of the past. I cannot go so far as to read the intentions of the people involved.

A higher god than myself, such as D, might be able to see even that, but I cannot.

God though I may be, there are things I can and cannot do.

Even so, there is one thing I do know.

The people who made these weapons had their backs against the wall.

Otherwise, they would not have created these terrible weapons that even Potimas was surprised to hear they had built, so cost-inefficient and impractical that using them would lead to their own destruction.

Surely they must have realized what would happen if they created and used such weapons.

The GMA bomb can blow away an entire continent, and even the G-Meteo has the potential to destroy the very planet.

If these people had even the slightest bit of sense, they would have realized what would happen to them if they used these.

And yet, their situation was such that they had no choice but to make them anyway.

For they were fighting an enemy who could not be defeated by any half-baked measures.

After all, their opponents were dragons like me.

They must have placed the last of their hopes on these weapons.

Yet, clearly they had a change of conscience or else simply did not complete them in time, for in the end, these weapons were buried underground without ever seeing the light of day.

Most likely, this was for the best at the time.

If the buried weapons had been used, they would have plunged the world into even greater chaos.

But the fact that this peril has come to pass in our current day instead is truly grave.

At the time, there were other gods such as myself who could have dealt with the weapons.

But now I am the only one left.

Which is why I had no choice but to accept Potimas's proposal that I go into space to deal with the G-Meteo.

I know this was the only choice. Nobody else could possibly fight in outer space.

Knowing Potimas, it is possible that he was concealing a weapon that could have done the job, but of course he would never admit it.

I have no doubt that he deliberately sent me away so that he could attempt something while I am gone.

He has always been this way.

Whenever something unexpected happens, that man attempts to use it to manipulate things in his favor.

Even if he himself was not expecting it, he is cunning enough to find a way to profit from it in the end.

I am sure that this situation, too, was not something he anticipated.

But it was all too clear that he is trying to use it to his advantage, nonetheless.

Since I had no choice but to go along with his wishes, I must curse my own inadequacy.

But it irritates me that he thinks he holds everything in the palm of his hand.

Up ahead, I can see my target.

The frightening weapon with the ability to capture meteors and intentionally drop them onto the planet.

The results would likely depend on the size of the meteor, but in the worst-case scenario, this weapon has the potential to destroy the entire planet.

Yet, despite how alarming its power may be, the weapon's appearance is rather foolish.

Its main body is spherical with propulsion devices attached, and it is equipped with eight arms for the purpose of latching onto meteors.

From some perspectives it may look like a strange sea creature, but as the sphere emits flames to propel it along, its appearance is more humorous than anything.

Though I suppose that makes sense, considering its designer.

Potimas is concerned only with mechanical efficiency and pays no attention to appearances.

This foolish-looking shape must be the result of another efficiency-focused design.

And since its emphasis is on such efficiency, no doubt there is far more to this weapon than meets the eye.

The G-Meteo, perhaps noticing my approach, begins shooting light bullets.

Outer space does not decrease the power of these optic weapons.

If anything, the vacuum only makes them stronger.

However, a weapon made by man cannot affect a god.

I proceed forward, not bothering to dodge the bullets.

My barrier neutralizes them instantly, so, far from injuring me, they cannot even slow me down.

As a true dragon, I have a barrier far more potent than any created by a system-based skill.

A true dragon's barrier is limitless, blocking both physical and magical attacks.

Not Potimas or even D could completely reproduce this unique ability of dragons.

D created an inferior version using skills, and Potimas developed a barrier that wards off magic, but neither of them comes close to the original.

It is the existence of this barrier that makes it so difficult to defeat dragons.

Even if one did instigate a disaster that destroyed the planet, it's still not certain whether the true dragons would be harmed.

All of that effort for only the possibility of putting a scratch on a dragon.

Even that would not be enough to break through a dragon's barrier.

That is the real difference between man and the godly dragons.

The humans of the past knew this, but they did not understand it.

Which is exactly why they created these weapons, believing they were their last hope.

And now, I crush that hope of the past.

The G-Meteo is destroyed in no time.

The now-meaningless hope from a bygone era, reduced to so much garbage in space.

I cannot help but feel the slightest twinge of sadness at the sight.

Perhaps it is because I, too, am a thing of the past, clinging to a purpose that may no longer have meaning in the present.

For I am just like man.

I continue to struggle for the sake of accomplishing my personal desires.

It is unlike a dragon, which is exactly why I am here.

Of all the dragons who once abandoned this planet, I alone remain.

This is the only place I can be.

As the remnants of the G-Meteo drift around me, I put aside my emotions and turn back.

If I hurry, I can still go to the aid of Ariel and the others.

The GMA bomb has not yet been dropped.

If a dragon such as myself appears in front of the G-Fleet, it may drop the GMA bomb, but even then, I would be able to handle such an event.

I am far more certain to be able to resolve this situation than Ariel and the others.

No matter what Potimas might try to do.

Whatever he is planning, I shall crush his attempts without mercy.

"Splendidly done."

The voice instantly takes the wind out of my sails.

Even in space, this voice reaches my ear effortlessly.

It's coming from a thin device floating directly in front of my face.

Even I did not notice the appearance of this object.

That alone shows the difference in power between myself and the being who sent this device to me.

And there is only one being who would contact me at a time like this.

"What do you want, D?"

I open my mouth so that my voice will reach my opponent.

For a god, it is a simple task to produce sound in space.

D: the evil god, the final god, the god of death.

The being who reigns as the most powerful of all gods has many names.

Normally, such a being would not bother speaking to a lesser god like myself.

And yet, this voice speaks to me quite freely.

A human who worships D might see this as the greatest joy imaginable, but for me, it brings nothing but a bad premonition.

"Hello to you, too. Your role in this particular incident is now over. So please watch the rest from here, if you will."

And my premonition is correct.

D is telling me to stay here and do nothing.

But I don't understand why.

Surely D would not want the GMA bomb to put an end to this little performance.

"Why?"

"Because it will be more entertaining this way," D responds unabashedly.

D wants to let the world remain in danger, simply because it will be more amusing.

The nerve of this god is unbelievable.

But she's being completely serious.

People's actions are based entirely on their personal whims.

And this god thinks and acts in a very similar way.

D acts purely on whether something will be amusing or not.

Everything she does is for the simple purpose of her own entertainment.

If it amuses her, she'll do anything—no matter who might be hurt or what might be broken.

That is the true nature of D, the being often called an evil god.

And since she's making this demand of me now, she must have decided that things will be more amusing if I don't return.

She wants the people down there to resolve this situation of their own accord, without my help.

No doubt D considers that highly entertaining.

But for me, it's not entertaining in the slightest.

"But…"

"Just stay where you are for now, please."

I attempt to protest, but D cuts me off with an order.

Her tone is polite but carries a firm undertone that suggests she will not allow me to act against her wishes.

Such a prideful, selfish will.

She really is just like her.

Their inclinations may be different, but the girl in white displays that same shameless drive to follow her own base desires.

She puts herself first and will gladly wreak destruction if it means getting what she wants.

That's precisely what concerns me so much about that girl.

I fear that drive of hers will someday bring about a serious situation.

However, I'm currently conversing with someone far more dangerous than that girl.

If D wished it, she could easily end even me.

"All right."

That's the only response I am permitted to give.

Because if I spoil D's mood, I will not be the only one to suffer the consequences.

As long as D's beloved girl in white is around, I doubt she will cause any serious harm to this world, but she certainly has the power to do so if she wishes.

And it is not within my power to stop her.

"Good answer."

The device that was producing D's voice is already gone.

Once she's said her piece, she simply goes on her way.

Now I have no choice but to stay here and watch the battle unfold.

Even if Ariel's life is in danger or if Potimas is on the verge of a pompous sneer.

No matter what the end result might be, D will most likely not intervene.

Because that simply would not be entertaining to her.

D has such overwhelming power that she could do just about anything if the mood strikes her.

Which is why she simply watches and rarely does anything at all.

Regardless of the outcome.

In the darkness of space, I clench my fists tightly at my own helplessness.

Please find a way to survive this.

12   The Bomb Squad's Explosive Progress

Following Potimas's guidance, we proceed through the gigantic UFO.

Now that the Demon Lord is going all in, we're moving along pretty quickly.

When she's serious, no number of robots or tanks can even pose a challenge.

A wild robot appeared!

Oh wait, it's dead already!

It's sorta like that.

She finishes them off so fast, my eyes can barely even follow her.

At this rate, even Potimas can't find a chance to attack her.

She's just destroying the enemies way too fast.

On top of that, thanks to Gluttony, the Demon Lord can fight for as long as she has to.

Exhaustion? You wish. She just has to munch up some metal with Gluttony and she's fully recovered.

I dunno if it actually tastes good, but she's going to town.

Seriously, this skill is so overpowered that I can't help but laugh.

It's like, why didn't you just get serious in the first place instead of worrying about Potimas?

But we're moving along just fine now, so I guess that doesn't matter.

The UFO's robot stockpile must be starting to run low, too, because the attacks have been getting less frequent.

That means we can move that much faster, so we're getting closer and closer to our goal.

Namely, the compartment containing the bomb.

As you might expect, the bomb is in the center of the UFO.

When it drops the bomb, it just ejects it right from there.

What's the problem with that? Well, this UFO is stupidly large, so it's kinda far from here to the center.

It doesn't help that the main gun was right on the edge of the circle, so we basically started from the farthest point possible.

And since the UFO's original purpose is to transport weapons, the robots and tanks inside keep coming after us, which obviously slows us down.

Considering the circumstances, we had no choice but to destroy the main gun and enter that way, but it's definitely eaten a lot of extra time.

The longer we take, the harder things get for our allies fighting outside.

Hyuvan and the other dragons won't go down easily, but some of the puppet spiders could easily kick it if they're not careful.

Like Sael, or Sael, or Sael!

I wouldn't put it past Riel to make a careless mistake and die, either.

The queens? Who would waste time worrying about them?

They're monsters of the same species as Mother, remember?

If they're in trouble, then everyone else is basically doomed.

Still, whatever I might say about the puppet spiders and Hyuvan and all them, they are decently strong monsters, so I'm sure they'll be fine.

The most worrisome bunch are the humans the pontiff brought.

Honestly, I'm already wondering how many of them are gonna be left alive.

Seriously, they're in waaay over their heads here.

It's like if ordinary civilians participated in a war for the fate of the world.

I mean, I know they're knights and all, but still... They're inevitably way weaker than everyone else.

It's a help to have them here, I'll admit, but it's almost like they're just meat shields.

Yeah. They really drew the short end here.

I'm guessing the pontiff knew that when he brought them here, so I suppose they're probably prepared.

But still, I feel bad for them, so I'd like as many of them to survive as possible.

I have no idea how the war outside is going right now.

Since the UFO's exterior is covered by the mystery barrier, I have no way of checking on things out there.

And having no idea what's going on outside is definitely making me uneasy.

It's like we're being forced to play a game with a time limit we can't even see.

But it's not like we're holding back in here, so as long as we keep doing our best, there's no real point worrying about it.

The best thing to do right now is forget about the outside and focus on our goal.

But that being said, I'm mostly just letting the Demon Lord do all the work.

My only real contribution right now is keeping an eye on Potimas.

And Potimas seems to be on his best behavior as our guide right now, so I guess you could say I'm not contributing at all.

Look, I don't need to help with small fry like this, okay?

I'm just letting the Demon Lord handle this, since she's the oldest, okay?

It's not because I'm totally useless here, okay?

I'm not mad that she stole the spotlight, okay?

Okay? Okay? Okay.

Huh?

Whoa, déjà vu.

I feel like I had the same thoughts recently, like maybe even earlier today.

What's up with that? Am I actually that useless?

Th-that's not true!

I'm getting warmed up right now!

I swear! I'm totally amazing when I try!

I-I'm sure I'll get a chance to shine.

I just know it!

I'm only saving my strength until that happens.

And making sure Potimas doesn't try anything suspicious!

So far, he's been leading us along without causing any trouble.

On top of being super-huge, this UFO is super-complicated on the inside, maybe because it's basically a flying military base.

The corridors themselves are big enough for the tanks to pass through, but there are tons of twists, turns, and branching paths, so you'd definitely get lost without a map.

I don't even know if we're going the right way, but I guess a cyborg like Potimas probably has some kind of memory folder in his brain.

He's mostly likely referring to the UFO's plans stored there to figure out where we need to go.

He has the Memory skill, too, after all.

There's no point doubting Potimas's memory anyway.

Frankly, it's not like I have any understanding of the inner workings of a UFO, so I wouldn't be able to navigate it alone.

Even Wisdom's mapping feature isn't working right now, probably because of the mystery barrier.

When you can't do something that you normally take for granted, you really realize how lost you are without it, in this case literally.

I guess that also means I should appreciate such handy features more.

But because I'm so accustomed to this particular feature, I don't pay attention to remembering where I'm going.

Hrm.

Will I be able to find my way back?

I guess I'll just have to hope the Demon Lord's memory is better than mine.

Yeah, I have no intention of letting Potimas guide us back.

As soon as that guy takes care of the bomb, I'm going to wipe him off the face of the planet.

Or at least have him take a hasty exit.

I'm sure this is just a remote-control cyborg body, so even if I destroy it, the real Potimas will be just fine.

As much as I wish he wouldn't be, for the sake of a peaceful future.

I'm sure the Demon Lord feels the same way I do, probably.

But I have no doubt Potimas knows what we're thinking, too, so I'm guessing he'll try something before he disposes of the bomb.

The Demon Lord and I want Potimas to destroy the bomb without a fuss so we can crush him afterward.

Potimas wants to destroy the bomb, too, but he's hoping to kill me and/or the Demon Lord first.

Talk about an awkward situation.

Why do people have to fight one another anyway?

It sucks that we can't just reach an understanding.

No, really, I'm being relatively serious.

The world is in danger, but the core members of this crew who have to save it are openly hostile toward one another.

We're basically doomed.

I have to make sure this doesn't actually turn into the end of the world.

With that in mind, I follow the Demon Lord, as she destroys more robots single-handedly, and Potimas as he takes the lead.

…When do I get to shine, huh?

We've arrived at our destination, and I still haven't gotten a moment in the spotlight.

The Demon Lord just carried us the whole damn way.

At this point, maybe I should let her do everything?

All jokes aside, though, there's an extremely heavy-looking door in front of us unlike any of the ones we've seen so far.

The room containing the bomb is on the other side.

Once we open the door, go inside, and have Potimas disable the bomb, our mission is complete.

"The GMA bomb is just on the other side of this door. I will begin locking the bomb's functions at once, but I do not know what defenses might await within. I must prioritize locking the bomb above all else. If there is any danger inside, I assume I can count on you two to deal with it."

Again with the "I assume." Can't you at least pretend to phrase it as a question?

You're saying it like it's already been decided.

Although I guess it's not like I have any better ideas.

According to Potimas, the room on the other side of the door is fairly small.

The bomb is in there, but for all we know, there might be robots or something, too.

Maybe there will even be stronger defenses than the robots, since this is supposed to be an important place, right?

I doubt they would put anything too dangerous right next to this mega-bomb, but considering they were reckless enough to make the damn thing in the first place, we can't be too sure!

No rational person would build a bomb strong enough to destroy a continent or a weapon that drops meteors down from the sky.

If they were that crazy, then they could probably mess things up in a way no normal human would ever even imagine.

Not to mention, Potimas's words sound suspiciously like foreshadowing.

There's gotta be something nasty waiting on the other side of that door.

Potimas unlocks the door by way of hacking.

I guess the guy who designed this system in the first place has no problem getting through electronic locks.

Despite its heavy appearance, the door opens without a sound.

So who's the final boss gonna be?

As I brace myself, I see a barren circular room before my eyes.

There's something in the middle that looks like a strange, clunky pillar of some kind.

Other than that, there's no robots, no nothing.

Come on—I figured there was gonna be some kind of high-performance super-robot, at the very least.

Bit of a letdown, to be honest.

"It can't be."

But compared to my disappointment, Potimas's reaction is very different.

His short murmur carries a tone of genuine surprise.

If this guy's surprised, then it definitely can't be anything good.

Sure enough, the pillar in the middle of the room begins to transform.

The weird structure opens up like a flower bud, forming countless muzzles.

And then it stands up.

What? It can stand?

All I can do is stare in dumb shock.

Seriously, a transformation?

It didn't merge with anything, but it definitely transformed.

And now that it's done, it's clear that it's some kind of weird robot.

The thing doesn't attack us, maybe because we haven't stepped into the room yet.

The pillar part forms the base, looking as sturdy as a tank or maybe even more so.

Then there are countless arms protruding from it with guns that appear to be exactly the same as the tanks' main guns.

And its propulsion system seems to be repurposed from a tank's treads.

Honestly, it kinda looks like a robot that was patched together from spare parts.

But since its weaponry appears to be made from those tanks, I know how strong it must be.

Well, it's not quite what I pictured, but I guess this is a robotic last boss, all right.

Although I feel like it kinda lacks the panache to be a last boss, among other things.

"A Gloria? But I did not give them those schematics. Where did they get this information?"

But while I'm a little let down, Potimas's expression is grim, and he's muttering to himself about something or other.

"Potimas, explain," the Demon Lord says shortly.

Like me, the Demon Lord doesn't seem overly threatened by the robot in front of us.

But Potimas's strange reaction has her suspicious, too, which is probably why she's demanding an explanation.

"That was developed based on the schematics of a different weapon of mine. However, I have never shared those schematics with anyone. I know not where they saw such a thing, but judging by its appearance, I believe it is not a perfect reproduction. However, it is impossible to tell how close this one's capabilities are to the original."

In other words, this last boss is a half-baked reproduction based on stolen glances of Potimas's secret weapon?

"So? How strong would the original be?"

"The original could easily destroy even an upper-class dragon. Ah, I mean the fakes, not the originals, of course."

Potimas's casual tone only makes his words seem more truthful.

Pardon me?

Is this guy serious?

An upper-class dragon—so like Hyuvan, you mean?

Ha-ha-ha. Good one, buddy.

You *are* joking, right?

But Potimas's expression is deadly serious.

And it's not like this guy would ever tell jokes in the first place.

Does that mean this thing is seriously strong enough to defeat a dragon?

No, wait, that's the original. This thing is just an inferior replica.

It can't be as strong as the original.

"And this might even surpass the original."

Sorry, come again?!

This super-shoddy-looking knockoff robot?

"This is the worst situation possible. I never imagined it would come to this."

"Hey. Can you share with the rest of the class, please?" the Demon Lord demands impatiently.

Potimas, on the other hand, just shakes his head with a sigh.

"What did we come here to do, hmm?" he responds in a condescending tone.

You never change, do you, jerk?!

I feel like I can see an enraged mask floating behind the Demon Lord.

But I ignore his sass and think about this rationally.

We came here to dispose of the bomb, obviously.

This final boss robot is the last barrier between us and victory.

Potimas seems super-stressed about this thing, but once we beat it, all we have to do is deactivate the bomb.

Wait. Deactivate…the bomb?

Huh?

Where *is* the bomb, exactly?

"Ha. It appears the white creature has figured it out."

Potimas smirks sarcastically, then shoots a mocking look at the Demon Lord, who doesn't seem to have realized just yet.

Not now, okay?

Now is not the time for crap like that.

The Demon Lord's rage meter is climbing like crazy, and she looks like she's about to smack Potimas down at any second, so I grab the end of her sleeve.

"What? I've got a noble mission to blow this guy away right now. Why are you stopping me?"

"Bomb."

The Demon Lord is practically popping a vein as she stares at me, and then the room beyond me, when I speak a single word.

And then she gets it.

Right away, she whirls toward Potimas.

"It is exactly as you imagine."

When Potimas confirms, the Demon Lord clutches her head and groans.

We came here to disable the bomb.

And the boss robot is our final obstacle.

But there's nothing else in this room except for that robot.

Hmm. So where could the bomb be?

Well, kids?

Do you see anywhere in this room where a bomb might be hiding?

Oh, and you can't say it was never in this room in the first place.

…Which means there's only one right answer.

The bomb we need to dispose of is somewhere inside that final boss robot.

"Strategy time!"

Since the final boss robot isn't attacking us yet, we can stand right in front of it and come up with a plan of attack.

Yep. That's not very nice.

But we really have to come up with a plan.

Who could've possibly predicted this?

It's so unexpected, it's not even funny.

Whoever came up with this idea is an evil genius.

Or maybe just a mad scientist.

Who would think to put a bomb that could blow away an entire continent *inside* a robot?

No wonder Potimas muttered, "It can't be."

"Potimas, are we absolutely sure the bomb is inside that thing?"

"There's no doubt. This body's internal measuring instruments are reacting to it."

The Demon Lord slaps a hand to her forehead and looks up at the ceiling.

I'd like to take the same pose, to be honest.

This is horrible.

Our goal is to disable the bomb.

The bomb is inside the robot.

That means we have to do something about the final boss robot before we can disable the bomb.

That in itself is no different than if the bomb were outside the robot, but since it's inside, we have to defeat that robot without causing the bomb to explode.

That bumps up the difficulty level quite a bit, I'd say.

On top of that, Potimas says this weapon might be even stronger than the original.

It might look like a shoddy knockoff, but this boss robot has one key difference that would make him say such a thing.

It's using the bomb as a power source.

In other words, the bomb's not just stuck in there—it's actually connected to the robot.

As one of its weapons.

"What do you think?"

"I can't imagine it's set up such that destroying it would cause the bomb to explode... Or at least, I certainly hope not. If that was the case, it would destroy the G-Fleet along with it. Thinking logically, no one would ever construct things that way."

Always quick with the *Do I really need to explain that to you?* comeback, Potimas responds smoothly to the Demon Lord's short question this time.

I can't help noticing that the Demon Lord looks a little annoyed about that.

No doubt she was hoping he would hesitate long enough that she could say, *Do I really need to explain this to you?* back to his face.

He's always snarking at us, so I understand the desire to get him back.

He sure sidestepped that attempt, though.

At any rate, I'll just stay quiet and pretend I didn't see anything.

Poking fun at her certainly wouldn't lead anywhere good.

"Unfortunately, we cannot say for certain that it's not the case." Potimas sighs.

He's right. Normally, you'd assume it wouldn't be constructed that way, but we have no way of knowing for sure.

That's the problem.

The bomb inside the final boss robot is stupidly powerful enough to destroy an entire continent.

Obviously, if it explodes on this ship, the UFO itself will be blown away, too.

There should probably be some kind of secure lock in place to prevent that from happening, but it's possible that the lock could come undone by certain circumstances.

Like vibrations from the robot being destroyed, for instance.

So in other words, if we're going to destroy this final boss, we have to do it veeery gently.

That just makes this even more difficult!

And what if there's actually a mechanism that makes the bomb go off if the robot is destroyed?

Then, we can't even destroy the robot at all.

No one in their right mind would design it like that, of course.

But at this point, we have to seriously doubt whether the person who did all this was really in their right mind.

Would whoever developed all this destructive technology really be rational about it?

There's no way of knowing for sure.

And we can't act based on wishful thinking alone.

The fate of the world depends on it.

We've got to be extremely careful and come up with a foolproof strategy.

But what are we going to do?

"..."

"..."

"..."

All three of us sink into silence.

Uh-oh.

I know I'm stumped, but the fact that the Demon Lord and Potimas aren't even suggesting possible plans is kinda scary.

But I guess I can't really blame them.

If we want to dispose of the bomb, we have to do something about the final boss robot.

But if we do that, then the bomb might explode.

We're between a rock and a hard place, dammit.

Of course, it's possible that we can destroy the robot without the bomb going off.

If anything, considering how powerful that bomb is, I think it's much more likely that it wouldn't explode from that.

If the robot is meant to guard the bomb against thieves who might infiltrate the ship, it wouldn't make sense for it to explode if the robot was defeated.

What kind of moron puts the bomb a guardian's supposed to be protecting *inside* the guardian anyway?!

That only makes the thing you're trying to protect even more dangerous!

I guess that's not the worst strategy, but who would even think of that?!

What if the bomb blows up by mistake?!

Seriously, what a mad scientist.

Considering that the culprit thought of this insane idea, it wouldn't be too out of character if the bomb really did self-destruct as soon as the robot was destroyed.

Yeah. We gotta tread lightly here.

Wouldn't it be better to let Güli-güli handle this?

We could just keep an eye on the bomb until Güli-güli gets back.

Pretty good idea, right?

I nod to myself in satisfaction.

Some of my hair falls onto my face, so I nonchalantly tuck it behind my ear.

And then there's a smartphone in my hand.

"No one's coming to help."

A beautiful yet unsettling voice comes through the phone.

I know of only one person who can do things like that and who sounds like that.

The self-styled evil god, D.

A chill runs down my spine.

How long have I been holding this smartphone?

Normally, it just appears out of nowhere, which means I can't detect it coming.

That's all well and good, since that's how it always goes.

But why am I *holding* the phone this time?

It was a coincidence that hair fell into my face.

And the fact that I tucked it behind my ear was nothing but a thoughtless, automatic reaction.

My hand just happened to be in the perfect position to be holding a phone to my ear.

That's all there is to it.

Yeah. That's it.

I just so happened to coincidentally be in a position like I was holding a phone, so D snuck the phone into my hand.

That must be what happened, right?

…Yeah, I don't buy it, either.

How long?

When did D start controlling me?

That's the only possible explanation.

Otherwise, I wouldn't be holding this smartphone like this.

Even now, I want to throw it onto the floor, but my body won't move an inch.

I feel sick to my stomach at the realization.

The owner of this phone is controlling me so completely that even I didn't notice.

"Oh, don't be so frightened."

I'm not frightened, okay?

I'm just mad.

I am me. I'm nobody but myself, and I'm nobody's puppet.

Of course I'd get mad if someone tried to control me.

That's what led to me fighting against the Demon Lord in the first place.

More than anything else, I refuse to bend on this subject.

Anyone who tries to control me is my enemy!

"Ahhh, you really are so entertaining."

Despite the voice's emotionless tone, it somehow conveys a sense of joy.

I force down the rising fear in my heart.

Be strong! Don't get overwhelmed! Stand up to your enemy, if only out of spite!

"Do not worry. Aside from the instance of light tampering just a moment ago, I have never interfered with your personal actions."

I focus all my brainpower on the words coming from the smartphone.

I don't want to miss a single syllable.

I'll even ignore the fact that D is reading my mind as if it's the most natural thing in the world.

If these words are to be believed, the only time D has ever controlled my actions is when I was made to hold that smartphone naturally just now.

But the words "your personal actions" sound suspicious to me.

"Very astute. I have not meddled with you personally, but I did provide your weapon with a few extra perks."

At D's words, my eyes automatically move to the scythe in my other hand.

"Still, it is nothing too remarkable. I simply made it so that its abilities will improve to correspond with your own growth. The fact that it seems to be developing of its own accord is likely due to the effect of the Parallel Minds skill. I believe an extra framework caused by an irregularity is affecting the weapon."

An irregularity? Does that mean the former body brain, the Parallel Mind that fused with the Demon Lord?

My Parallel Minds skill is level 10, but I can produce only nine Parallel Minds.

The last one, due to various circumstances, wound up in the irregular situation of being fused with the Demon Lord's soul.

Since it's basically been absorbed by the Demon Lord, that means I lost a Parallel Mind. So does that mean this "extra framework" is essentially giving the scythe a mind of its own?

"That is correct, more or less."

Guess I was right.

"The scythe, which was made from part of your own body, is still a part of you now. That is why it has developed unusual properties. And as it is a part of you, it will not betray you in any way."

I wonder about that.

My Parallel Minds were supposed to be part of me, and they still managed to betray me.

Who's to say this scythe won't betray me, too?

"My, but you are cautious. Well, what you do with that information is up to you. I *simply wanted to give a bit of a special present to one of my favorite people. You get to decide what you do with it.*"

Oh yeah?

Well, this scythe is useful.

Really useful, in fact.

I'm not sure if I can take D's words at face value, but I don't want to give up the scythe, either.

At the very least, I'd like to keep using it until this particular incident is settled.

"*I'm terribly pleased it seems to be to your liking.*"

Ugh. Having my mind read is seriously a pain.

No matter what excuses I try to make, you'll always know what I'm really thinking.

Fine, then, I'll admit it.

I like it, okay? I reeeeally like it!

This thing is just crazy convenient, all right?!

It's strong! Insanely strong! Sooo freakin' strong!

And I made it with my own hands, out of my own body, so yeah, of course I love it!

You got a problem, dammit?!

"*Now then, as I was saying, no one is coming to help.*"

…Wow. Totally ignored me.

Uhhh. Okay. Fair enough.

No waaay.

So, um, what was that about no one coming to help?

Why is that, exactly?

"*I thought it would be more entertaining this way, so I stopped him.*"

What?!

So it's *your* fault?!

I was a teensy bit worried that something might have happened to Güli-güli, but clearly I was wrong!

In fact, this might be even worse in a way!

You damn evil god! You're seriously evil!

Who the hell would take the safest option off the table when the fate of the world's at stake just because it'd be more entertaining?

Only the worst gambler ever!

I mean, I guess it doesn't affect D much either way, but for those of us with our necks on the line, this seriously sucks.

I guess if you're just a spectator, then sure, watching us struggle against all odds would be way more interesting than Güli-güli just poofing the problem away!

But put yourself in my shoes for a second here!

I don't even know if it's possible for us to solve this on our own!

"At any rate, you're on your own, as you can see. Do your best to bring home a win, okay?"

You've gotta be kidding me!

Just like that, the phone in my hand disappears.

As usual, D sticks around only long enough to say her piece.

I bring the hand that was holding the smartphone in front of my face.

I'm guessing my expression is fairly different for once.

"What's up, White?"

See? The Demon Lord noticed, too.

…Hmm?

I raise my head, peering at the Demon Lord and Potimas.

The Demon Lord looks bemused, and Potimas looks composed as usual.

Neither of them makes any reference to the smartphone I was just holding a second ago.

That's odd.

They're acting like the phone conversation I just had never even happened.

I guess for all I know, it really didn't.

"Phone."

"Hmm?"

I say the word *"phone"* as an experiment, but the Demon Lord just tilts her head, clearly having no idea what I'm getting at.

Potimas doesn't respond, either, but I'm guessing he doesn't get it, either.

Neither of them must have sensed my conversation with D.

In fact, it didn't seem like they moved at all during the conversation, so maybe time was stopped or something.

Somehow, D sent me a message without either of them even noticing.

Once again, I'm reminded how unusual D really is.

A real god, an evil one.

No wonder D sees a possibly world-ending threat as nothing more than a source of amusement.

D lives in a different world in many different ways.

Physically, mentally, and in terms of power.

"You okay, White?"

The Demon Lord seems concerned about my unusual state.

Ahhh, after talking with D, that kindness heals my wounded heart.

Describing a demon lord as a healing force seems sorta wrong in various ways, but for now I'm just gonna lean into it.

Moving on some weird impulse, I end up giving the Demon Lord a hug.

"Huh? White?"

Now she's even more confused.

Hrm. Because of our size difference, this isn't quite the kind of hug I was going for.

I kinda wanted her to comfort me, but instead it feels like I'm picking up and reassuring a child.

Oh well, I guess that's fine. Going along with it, I pat her head, since she's at just the right height.

"Wh-whaaa—?"

The Demon Lord voices her confusion again, but she isn't trying to pull away from me.

She's just letting me do it, even though I'm sure her head is full of question marks right now.

I suddenly started hugging her and patting her head, so I can't really blame her.

I'm the one doing it, and I don't know what's going on, either!

The fact that she's not shaking me off in this weird situation is just further proof that the Demon Lord is a freaking saint.

How is she so tolerant?

Seriously, why is this person a demon lord?

It's like one of the Seven Wonders of the World at this point.

"Could you put an end to this foolish charade already?"

On the other hand, the man who's watching us coldly is absolutely the devil.

How is he so evil?

This guy stinks to high heaven! Or should I say to hell?

But I guess in this particular situation, Potimas is probably right.

We can't just run away from reality forever.

I reluctantly let go of the Demon Lord, feeling like a child who's been forced to put down their stuffed animal.

Not that I ever had a stuffed animal, in this life or the one before it.

"All right. Since White seems to have calmed down, let's get back to our strategy, shall we?"

The stuffed animal in question, the Demon Lord, calmly resumes our strategy mission as if that never happened.

Oof. Gotta admit, that borderline indifference hurts a little.

"Problem is, I can't think of a single way to approach this. I'm stumped." The Demon Lord throws up her hands. "If we just had to destroy that machine, that'd be one thing, but if we have to make sure nothing explodes in the process…"

She sighs and glares at the final boss robot.

I guess she's just as flabbergasted by this disastrous bomb-in-the-robot situation as I am.

"Honestly, maybe our best bet is to wait until Gülie gets back?"

"Most likely."

What's this?

Did Potimas just *agree* with the Demon Lord?

The Demon Lord seems as surprised as I am; she stares at the elf in blatant shock.

"Obviously, I do not desire any situation in which the GMA bomb explodes. Attempting to kill you two was, in the end, a secondary objective. If I can, I will, but if not, I care little. You are not important enough to be higher priority than a situation like this."

Aaargh!

Can't we just kill this guy already?

He's definitely picking a fight with us, right?

But sadly, we probably shouldn't kill him, at least not right now.

"Ignoring how obnoxious you are for the time being, shall we agree to wait for Gülie to come back?"

"Indeed."

The Demon Lord and Potimas seem content to wait until Güli-güli gets back.

Unfortunately, that means I have to tell them what I know.

"Not coming back."

"Hmm? What was that, White?"

"He's not coming back."

When I repeat myself, the Demon Lord looks puzzled.

But there's also concern on her face.

"Did something happen to Gülie?"

A flicker runs across Potimas's face at that.

Hmm. How should I answer? Something did happen, but Güli-güli isn't hurt or anything...

"Yes. But he's fine."

That's all I can think to say.

"What does that mean? Explain yourself."

Yeah, that's what I expected.

Even I would've been surprised if they actually accepted that answer without a peep.

But you're asking *me* to explain this?

Do you know who you're talking to?!

If I could manage talking well enough to explain in detail, I would've done that in the first place!

Can't you tell that was the best explanation I was capable of?!

Ugh, this is a problem.

How am I supposed to explain all this?

Dammit, the fact that D told only me about this is a pain in the butt.

I wish this guy would've shared that information with the Demon Lord and Potimas, too...

Wait a minute—was this on *purpose* so D could watch me embarrass myself trying to get through to them?!

No waaay... But actually, knowing D, that's entirely possible.

"I'm not sure what's going on, but if White says Gülie is fine but can't come back, that's probably how it is. Even if we press her, I don't think she's gonna explain any more than that, right?"

As usual, the Demon Lord comes to my rescue.

She gets me so well that I kinda want to hug her again.

I guess she has known me in this life longer than anyone else!

Potimas shoots her a look, silently asking what the deal is, but the Demon Lord just shrugs.

Now it's like she really did get him back with his favorite *Do you really need me to explain it to you?*

Although it's not exactly a perfect revenge, since she doesn't really know what's going on, either.

Potimas doesn't seem satisfied, but he seems to be forcing himself to go along with it for now.

His eyebrows furrow, but he doesn't say anything else.

"So, White, is it safe to assume that Gülie is unharmed but he can't come to our aid right now?"

I nod vigorously.

"In other words, we have to find a way to deal with that thing ourselves?"

She's pointing at the final boss robot, so I nod again.

At that, both the Demon Lord and Potimas lapse into silence.

They're probably racking their brains for a solution to this predicament.

Me? My job is to stand around staring blankly until one of them comes up with a plan.

What? Come on—I can't think of anything.

If this was a monster I could Appraise, I could come up with all kinds of strategies, but this is a totally unknown opponent.

Machines are waaay out of my wheelhouse here.

There's no point even trying to think about it.

And I make it a rule not to do anything pointless, so I'm just gonna leave this one to the professionals.

"I had hoped to avoid doing this, but I suppose I have no choice."

Sure enough, Potimas seems to have come to a decision.

"There is one way. If it succeeds, we can silence both the GMA bomb and that fake Gloria."

Potimas looks at us, waiting to see if we'll go along with his plan.

"What is it?"

The Demon Lord wants answers before she agrees to anything.

We obviously can't trust Potimas enough to consent to his plan without at least hearing what it is first.

"The body I am currently using is equipped with hacking functionality."

He extends the pointer finger of his left hand, and it just…stretches.

The finger, which has transformed into a cord, must be the part with the hacking functionality he mentioned.

"I will insert this into that thing so that I may hack into its controls. If I succeed, I should be able to deactivate both the fake Gloria and the GMA bomb."

Potimas keeps calling the final boss robot a "fake Gloria."

Gloria must be the name of the original weapon, though it's clear from his expression when he says "fake Gloria" that he isn't too happy about the knockoff.

He must feel like an artist who's been shown a counterfeit version of his own work.

"However, the hacking will take some time, and I will be vulnerable while I do so. If it attacks me while I am working, I will be unable to defend myself, and of course the cord will disconnect and the hacking will fail."

Right. I can see why Potimas didn't want to do this.

I'm sure being defenseless in front of the Demon Lord and me isn't high on his bucket list.

"I will extend the cord from here and begin hacking into the fake Gloria. In the meantime, you two will protect my body and the cord."

Immediately, the cord extending from Potimas's finger begins to slither inside the room.

Hey, at least wait for us to agree!

But since he's already started, I guess we don't have much of a choice.

It's not like we had any other plans anyway, so we're stuck doing what Potimas says.

The Demon Lord seems to reach the same conclusion as I did; she heaves a loud sigh and keeps an eye on the cord as it moves.

I'm sure Potimas deliberately started without waiting for an answer, knowing we would have no choice but to accept it.

"White, you protect Potimas. I'll cover the cord."

The Demon Lord keeps her eyes on the cord as it moves toward the final boss robot.

Sensing its approach, the robot slowly shifts into action.

The final battle for the fate of the world has begun.

13 FINAL BOSS WALK-THROUGH

The final boss robot moves its multitude of arms, pointing its guns at the intruder.

The intruder in question, Potimas's hacking cord, continues moving forward anyway, slithering silently along the floor like a snake.

Maybe that made the robot feel threatened, or more likely it was just set to attack anything that entered the room without permission, but either way it began attacking mercilessly.

All the guns unleashed balls of light at the same time.

Each of them was around the size of a cannonball, like the tank's ammunition, so when all of them fired at once, it was like a blinding flash of light.

And it was clearly powerful enough to hurt a lot more than just my eyes.

A single shot was able to pierce the puppet spiders' five-digit defenses, so a countless number of them?

If they hit that thin cord, they won't just break it, they'll evaporate it into nothing.

The rain of bullets, which is more like a wall of light at this point, zooms toward the cord, until the Demon Lord eats it all up in one bite.

She moved from outside the room to in front of the onslaught in an instant, then used Gluttony to consume the entire attack in order to defend the cord.

...What a cheater.

You really staved that off without a scratch, huh?

Would I have been able to do the same, I wonder?

Defend myself from the light without a scratch... Yeah, I could probably manage that.

But do it while keeping the cord safe, too?

Yeah, I don't think so.

She definitely chose our roles correctly. I wouldn't be able to keep that cord intact for very long.

The Demon Lord continues easily gobbling up the bullets that fly toward her and the cord.

It's a fairly intense barrage, too, probably because the robot is powered by that bomb's energy.

And yet, the Demon Lord's not even breaking a sweat.

Wow, she's amaaaazing.

I can just sit here in safety and watch her.

...Oh, maybe I spoke too soon.

Several of the arms turn their muzzles this way.

There are a whole lot of them.

That means they can shoot at me while still attacking the Demon Lord and the cord at the same time.

And since Potimas is operating the cord, he can't move.

Light bullets shoot straight toward the immobile Potimas.

This is my chance!

It's my time to be in the spotlight and the chance for an underutilized skill called Shieldsmanship to make its debut, too!

I spring out in front of Potimas, holding up my shield.

The bullets hit the shield, but since it's been strengthened with Energy Conferment and Magic Power Conferment, they don't do a thing!

Huh? Where did I get a shield like that, you ask?

So I just happened to find some convenient materials and repurposed them into a shield, so what?

Specifically, the crazy-sturdy-looking door that was blocking our path into this room before.

Heh, even a door that thick is no match for my special scythe.

But it's sturdy enough to make an excellent shield.

As you can see by the bullets bouncing right off it!

Not a chance! It'll never work!

So yeah, I can protect Potimas without a problem over here.

If anything, I'm more worried about the Demon Lord.

She's having no problem protecting the cord right now, but it needs to make contact with the robot in order to hack it.

And she has to make sure it doesn't get cut while it's connected.

I'm sure the boss will put up a fight against the hacking, which could mean big trouble for the cord when it's physically attached.

What is the Demon Lord going to do about that?

As I watch and worry, the end of the cord finally reaches the boss robot.

It glows for just a second, then plunges right into the robot's body with brute force.

I guess that answers my question about how it was going to connect.

The cord makes its way farther into the final boss robot.

The robot tries to fight against it, of course, but its movements are slow.

Because its body is bound by tons of thread.

The Demon Lord's thread has rendered the robot all but motionless.

Pretty sharp handiwork, if you ask me.

Now the boss robot can barely move at all.

It's easy to get caught up by the Demon Lord's Gluttony skill, but she's got plenty of other overpowered abilities, too.

Our thread-related skills are the same level, but I don't think I can use them nearly as well as she can.

Tangled up in the thread, the boss robot nevertheless tries to fight back with a barrage of bullets.

But since the arms holding the guns are also tied up in thread, the light bullets go flying in random directions, nowhere near the cord or Potimas.

Yeah, I don't think it's getting out of that mess.

Even I probably couldn't escape unless I used Teleport.

Now we just have to wait for Potimas to finish his hacking.

Hey, this was easier than I thought.

I was expecting a tougher battle, but I guess I worried for nothing!

Like, after all that ominous stuff Potimas said, I gotta admit I was scared about this final boss robot.

But at this rate, it'll be over before you know it. Kinda makes you wonder why we spent all that time strategizing.

Honestly, it's a little anticlimactic.

But that's just because it's the Demon Lord who ended up taking on the boss robot.

I couldn't do the same thing all by myself, that's for sure!

The Demon Lord herself is like a big overpowered cheat, so maybe the boss robot is actually insanely strong, and she's making it look easy.

The Demon Lord is just a crazy exception. I'm sure the boss robot actually has strength befitting a final boss, probably, maybe.

Yeah. That's gotta be it!

For some reason, I'm making excuses for the final boss robot now.

I guess I just relaxed a little because this whole incident wrapped up more easily than I expected.

But I was forgetting something important.

That there's someone here who's way more dangerous than any final boss robot.

"White!"

I hear a sudden cry.

But by the time the voice reaches my ears, it's already begun.

First, I'm getting an intense feeling of discomfort.

Like the world has changed around me or my very senses have been rewritten.

I've felt this dreaded sensation once before.

It's what I felt when I was caught inside Potimas's barrier.

And behind me is Potimas, the man himself.

The giant door in my hand, which I was using in place of a shield, suddenly feels terribly heavy.

That means my skills and stats have stopped working.

But one of the few that continues working, High-Speed Processing, makes the world around me move as if in slow motion.

Since my stats have gone down, my body won't move the way I want it to.

I feel sluggish, like I'm trying to move underwater or maybe in a dream.

Even in the slowed-down world, the Demon Lord still moves quickly as she runs toward me.

Behind me, I can tell Potimas is moving.

But my body is frozen in place, unable to react.

Then the Demon Lord crashes into me, and a beam of light pierces her body.

As my eyes take in this unbelievable sight, various thoughts float through my mind.

Like *Oh right, Gluttony is a skill, so she can't use it inside the barrier.*

And *Shit, I knew Potimas was going to betray us; I shouldn't have let my guard down.*

And *Now you've done it, you bastard! I'll kill you!*

But of all the thoughts that circle my brain in that moment, one is far louder than the rest.

She protected me.

She protected me.

She knew I pretty much can't die, but she protected me.

SHE PROTECTED ME!

"Oh-ho. What a delightful surprise."

Holding in one hand the gun that just shot the Demon Lord, Potimas stares coldly.

His voice is as cool and emotionless as ever, but I can still detect a little bit of triumph.

Potimas points his gun at the Demon Lord as she falls.

At the same time, the boss robot frees itself from the thread and points its guns at the Demon Lord, too.

Potimas's goal is deadly clear: He wants to use this opportunity to bury the Demon Lord once and for all.

From the start, he must have been waiting for the moment the hacking succeeded to activate the barrier and shoot me from behind.

But since the Demon Lord unexpectedly protected me and got shot instead, she's become his primary target.

If she gets wounded any further inside this barrier, even the Demon Lord will die.

She doesn't have any moves like mine to narrowly escape death.

Potimas was right to prioritize finishing the Demon Lord before me.

Anyone could tell that she's more dangerous than I am.

This is a one-in-a-million chance to kill the dangerous Demon Lord.

In order to make sure that chance doesn't slip by, Potimas is pointing both his own gun and the guns of the robot he's hacked into right at the Demon Lord.

Totally ignoring the fact that I'm even here.

I can't say that I don't feel anything about that fact.

But the emotion I'm feeling most strongly is indignation toward the Demon Lord.

Why did she protect me?!

Aren't we still low-key enemies?!

As far as I know, the Demon Lord doesn't know the secret to my immortality.

So she would have no way of knowing that I might actually be able to die inside this barrier.

What's the point in protecting someone you think is immortal?

More importantly, why would she protect me when we're allies only because we had no other choice?

And yet, she took a bullet for me.

Just like when she rescued Sael from that tank without hesitation.

She protected me without a second thought.

And because of that choice, she's now in serious trouble.

At this rate, the Demon Lord will die.

No way. I can't allow that!

Potimas's gun and those of the final boss robot fire at the same time.

Without a moment's hesitation, I move to stand above the fallen Demon Lord, warding off both attacks.

I slice through Potimas's bullet with my scythe and block the barrage from the boss robot with my giant door shield.

Without the strengthening of my skills, the shield starts to buckle with each hit.

C'mooooon!

Let's see some action, Shieldsmanship!

If you don't come in handy now, when are you ever going to be useful?!

I keep holding off the boss robot's merciless barrage with the shield in my

left hand, while attacking Potimas on the opposite side with the scythe in my right.

Since most of my skills aren't working, this is pretty tough.

But I'm no ordinary human, you know!

I'm a half-human, half-spider arachne!

I use my spider legs to grab a certain something.

Since my spider legs end in claws, they're not exactly dexterous, but if I use more than two, I can still grab things if need be.

And then I give the thing I grabbed a sharp tug—the cord connecting Potimas to the boss robot.

"Wha—?!"

Potimas gives an exclamation of surprise at my unexpected move.

Yanked along by the cord, Potimas's body flies through the air above me.

Right into the onslaught of bullets being fired by the boss robot.

On the other side of my shield, I hear the sound of something being smashed.

In the same instant, the discomfort enveloping my body disappears.

Potimas's barrier has been deactivated!

Time to supply my half-busted shield with energy and magic again!

Still holding the shield in front of me, I push forward.

Soon, I'm charging in a perfect shield bash!

I slam right into the boss robot along with my shield, knocking it over!

The attack sends the giant robot flying right into the wall.

Unfortunately, the attack also crushes my already half-broken shield.

Thank you, door shield. You served me well.

Tossing the broken shield aside, I chase after the boss robot.

As it hits the wall with a dull *bang*, I swing my scythe down for another attack.

My scythe neatly slices the robot diagonally in two, and its gigantic body disintegrates into dust without a sound.

But for some reason, a round object remains intact in the dust.

It's a small sphere that could fit in the palm of my hand... Could this be the bomb?

Oh crap.

I got so worked up that I forgot all about the damn bomb.

It's not gonna explode, is it?

I cautiously lift up the sphere, but it doesn't seem to be doing anything strange.

Phew. I think we're okay.

Putting a hand to my chest with a sigh of relief, I quickly turn around.

There, I see the Demon Lord standing up while clutching her side and the head that's all that remains of Potimas's cyborg body.

"Hmph. You got me this time."

"That's our line, you bastard."

The Demon Lord plants her foot on Potimas's sour-looking head.

Considering that he's been reduced to a talking head, that was a pretty bland remark.

He shouldn't even be able to talk without lungs, but I guess cyborgs must have vocal organs that work differently than humans'.

I wonder if I could use a mechanism like that for the puppet spiders... Oops, my mind is wandering a little.

"I thought for sure that plan would work. You ruin everything, don't you?"

"Too bad for yoooou! Nothing you do can top the power of our friendship!"

The Demon Lord cackles, grinding her foot into Potimas's head.

Power of friendship, huh...?

That little turn of phrase makes it all too clear why the Demon Lord protected me.

She did it out of pure reflex, without any calculations or ulterior motives.

Like she was protecting a family member.

On the other hand, I protected the wounded Demon Lord because I felt like I should return the favor.

Technically, I could've just let her die.

Since I see her as a potential threat, that might have even been the more sensible option.

But at the time, that didn't even cross my mind for a second.

She protected me, so I had to protect her in return.

That's all I was thinking at the time.

But I think that's for the best.

There's no way I could've just let the Demon Lord get killed right in front of me.

If I let her die without paying her back for protecting me, that would've been totally shameless.

So this was for the best.

"Thanks for saving me, White. I would've been a goner without you!"

Oh, come on!

You can't give me such an honest, carefree smile when I'm trying to make up some phony reason for saving your butt back there!

You're making me look like an idiot for coming up excuses over here!

Ugh, fine! You win!

"Thank you, too."

When I give a prompt response for once, the Demon Lord stares at me wide-eyed.

D-don't look at me like that!

It's embarrassing!

Don't get the wrong idea, okay?!

I protected you only to return the favor—that's it!

There weren't any other gross feelings involved.

Not a single one! I swear!

Ughhh!

"Could we move on already?" Potimas asks coolly.

"Move on? To what?"

"Our next course of action. You two are to take me to the G-Fleet's control room. There we will seize control of the ship and make an emergency landing."

…Does this guy switch gears fast or what?

He just tried to kill us, and he's already giving us orders?

Talk about shameless.

"You win this round. Obviously, I cannot do anything in this form. So now all that is left is to finish resolving this situation, as was the original plan."

Sensing our disbelief, Potimas explains himself without being asked.

He can actually be pretty good at guessing what people are thinking, but I wish he could find a better use for that ability.

Ugh. Well, I suppose it's true that Potimas's top priority from the beginning has been dealing with the UFO and the bomb, and trying to kill us was just a bonus.

Like a side quest he was hoping to maybe complete but didn't really care if he didn't.

Although, knowing that my death was just a secondary goal is pretty infuriating.

Anyway, I guess he's saying that since that's not possible now, he's just going to do his best to deal with the UFO situation.

Well, I guess it's not like he can do much else, since he's just a head now.

And if we're going to try to take control of the UFO, I guess having his advice would be useful for that, as annoying as that is to admit.

"I guess that's fine. But is that thing White's holding the bomb?"

The Demon Lord points at the sphere in my hand.

"Indeed."

I knew it. So it really is the bomb.

"Are we sure it's not gonna explode now?"

"Fear not. I have already locked it."

Apparently, he was doing his job even as he pointed his gun at the Demon Lord and me.

I guess he hacked the boss robot and even accessed the bomb to prevent it from exploding.

"It would be best to hand that over to Güliedistodiez. He will be able to dispose of it safely."

Yeah, I guess leaving it to Güli-güli is the safest thing to do.

"You're being surprisingly cooperative."

"I told you, did I not? You have won this round. I am simply acknowledging my defeat and yielding to the victors, as is proper in such a situation. If I could have secured the GMA bomb and obtained the energy within, that would have been ideal, but clearly that is beyond my power in this state. I would have liked to seize the G-Fleet itself, too, but I have given up on that now."

Oh yeah.

This guy sucks, all right.

I'm glad he's being so gracious and all, but he was seriously planning to steal the UFO itself as well as the bomb?

Talk about greedy.

Ah, no wonder he conveniently had a hacking function!

He probably could've pulled it off, too.

If we made one wrong move, the Demon Lord and I would both be dead, and the bomb and UFO would've fallen right into this guy's hands.

Just thinking about that is scary.

"At any rate, first we—?!" Potimas suddenly stops mid-sentence. "Interference from outside? No!"

For the first time ever, I can hear actual panic in his voice.

But I have no time to be surprised about that.

The bomb in my hand has started glowing.

"Is it going to explode?!" the Demon Lord practically shrieks.

"The G-Fleet is attempting to remotely unlock it. Wait—it's actually providing it with more energy. Damn it all! It's going to self-destruct!"

"So what do we do?!"

"It's no use. We can't stop it in time."

My eyes zip back and forth between Potimas and the Demon Lord as I try to wrap my head around the situation.

Okay, uh, the UFO is trying to remotely detonate the bomb, and it's even pouring its own energy into the damn thing?

The UFO and the bomb aren't physically connected, but maybe they're using runes or something?

Wait, that doesn't matter right now!

Is it gonna explode?!

Seriously?!

Potimas's hopeless tone sounded way too real.

Dammit.

No, no, no, no, no, no, no, no, no!

Sometimes, when people panic, they do things so strange that even they don't know why they did them.

I witnessed that myself on this day.

No, I *did* it myself.

I don't know what I was thinking, but as the bomb emitted that suspicious light, I went ahead and swallowed it.

"Wha—?! White, did you just EAT that?!"

The Demon Lord is panicking.

And so am I.

What the hell did I just do?!

What good is eating it gonna do anyway?!

I acted in a total panic, and now I'm panicking even more about what I just did!

Aaargh! Fine, I'll just digest the damn bomb before it can explode!

Still in a panic, I come to a ridiculously panicked conclusion.

The Demon Lord's Gluttony skill comes to mind.

The skill that can swallow up and absorb anything.

With that in mind, I try to imagine myself absorbing the bomb I stupidly ate.

<Experience has reached the required level.

Skill [Divinity Expansion LV 9] has become [Divinity Expansion LV 10].>

<Condition satisfied. Commencing deification.>

Right after I hear this message, intense pain assaults my body.

For a second, I think the bomb is exploding inside my stomach.

But that's not it.

It didn't explode.

So why is my whole body in pain?

It's so excruciating that I can't even tell what hurts anymore.

Pain unlike anything in this world runs through me, as if I don't have the Suffering Nullification skill at all.

This pain is familiar to me.

It's like how my head felt back when I couldn't control Detection but forced it to activate anyway.

But even if the nature of the pain is similar, the degree is exponentially worse.

It's like my whole body is going to break into pieces if I don't keep it together.

And my instincts are screaming that that's exactly what's happening.

If I can't handle this pain, I'm going to die.

That much is horribly clear.

Trying to bear it, I tighten my grip on the scythe in my hands.

The pain starts to flow into the scythe, relieving me ever so slightly.

Using that same principle, I try to keep scattering the source of the pain.

I can sense that the pain I'm pushing away is going into some other distant *something*, but I'm not conscious enough to figure out what that is.

The pain continues to assault my body.

"Better take emergency measures."

I feel like I hear a voice, but I don't have the energy to focus on it.

I don't want to die yet.

I want to keep living.

So I'm not going to lose to this stupid pain!

I try to strengthen my resolve, but the onslaught of pain seems to melt it away.

And my consciousness begins to slip, too...

\<Resetting skills.\>

\<Resetting stats.\>

\<Resetting titles.\>

\<Resetting skill points.\>

\<Resetting experience.\>

\<Installing D's special [Basics of Godliness].\>

\<Deification complete. You will no longer receive any support whatsoever from the system. Thank you for your patronage.\>

UFO

HP

error / error

MP

error / error

SP

error / error

error / error

status

Average Offensive Ability : error
Average Defensive Ability : error
Average Magic Ability : error
Average Resistance Ability : error
Average Speed Ability : error

skill

error
error error error error error error error error error error
error error error error error error error error error error
error error error error error error error error error error

A weapon that was kept in the ancient ruins. Its official designation is the G-Fleet. It is equipped with a High-Powered Type-9 Light Cannon as its main gun, 314 High-Powered Type-7 Light Cannons as its secondary guns, and many other weapons. However, these are only the external weapons, with its most powerful one being the GMA bomb carried on board. Because its armor is constantly producing an anti-magic barrier, it is highly resistant to magical attacks. Most of its power is provided by MA energy, and since it can also extract that energy independently, it can function indefinitely as long as it is not destroyed. It is essentially a flying fortress: It carries weapons such as G-Tetras and G-Tris in large numbers and deploys them for battle. It is equipped with some facilities for repairs but no production plants. Though it was developed as an anti-dragon weapon, it caused far too much damage when actually used, so it was stored away in the underground ruins. In the present day, the seal has been broken, and as it has no target to defeat, it is instead beginning to go on a rampage.

14 Unidentified Flying Objects Are the Vehicles of Gods

"You really are quite entertaining."

I hear a beautiful yet deeply unsettling voice from somewhere very close to me.

"Who would have guessed you would *eat* the thing? That surpassed even my expectations."

It's a very level voice with no hint of emotion.

Potimas's voice is fairly emotionless-sounding, too, but you can still pick up on what he's feeling a little bit.

This voice, though, is so devoid of feeling that it's like you're either talking to a machine or some superpowered being beyond human imagination. In this case, it's probably the latter.

But what is that being doing here?

And where *is* "here" anyway?

"There was a possibility that the bomb would explode, so I temporarily evacuated you to my location. However, it seems you have absorbed its power safely, so perhaps that was an unnecessary precaution."

Explode...?

Oh yeah! I ate the bomb, and then I was in a ton of pain.

What happened after that?

"Do not worry—your little world is safe. Please rest here a while so that you can adjust to your power a bit more. Now that your power has temporarily left you, we must return it from the egg to your body."

Egg?

"One of the spare vessels you used for what you call egg revival. You subconsciously let your power flow into it, like a source of external electricity. I am in the middle of returning that to your real body now."

I'm not sure what's going on exactly, but it sounds like the eggs I left lying around came in handy.

"The scythe, on the other hand, is probably better this way. I am sure it will continue to be of use to you in the future."

The scythe?

Now that you mention it, my scythe's not in my hands anymore.

In fact, I can't really tell what's going on with my body right now.

It's like I'm in a dream or something.

But one thing is clear: A certain someone is right behind me.

The being I've only ever spoken to through a smartphone is now right under my nose.

But I can't turn around.

If I turn and see that face, I... I...!

"Welcome to the domain of the gods. I have awaited you, O nameless spider."

For some reason, my heart pounds upon being called a *"nameless spider."*

Even I don't know why it agitates me so much.

Or maybe I don't want to know.

"It is hardly convenient for you to remain nameless forever, so perhaps I shall give you a name now. Consider it a modest gift from yours truly to congratulate you on becoming a god."

Alarm bells go off in my mind.

If I pass this point, I'll never be able to go back.

But there's nothing I can do about it.

I have no choice.

"Shiraori. The White Weaver. That shall be your name. A fitting moniker, if I do say so myself."

With that, D snickers.

There's still no emotion in that voice, but it definitely sounded like a snicker to me.

Wanting to confirm D's expression, I turn around.

And then I see it.

That face.

The face I was never supposed to see.

Ugghoargh.

As I open my eyes, my vision is filled with white walls.

No, not walls. Something…silkier?

It looks like I'm wrapped in a cocoon, and an extremely tight one at that.

I try to rip through it with my hands, but it's way too sturdy.

As I struggle and flail inside the cocoon, it abruptly rips from the outside.

My eyes meet with the person who tore open the cocoon.

"White?"

Why'd she phrase it like a question?

The Demon Lord stands before me, looking bewildered.

I don't know what she's so confused about, but first, I just need to get out of this cocoon.

Why am I even in this thing anyway?

This is all very strange.

But when I try to stand up and get out of the cocoon, I fall into an even stranger situation.

Literally. I fall right on my face.

My upper body is outside the cocoon now, but my lower body got stuck on the cocoon, so I just tipped forward.

Face, meet floor!

Ow! Owww! My nose hurts!

…It hurts?

But what about my Suffering Nullification skill?

In that moment, my memory of everything that happened before I passed out comes flooding back.

I swallowed the bomb inside the UFO.

My whole body was subjected to excruciating pain.

And then I met D…

As it all comes back to me, my consciousness is suddenly sharp and clear.

Like when you wake up from being half-asleep.

And that's when I notice.

My lower body feels strange.

Turning to look at my lower half, still stuck in the cocoon, I get a major shock.

Instead of the spider body I'm used to seeing, my eyes fall on two human legs.

Where did my spider body go?!

No wonder my vision feels so weird!

Normally I see through both my spider and human eyes, but now I've got only the human view!

Wait, why didn't I notice this as soon as I woke up?!

I should've picked up on a huge change like this right away!

And as a little extra bonus change, I'm totally naked right now!

"So you're awake?"

And now this guy just strolls on over?!

"Gülie! Not right now! Face the other way!"

The Demon Lord hurriedly turns Güli-güli around.

"But I do not feel anything when I see a woman's body..."

"You might be fine, but *we're* not! Really, you're so indelicate! No wonder you could never get Lady Sariel to look your way!"

Her harsh words do some serious damage to Güli-güli; even from behind, I can tell he's down in the dumps now.

"Let's get some clothes on you, okay?"

Obediently, I pull myself out of the cocoon.

Oh, my scythe is in there, too.

Once my legs are freed, I stand up.

But then I lose my balance and fall.

Again? Really?!

How many times are we gonna have to do this, body?

I try to stand up again but lose my balance a third time and fall back on my butt.

"...White?"

Oh geez.

How do you walk on two legs again?

After many more attempts to stand up that end in my falling over, I finally manage to shakily stay on two feet.

Hrm. This isn't as easy as I remember.

Seriously, why do humans have only two legs?

It's so unstable and stupidly inconvenient!

Obviously, having eight legs is way better!

"Are you all right? Think you can stand now?"

The Demon Lord looks concerned, so I nod, then promptly fall over again.

Arrrgh!

"All right, no need to push yourself. Let's just get you dressed for now, okay?"

Nodding in agreement, I try to pull some clothes out from Spatial Storage, but I can't.

Huh? How do you use Spatial Storage again?

Normally I can just manipulate space without even thinking about it and pull out whatever I need, but now I have no idea how to do it.

Then I figure I'll just make some clothes out of thread, but I can't figure out how to make thread, either.

The blood drains from my face as understanding hits me.

"White? What's wrong?"

The Demon Lord's concerned voice goes in one ear and out the other.

I can't use my skills.

Not this one, or this one, or that one!

I can't use a single one of my skills!

Feeling lost, I look up at the Demon Lord's face.

She's tilting her head, looking at me in uncertainty.

Normally, High-Speed Processing would make everything look like slow motion, but now it's all happening at normal speed.

My vision's not enhanced anymore, either, so I can't see into the distance very clearly.

And I can't use Detection to grasp what's going on around me.

It's like I'm in Potimas's barrier... No, I'm even more powerless than that now.

"Can you not use your skills?"

Still looking the other way, Güli-güli poses the question.

I'm so dumbfounded, I can't even respond.

*   *   *

After that, I stay in a stupor for a while, so the Demon Lord, Vampy, and the puppet spiders bring me into a tent and play dress-up using my body for a while.

Taking advantage of the fact that I'm not resisting, they put me into outfit after outfit, mess with my hair, and even put makeup on me.

Somewhere along the way, the Demon Lord catches me up on the situation. Turns out the UFO's been brought down successfully.

In fact, since all of its energy was absorbed into that bomb, it just fell on its own.

While that was happening, I was apparently teleported somewhere else.

I was in too much pain to do that myself, so I think D probably teleported me instead.

Actually, that shouldn't have even been possible because of the barrier around the UFO, but leave it to D to go ahead and do it anyway.

The Demon Lord then made a daring escape from the falling UFO, which she described to me in dramatic detail, but the reality is that she just booked it out of there.

I mean, running was probably the only way to escape that UFO.

She did bring Potimas's head out with her, but by that time his consciousness had already gone back to his main body anyway.

That guy sure is quick to make his escape.

"If he *was* still conscious, I would've beaten the crap out of him."

You and me both.

Potimas is the biggest piece of shit I've ever met.

"He's such a child. No matter how long he lives, he never grows up. That's why he can't even cooperate with people properly. You have to scold a child so they grow up, right? But that bastard never learns, so there's no point in even trying. The only way to stop that guy is to kill him."

For some reason, the Demon Lord's words make all too much sense.

Potimas really is a child.

He's always chasing an unattainable dream, only ever caring about himself.

"Good kids have to learn what's right and wrong so they grow up, okay? Otherwise, you'll end up just like Potimas."

This particular threat seems to be pretty effective.

Vampy and the puppet spiders all nod emphatically.

As for the rest of the battle, it sounds like the ground forces eked out a narrow victory.

All of Potimas's machine soldiers were destroyed.

The pontiff's Word of God army suffered a lot of losses and injuries, too.

The Demon Lord didn't know the exact number, but it sounds like it'll definitely be a huge blow to the Word of God's future prospects.

As evidence of this, the pontiff rushed back to his home nation as soon as the situation was resolved. I'm sure he'll have his work cut out for him for a while.

The pontiff requested that the Demon Lord pass along his regards to me.

He praised my success in dealing with the bomb and said he regretted he wasn't able to thank me directly before leaving.

As for Hyuvan and the other dragons, they've scattered across the wasteland.

Basically, a bunch of humans have been coming to get a closer look at the UFO they saw in the distance, so the dragons are on patrol chasing them away.

The crashed UFO is too big to dismantle right away.

They can't let it fall into the hands of oblivious humans, so the dragons are going to get rid of it and the rest of the underground ruins little by little.

Until that's done, humans are still banned from the area, which is why the dragons are extra eager to keep them out right now.

Man, these poor chumps just wrapped a difficult battle, and now they're being put to work again already.

Sucks to be them.

I'll never forget you, though, Hyuvan.

(Yeah, I know, the guy's not dead.)

Anyway, the only side that made it out without any losses whatsoever is Team Spider over here.

The puppet spiders and the queens all made it through alive.

Sounds like they were both pretty instrumental in the ground battle, too.

Ael came up to me, obviously looking for praise, so I patted her on the head.

Then Fiel joined in on the bandwagon, then Riel, then the hesitant Sael, and finally even Vampy for some reason, which means I somehow wound up patting every one of the little tykes on the head.

Oh, that's right. Güli-güli went and picked up Vampy and Mera.

I was unconscious, so I couldn't Teleport there to get them myself.

I'm glad Güli-güli was kind enough to take care of them for me.

Otherwise, they would've been stuck in the Great Elroe Labyrinth this whole time.

By the way, turns out it's been forty-seven days since the whole UFO incident.

I still can't believe I slept that long.

And did these guys just stay in the wasteland with me the whole time?

"Yeah, it was pretty rough. You suddenly came back in that cocoon thing, and we didn't want to risk moving you, sooo…we've been camping out in this empty freaking wasteland for ages."

Geez, sorry about that.

"We were all really worried, you know? Especially little Sophia here. When Gülie came to get them instead of you, she thought something had happened to you and was totally freaking out—"

"Waaah! Stooop!"

Vampy rushes to cover the Demon Lord's mouth, but it's a little late for that.

Awww. So Vampy was worried about me, huh?

"I was worried, too, of course."

Yeah, yeah.

"Seriously. You just teleported away before my eyes, so I thought maybe you'd gone into another dimension to sacrifice yourself by blowing up there. I was freaking out, too."

Her unexpectedly serious voice catches me by surprise.

"I'm glad you're all right. Really."

…What's going on here?!

Is it just me, or is this, like, super-embarrassing?!

Come on—I'm blushing over here!

Speaking of which, the makeover's done now.

Ael grins triumphantly as she shows me the mirror.

Looking into it, I see… What the hell?!

On the whole, my face hasn't changed.

But one part is definitely pretty weird.

My eyes.

I have waaay too many pupils.

Each of my two human eyes contains four small arachnoid pupils, which is pretty damn freaky.

Overall, it makes it look like I have five eyes on each side, making ten altogether.

That's the number of a spider's eyes plus a human's.

Also, it's creepy.

Like, super-creepy.

No wonder the Demon Lord looked so confused when she first saw me.

I thought she was just startled that I have human legs now, but it must've been these weird eyes that surprised her so much.

So now I've got normal human legs, my eyes are super-creepy, and I can't use my skills anymore.

What the hell happened to me, exactly?

"Are you almost ready?" Güli-güli's voice comes from outside the tent.

The Demon Lord opens the tent's front flap, allowing Güli-güli and Mera to come inside.

And then Güli-güli gives me the biggest shock of all.

"She turned into a *god?*"

"That's right."

Güli-güli nods at the Demon Lord's incredulous question.

"This said… Allow me to call you White. During the incident, White took the GMA bomb into her body, absorbed its energy, and evolved as a result. Evolution that turns one into a god: deification."

Turns out I unconsciously absorbed the energy from the bomb and used it to forcibly evolve.

"As a result, White has surpassed the limitations of a living being and become a god like myself. However, this means she is now outside the scope of the system, so she can no longer use skills. In fact, the system will no longer affect her in any way."

Come to think of it, before I passed out, I did hear some kind of announcement to that effect.

No waaay. So I've finally become a god?!

Wait, but that means my skills and stats are gone?

No wonder I can't use any of them and my body feels so heavy.

Without stats, my body's even weaker than that of a normal human.

Huh? If I'm a god now, why does it seem like I've gotten a major *down*grade?

"What does that mean?"

"White is now just an ordinary person with a great deal of energy."

Whaaaat?!

"So what do we do?"

"Well, skills and stats are essentially a simplified method to expend energy and create magical effects using the support of the system. If she can learn to use magic without that support, she will be able to manifest power just as strong—no, judging by the amount of energy, even stronger than before."

Excuse me, Professor! I'm almost certain I can't do that!

"A god is essentially a being who has full control over magic. Since White has used the power of the system to become a god through irregular means, it will likely take considerable time for her to learn to use magic effectively on her own."

Yeah, I figured.

It doesn't exactly sound like the kinda thing I can pick up overnight.

Basically, I've been zipping around on a bike with training wheels this whole time.

But now, it's like I've suddenly been plopped onto an oversize motorcycle.

That's a really basic analogy, but you get the idea. No way I can start riding that easily.

I didn't even get to take the training wheels off the bike first. I just jumped up several degrees of difficulty.

The specs of my vehicle have greatly improved, but if the rider doesn't know how to ride it properly, she's not gonna be able to get around.

In the same way, my specs are now higher than ever, but I have no way of putting them to use.

"I see..."

Crap. Am I basically just a burden now or what?

In fact, if I'm the same as an ordinary person without stats, that means I've got no Immortality and no egg revival, so I'm basically just an NPC who can get killed with a single blow!

If the Demon Lord feels like it, she could kill me whenever she wants!

"Well, it's not like she can change back now. We'll just have to look out for White until she gets her strength back."

The Demon Lord doesn't even consider killing or abandoning me. Not even for a second.

Seriously, are you a demon lord or a saint?

Ughhh, fine.

If you're gonna be this nice to me, I have no choice but to give in already!

No matter how hard I try, I just can't think of this person as an enemy anymore.

But I guess I already knew that.

It hit me the moment she protected me in the UFO.

I tried making excuses to myself about why I protected her in return, like how I was paying her back or whatever, but really there was only one thought in my head at the time.

I don't want the Demon Lord to die. That's it.

I guess somewhere along the line, the Demon Lord won me over with her kindness.

And it looks like she isn't even thinking about trying to kill me anymore, either.

In that case, there's no point being stubborn about it at this point.

So, on that note, please look after me until I learn to do magic on my own!

Thus, having received a power-up that instead made me super-weak, I resolve to leech off the Demon Lord for a while.

SHIRO

True name: Shiraori. A former spider monster who was born in the Great Elroe Labyrinth and a reincarnation who retains memories of her life in Japan as high school girl Hiiro Wakaba. After absorbing the energy of a bomb said to be able to destroy a continent, she underwent deification—evolution into a god. At that time, D gave her the name Shiraori. However, as a result of becoming a god, she has transcended the system, losing all her stats and skills, and currently does not know how to use her power. Though she is a god whose body contains an immense amount of energy, her current state is as weak as an ordinary human's, so she will be continuing her journey under the care of the Demon Lord, Ariel.

Final Chapter

THE ETERNAL CHILD'S SOLILOQUY

My monitor displays the girl in white.

For some reason, the head that belonged to the body destroyed in that incident is still intact, being carried around by Ariel. My consciousness has already left it, but it can still record video perfectly well.

I've been using it to monitor their movements, and now it appears the white one has awoken.

Not only that, but she's become a god.

How very vexing.

I have strived to become a god myself for so long and have yet to attain that status, yet this girl comes from nowhere and achieves it just like that?

I should have made sure I killed her back there, no matter the cost.

"L-Lord Potimas?"

One of the expendables calls my name in a quavering voice.

"What is it?"

"I—I thought you might wish to place the blame for this operation's failure on Auries."

Failure?

Ah, this expendable is assuming I'm in a bad mood because the operation failed.

And he is contriving to place the blame on another expendable to protect himself.

How pathetic.

His premise is wrong from the very beginning.

"This operation was not a failure."

"Pardon?"

Honestly. Do I really need to explain every little thing for these people to understand?

"The goal of this operation was to silence the G-Fleet and deactivate the GMA bomb. We succeeded on both these points. Therefore, the operation was a success, not a failure."

The bare-minimum goals that absolutely needed to be accomplished were met.

I simply wasn't able to accomplish my secondary goals, but the operation itself was still a success.

It's not the ideal situation, but it's still a positive outcome.

Yes, the Gloria type-Bs I sent were all destroyed and my body was severely damaged.

Almost all my forces were destroyed, and I have nothing to show for it.

I can understand why an expendable would deem this a failure.

However, I have no shortage of Gloria Bs.

Since my body was equipped with an anti-magic barrier, I've incurred a considerable cost, but I can simply make another.

A trivial expenditure, all in all.

Indeed, that was only a small fraction of the military strength I have in reserve.

If I wished to do so, I could easily bring down a G-Fleet with my forces alone.

A relic of a bygone era poses no threat to me.

Even if the GMA bomb did explode, we elves would not be injured in the slightest.

If anything, it might be more convenient for us if that was to occur.

Which is why I sent only a small force.

I thought I had calculated just enough to pull off a narrow victory, but considering that none of Ariel's kin was harmed, perhaps I should have sent a trifle less.

Still, at least I was able to put a severe dent in Dustin's forces.

However, I simply must kill that white creature.

In the most gruesome way I can imagine, just as I promised.

"There is no need for anyone to take the blame. Instead, please prepare the troops."

"Yes, sir!"

"Chase Ariel down. And kill her."

"Of course, sir!"

Then an excellent idea strikes me.

I call out to the expendable who is scurrying off to carry out my orders.

"Ah, one more thing. Bring Oka with you."

"What? Lady Oka?"

"Yes."

Oka.

The reincarnation who was born as my daughter.

The foolish girl who was the reincarnations' teacher in their previous world.

"I shall speak to her about it later. Make arrangements for enough forces to protect her."

"Y-yes, sir!"

I watch as the expendable scurries away.

Now, how will I talk Oka into this?

Having the reincarnations kill one another...

Now that would be delightful.

I do not know how close White was with Oka, but it would surely cause them both distress.

"Hmm. It would be a shame not to witness this in person."

Perhaps I should go along in case of any extenuating circumstances.

A smile rises unbidden to my lips.

I feel my mood improving for the first time in quite a long while.

Just imagining White suffering in anguish is enough to relieve my frustration.

"Just you wait. I shall stage the greatest death imaginable for you."

AFTERWORD

Hello, I'm Okina Baba.

In the blink of an eye, this series has already reached Volume 7.

Lucky number seven!

And *seven* brings to mind everyone's beloved catfish.

You might not remember, since it was way back in Volume 2, but the catfish monsters' official name was the Elroe guneseven.

They might not ever make a reappearance in the novels, but they're a major player in the manga Volume 3, so make sure you check it out!

Anyway, now that I've managed to work in a manga plug, let's talk about Volume 7.

Since Volume 6 had way less action than any of the volumes before it, this volume makes up for it by being almost entirely action.

Really, I don't think I've ever written a volume that was full of so many battles from start to finish.

Not to mention, the opponent was unlike anything we've seen before.

And on top of that, even though they spent the whole volume fighting, less time passed than almost any other volume.

It's like, a certain amount of time passes between Volume 1 and Volume 6, but this one focuses on a single incident, so it's basically all within the span of one day.

Just like an episode of 24.

As for other changes, the notes about the reincarnations in the table of contents have changed from Shun's list to Ms. Oka's.

It contains different information from Shun's list, too.

So did you notice anything?

The location of Mirei Shinohara's name is different in this list from the old one!

Both lists are in Japanese alphabetical (A-I-U-E-O) order, yet Shinohara's in two different places.

To tell you the truth, that may or may not have been a mistake on my part.

See, originally, her name was going to be read "Mirei Urushibara."

But when I was adding the name meanings, I changed it to Mirei Shinohara and then didn't notice.

It slipped through proofreading, so it wound up that her name just changes somewhere along the way.

Thus, because of a fairly minor mistake, her name changed from Urushibara to Shinohara.

Still, I think Mirei Shinohara sounds better than Mirei Urushibara anyway, so I decided to just keep it that way instead of correcting it.

Which is why Shun's list still contains that mistake.

In the web version, she's like a barely mentioned nameless background character anyway, but in the novel version, she's become a regular part of the S story, so I'm sure you can forgive me.

What? You can't?

Come on—give me a break here.

Anyway, it's the masterful Kiryu's amazing illustrations that let me get away with stupid mistakes like that.

I cruelly requested covers without any human characters for the first three volumes, and even now none of them is actually a human, but Kiryu's art makes it all work!

So I've been recklessly putting faith in that, and even in this volume, I keep making impossible requests like the devil I am.

Just look at how many machines are in this volume's illustrations!

Look upon this cruel author who asked Kiryu, an expert on drawing monsters, to draw a bunch of mecha instead!

Really, Kiryu, thank you so much.

Speaking of which, let me say my thanks here.

Starting with Kiryu, of course, for drawing those mecha I so heartlessly requested. Thank you again.

Thank you to Kakashi, who draws the sometimes serious, sometimes hilarious, always amazing manga adaptation.

Volume 3 of the manga even includes a bonus manga about the aforementioned Mirei Shinohara, so be sure to take a look.

Thank you to my editor Mr. K and everyone else who helped bring this book into the world.

And to everyone out there who picked up this volume.

Thank you very much.